The Flame Tree

E DUE

The Flame Tree

by Richard Lewis

SIMON & SCHUSTER BOOKS FOR YOUNG READERS
New York   London   Toronto   Sydney

For my mother and father

SIMON & SCHUSTER BOOKS FOR YOUNG READERS
An imprint of Simon & Schuster Children's Publishing Division
1230 Avenue of the Americas, New York, New York 10020

SIMON & SCHUSTER BOOKS FOR YOUNG READERS is a trademark of
Simon & Schuster, Inc.
Book design by Mark Siegel
The text for this book is set in Garamond.
Manufactured in the United States of America
10 9 8 7 6 5 4 3 2 1
Lewis, Richard.
The flame tree / by Richard Lewis.—1st ed.
p. cm.
Summary: Just before the September 11, 2001, terrorist attacks, an
anti-American Muslim group gains power in Java and Isaac, the
twelve-year-old son of American missionary doctors, finds his world
turned upside down.
ISBN 0-689-86333-0
[1. Islamic fundamentalism—Fiction. 2. Americans—Java—Fiction.
3. Friendship—Fiction. 4. Christian life—Fiction. 5. September 11 Terrorist
Attacks, 2001—Fiction. 6. Java (Indonesia)—Fiction.] I. Title.
PZ7.L5877 Fl 2004
[Fic]—dc22
2003009672

Acknowledgments

When I was a kid, I imagined that novelists scribbled away in isolation, their novels seeing print in a deus ex machina sort of way. Nothing like that happened to me. My scribbling wouldn't have amounted to much if it weren't for my wife's belief in me and her loving encouragement. Christie Golden and John Ruemmler of the Writer's Digest School, Brandi Reissenweber of the Gotham Writers' Workshop, and Lil Copan all taught me both the craft and the art of writing fiction. Laurie Rosin read an early draft and gave me not only an excellent critique, but also timely encouragement. Thanks also to my online writing friends at Zoetrope.com, who provided me a sense of community. Many thanks to Ed Borass, Darryl Hadfield, Mas Sugeng, Bapak Haji Taone Umar, and Aziz Bellotadz Yala, who patiently fielded pestering questions. John Kaltner provided much-needed help with the Arabic transliterations. Whatever errors remain are my fault. I am forever indebted to my agent, Scott Miller, who took a chance on an unknown writer halfway around the world and who also provided a critical reader's eye. Thanks also to Jessica Yerega, who made the introductions. I am particularly grateful for my editor, David Gale, whose enthusiasm and support and gentle shepherding not only came when most sorely needed, but also gave me courage to keep at this difficult business of writing fiction.

Author's Note

This is a work of fiction. While there is a Brantas River, the town of Wonobo is fictional, as is its Immanuel Hospital. The Union of American Baptists and the Nahdlatul Umat Islam are fictional organizations. Apart from obvious historical characters and events, all other characters and events in the novel are drawn from the imagination.

A glossary of foreign terms appears at the end of this book.

The Flame Tree

Chapter One

THE TUAN GURU HAJI Abdullah Abubakar first appeared in twelve-year-old Isaac Williams's largely untroubled life on a Saturday morning in late August.

Isaac sat thirty feet above the ground in the flame tree by the school wall, waiting for his best friend Ismail, who lived in a *kampung* on the other side of the Muslim cemetery. Three overlapping branches the size of his wrist, each carved with his initials, made a natural seat in front of an oval gap in the foliage through which he could observe a wide swath of the neighborhood before him.

Behind him was his other world. The American Academy of Wonobo, Java, a boarding school of the Union of American Baptists, offered a rigorous, godly education from first through ninth grades. Above the school's main doors, sternly carved on the sandstone gable pediment, was a verse from the Psalms: TEACH ME GOOD JUDGMENT AND KNOWLEDGE. Isaac did not board in the dorm there. He lived with his parents in a house on the residential side of the tangerine trees and hibiscus hedge that divided the large mission compound. Graham and Mary Williams were doctors at the Union of American Baptists' Immanuel Hospital, a four-story building that was the tallest for miles around and took up a good portion of the skyline to Isaac's right.

Isaac had just returned from a six-week summer trip to the States, most of that time spent with his family at the Connecticut gentleman's farm his grandpa Tarleton owned. His sixteen-year-old sister, Rachel, had stayed behind to go to a Christian boarding school in Virginia for her tenth grade. Such a fate was looming for Isaac, but he did his best not to think about it. Boy, it was great to be back home, even if his perch was smaller than he remembered and the top of the wall beneath him not as far away. The mission walls, quarried limestone blocks two feet thick and stacked eight feet high, kept the compound a world unto itself. The flame tree grew by the northern wall, shading a good part of the playground, but several of its branches thrust out over the wall and the public sidewalk of Hospital Street beyond.

Flame-of-the-forest trees, like American boys, are not native to Java, but flame trees and white boys born on the rich Javanese soil sink deep roots. This particular flame-of-the-forest had been planted thirty years ago as a promise tree, when the Wonobo Medical Mission had first opened its doors. The tree had grown with the mission, sprouting seedpods about the same time the mission added a school for the doctors' children. The tree grew and so did the school, which began accepting boarding students. When the tree could grow no higher, it grew thicker and wider. It seemed to Isaac that the tree had been there since the time of Creation and would be there until the Day of Judgment.

On the two-lane but occasionally four-way Hospital Street trishaws, bicycles, mopeds, motorbikes, sedans, public transport jitneys, and a sugarcane cart pulled by two oxen rattled and

Richard Lewis

rumbled and tooted and clopped. Pedestrians ambled along the cement brick sidewalks, many heading for the hospital's public gates a hundred yards to Isaac's right. Across the street the neighborhood mosque had new tin sheets on the roof and a new plywood facade of Moorish arches on the sagging front porch. The minaret displayed new speakers, with four of the six aimed at the school and hospital. The new Imam squatted on the front porch, a storky, beady-eyed man who wore white robes and the white cap of a haji who'd made the pilgrimage to Mecca. The old Imam had been fat and jovial; this one gave Isaac the shivers.

Sometime that morning a green banner had been stretched across the mosque's freshly painted wooden picket fence. Its ornate calligraphy proclaimed the mosque to be an official post of the Muslim society of the Nahdat Ummat al-Islam, or, according to the Indonesianized version of the name printed below it, the Nahdlatul Umat al-Islam. Isaac had never heard of it before. Printed on the banner was a portrait of the society's leader, an ancient man in robes and turban, with sunken eyes, tombstone cheeks, a white tuft of a beard, and exorbitant eyebrows. TUAN GURU HAJI ABDULLAH ABUBAKAR, the portrait's title said. If the Imam gave Isaac the shivers, then this old man's lifeless gaze chilled his soul.

Underneath Isaac's dangling right foot the sidewalk arced around an ornamental stand of head-high, yellow bamboo that clumped up against the compound wall. The ripe scent of aged urine floated up from the bamboo. A man in black trousers and white shirt broke his stride to step into the stand, where he unzipped his trousers and peed against the wall. His groan of relief rose as clear as a gamelan gong.

There was something different about the bamboo that caught Isaac's attention. The shoots closest to the wall had been cut down. From his elevated angle, something was off-kilter about the wall, too. Curious, he scrambled down the tree and slipped into the stifling shade of the tangerine tree that hid this section of wall from ground-level view. He brushed off a sweat drop trickling down his forehead, frowning at the thick sandstone bricks like he would at an algebra problem. Then he saw the gate. Somebody had cunningly detached a four-foot-square section of wall and then rebricked it within a thin frame of steel strips painted the same color as the stone. The frame was in turn attached on its right side by inset hinges to a stouter I beam inserted behind a facade of sandstone brick. A small gate, but nonetheless one that would allow even a large man to leave the compound.

Or enter.

I wonder if Tanto . . . But even as the question formed in Isaac's mind, there came from the large lawn on the far side of the residences the blatting of the gardener's mower. Tanto was a hard worker. When would he have had the time to make this gate? Not only that, he was security-conscious. The previous year he had caught a thief climbing over the wall with a bundle of clothes taken off the Higgenbothams' drying line, and he'd nearly bludgeoned the man to death.

It took Isaac a minute to figure out the latching mechanism, cleverly hidden inside a loose brick. With just a touch, the gate

Richard Lewis

opened silently outward. The inch-wide gap beckoned as alluringly as a hole into another universe.

I should tell Dad.

Isaac pushed harder. The bamboo on the other side had been cut to allow the gate to swing open. He bent and stepped through the hole in the wall, scrunching his nose against the acrid stench of urine. Wouldn't anyone who used this patch of bamboo as a pissoir notice the gate? He closed it. On this side the gate was even harder to see.

Now it is really time to tell Dad.

Through a gap in the bamboo, he spotted Ismail darting across the street. Ismail halted underneath the flame tree and glanced up at Isaac's empty perch, his narrow brown face looking as lively as a crackling electric wire. Isaac grinned and slipped out of the bamboo stand. He came close to his friend and tapped Ismail on the shoulder.

Ismail whirled around, his mended shirt flapping loosely on his skinny bones. He was a foot shorter and half as heavy as Isaac, but his scrawny muscles were just as strong. "*Iyallah,* where did you come from?"

"I have mastered the art of teleportation," Isaac said.

"That so? Then teleport us down to the river."

Isaac waved his hand and intoned, "*Bim-sallah-bim.*"

Ismail looked with exaggerated wonder around him. "*Aiyah,* it almost worked."

Isaac returned Ismail's snaggletoothed grin with his orthodontically shining one. He wondered if he should tell his friend about the gate, but he decided to keep it his delicious secret for a while longer.

"You're fatter," Ismail said. "And your eyes are more blue."

"They're just the same as they were," Isaac said. "Let's go, we got treasure to find."

They dashed down Hospital Street, weaving around pedestrians. They ran past Pak Harianto's barbershop. The petite man lifted his hand clipper from a black-haired head to wave at Isaac. "Welcome back!" he called out. Isaac was a valued customer—the only blond among Harianto's clients. Above the barber's wall mirror was a plaque bearing an Arabic inscription, a phrase from the Qur'an: BISMILLAH AR-RAHMAN AR-RAHIM. This stand-alone phrase was so common, Isaac could recognize what the Arabic script meant on sight: "In the name of Allah the Compassionate, the Merciful."

On the corner opposite the hospital gates was the Toko Sahabat, or the Friendship Shop. A crowd of shoppers, mostly families of patients, milled around its entrance. The boys slowed to a twisting crawl to pass through the congestion. The owner, Mr. Ah Kiat, hovered behind the two checkout girls on the registers, snuffling his nose into a handkerchief while his sharp eyes kept watch on everything. He always had that handkerchief in hand. The other students called him "Ah Choo." Ah Kiat glanced out the doors at the discount clothes rack on the sidewalk and lowered his handkerchief to yell, "Udin, where are you? I've told you a dozen times to straighten out the sales rack."

From behind the rack, a voice muttered, "By Allah, what does the bastard think I'm doing?" A young man wearing a dirty Iron

Mike Tyson T-shirt and an Iron Mike frown stepped out, pushing Isaac to the side.

Isaac protested. "Hey! *Awas lo!*"

The older boy pointed the handful of coarse hairs on his chin at Isaac as though they were porcupine quills, his face one big bad mood. Isaac, knowing that teenage nastiness transcended cultures, lowered his head and scooted along. *Oomph*—he ran right into a barrel belly encased in a blue security officer's uniform. He looked up with a sinking heart at the broad black face and pale yellow eyes of Mr. Theophilus, the hospital's Irianese chief of security.

"You be going where, Isak?" Mr. Theophilus asked in his peculiar outer-island patois.

"Just down to Ismail's house," Isaac said.

"Your mother, does she know this?"

"Of course she does."

Behind the security chief, Ismail bounced from one foot to the other.

"And you are a Christian boy who tells no lies, is that so?"

"I always go out, she knows that. I wouldn't be out if she didn't know it."

Mr. Theophilus's eyes narrowed, but he stepped to the side. "This I will be asking her."

The boys ran around the corner onto Hayam Wuruk Avenue, wide enough for six intercity buses to race side by side on four marked lanes or for any rambunctious mob to spread its elbows. They ran and ran, and the world that was behind Isaac grew smaller and smaller, dwindling down to a memory no more consequential than a wad of Juicy Fruit gum stuck to the bottom of a tennis shoe. They ran past the flower shop with floral arrangements laid out in front like the life of man, from baby bouquets to funeral wreaths. They dodged the cutout cardboard Fuji girl who stood all green and smiles in front of the camera and photocopy shop. They sped up to pass the red-tiled house used as a children's Islamic study hall, where Ismail was supposed to be in present attendance, chanting Qur'an verses with the others. They slowed down to a hopeful trolling pace in front of Pak Heru's fruit shop.

Sure enough, Pak Heru called out, "Isak, wait." Isaac's dad had saved Pak Heru's skin, in the literal sense of the term, for Graham Williams was a dermatologist as well as the hospital's medical director. Pak Heru handed Isaac a tall tangerine slurp. He beamed at Isaac and waved away Isaac's thanks.

Isaac and Ismail walked on, passing the cup back and forth to suck on the tangy ice shavings. They strolled by the establishment owned by Muhammad Ali Benny, a formerly indifferent Buddhist and avid boxing fan who had recited in front of two witnesses the *shahadah*—the Muslim confession of faith that there is only one God and Muhammad is His prophet, and had so become a strict Muslim. He continued to serve all faiths as a poor man's dentist. He replaced the teeth he pulled with off-the-rack dentures made in Taiwan, enormous models of which were painted on a whitewashed window, huge pink things with painful-looking, beaver-size teeth. The *bismillah* sign in his dentist's office was one of the most appropriately placed *bismillahs* in all of Wonobo. How many patients had those monster chompers levered into place as they

Richard Lewis

tearfully stared at the plaque proclaiming God's compassion and mercy?

On one crumbling warehouse wall, posters had been pasted. The blaring red letters advertised a free *dangdut* show in the town square the following Sunday, with a silhouetted picture of a slinky female singer at the microphone.

"Hey, this ought to be fun," Ismail said. "You want to go?"

The show was scheduled for the first Sunday of Spiritual Emphasis Week. Reverend Biggs would be arriving from mission headquarters that day to lead the week-long event, and Isaac knew from past years that he would be preaching both morning and evening sermons. But there would be no church service in the afternoon, and Isaac now had a secret gate to sneak out of the compound. "You bet," he said. "Just remind me the day before."

"So how is America?" Ismail asked. "Any *dangdut* there?"

"America is funny," Isaac said. "You can drink the water. You don't have to take off your shoes when you walk into a house. But you want to know what's really funny?"

"What?"

"There's no people there. Not in the country, anyway. You can drive and drive and drive and hardly see anyone out walking or working. It's spooky."

They passed the dirty, legless beggar sitting on his four-wheeled trolley in the bus stop's dilapidated security post, a cup for coins placed beside the sidewalk. Isaac had no coins to give. He sucked up the last drops of the drink and tossed the empty cup into the gutter. Isaac Williams the American boy would have been horrified at the littering, but at the moment he was Isaac Williams the Javanese *bulé* out with his best friend. In Java you scoured your houses and yards clean as heaven, and the jinns and the government took care of the rest.

A public transport *bemo*, a tinny box on tiny wheels, avoided a minor traffic jam by driving up onto the sidewalk, nearly running the boys over.

"Another thing about America is that drivers will actually stop and let you cross the street," Isaac said as they started walking again.

Ismail's off-centered brows tilted even more in surprise. "Why would they do that?"

"Maybe because pedestrians are so rare, the drivers stop to stare at them."

Ismail laughed. "Like white bulés in Java. See, that driver is staring at you. Hey, by the way, I had my circumcision ceremony when you were in America."

"I'm sorry I missed that," Isaac said. "I would have loved hearing you crying and wailing."

Ismail looked offended. "I didn't make a sound." His expression turned sly. "So when are you going to have the blanket taken off your worm?"

Isaac said loftily, "Worms with blankets grow to be bigger snakes."

"Infidel," Ismail said, flashing his grin and punching Isaac's arm.

They came to a weary, wrought-iron fence. Beyond, ancient

Richard Lewis

frangipani trees sheltered the graves of the old Muslim cemetery. The boys squeezed through a rusted gap in the fence and began to run again through this silent, shadow-shrouded world. Isaac, who had a college vocabulary in his head, flipped through it. *Crepuscular, caliginous, tenebrous*: Fancy words to keep less fancy fears away, but not altogether successfully. The frangipani trees twisted up from the ground like skeletons rising from the graves. Isaac ran faster yet. At the far end of the cemetery he swung over the fence on a stout frangipani branch and dropped down onto the weedy verge of a narrow residential lane beside Ismail. They bent over with hands on knees, panting and laughing. Isaac wiped fat drops of sweat off his forehead with the sleeve of his T-shirt.

They hurried on, jumping over the lane's potholes. All the houses along this lane were square-planked and raised on stilts, with narrow front verandas and clay-tiled roofs. Ibu Hajjah Wida sat as usual in her veranda's rocking chair, a gilt-edged Qur'an open on her robed lap. A green herbal mask covered her face. Her head was swathed with the incorruptibly white scarf she'd brought back from Mecca three years previously. She read aloud, deaf to the quarreling of her three grandchildren around her feet, but she must have heard the boys, for she stopped reading and glanced up at them. She granted Isaac a benedictory smile. "*Al-salamu alaikum,* Isak," she called out. "Welcome home."

He dipped his chin. "*Alaikum as-salam,* Ibu Hajjah. It is good to be back."

She waved him toward her. Isaac glanced at Ismail, who made an impatient face. But Isaac was a polite Javanese bulé who respected his elders, so he opened the gate and stood at the foot of the veranda steps, keeping his gaze downcast, as was proper.

"How are your parents, young Isak?"

"They are fine, thank you."

"Good." She rocked some more, rubbing her gnarled, arthritic fingers across the gilt-embossed cover of the Qur'an. "They are people of the Book, doctors who help the poor. Tell your kind mother and your father they are safe. Tell them not to worry. Most people know they are good people."

Isaac looked up at her in surprise. Behind the green herbal mask her black eyes twinkled kindly. He cleared his throat and said, "Thank you, Ibu Hajjah, I will."

"It's black magicians like Adi the tofu maker who should worry," she said, and returned to her Qur'an.

Isaac rejoined Ismail. What had that been about? What had she meant, that his parents were not to worry, that they were safe? When somebody said something like that, the first thing you did was to start worrying when there had been no worry in the first place.

Ismail's house looked like it had too much of the local *arak* to drink. The whole of it leaned slightly to the right. Ismail, who was playing hooky, peered through the neighbor's hibiscus hedge to make sure his mother was not around and then darted into the yard to get the metal detector, which was behind the chicken coop. The detector was a battered metal spade with a cracked wooden handle. Ismail claimed that Adi the tofu maker had charmed the spade, putting a metal-detecting jinn into the iron scoop. Adi lived in this neighborhood and made charms and sold amulets to ward off evil influences. Isaac didn't see what was so black about his magic.

Several men, one in robes and turban, squatted on the veranda of Ismail's house, staring at Isaac without expression. He did not recognize them. Through the open door, Isaac saw, on a stand beside the small television, a framed picture of Tuan Guru Haji Abdullah Abubakar. He pointed the picture out to Ismail. "Who is that old guy?"

"The Tuan Guru? A strict Muslim. If he had his way, we wouldn't be able to watch any more *wayang kulit* shows, don't even mention Hollywood movies."

"Is your father a follower?"

Ismail frowned, his brows twisted with discomfort and embarrassment, an unusual expression on his normally vivacious face. "It gets easy to like a Tuan Guru who preaches against corruption when corrupt bosses steal your land. At least my father still has his job at the sugar mill, or we'd be really hurting." His face cleared and he smiled. "But maybe we'll find some treasure down by the river. Come on."

Several hours later all that the metal-detecting jinn in the magic spade had uncovered in the baked clay and moist muck of the nearly dry Brantas River was a rusted hubcap and an engine block. Isaac's T-shirt was drenched with sweat. A swim would have been nice, but because of the prolonged drought, the river was nothing more than scummy-looking ponds and a sluggish brown stream. A worm of guilt wriggled across his conscience—not only had his parents laid down a new rule that he had to ask permission before leaving the compound, they had specifically told him not to play down by the river because of mosquitoes and malaria. But Isaac wasn't really disobeying. The State Department warnings that had alarmed his parents were for stupid Americans who didn't know what they were doing, blundering around the country and ignorantly offending people. As for the river rule, that really applied only at sunset, when the mosquitoes swarmed.

"You'd think with the water this low, we'd find lots of things," Isaac said. "Like the Strangs are finding."

Ismail began strolling along the bank, spade extended to the ground. They'd walked far enough out of town that sugarcane fields lined both sides of the river. "The who?"

"The archaeologists."

"Oh, them. But they're still not finding any gold." The local villagers, not to mention government authorities, kept close watch on what the Strangs were finding.

Picar Strang and Mary Williams were good friends, which baffled Isaac. Imagine a weird New Ager yakking about work and family with his mother during their Saturday coffee klatches. His mother was not nearly so generous with her private time with anyone else outside the family.

Ismail halted. "The jinn sensed something here," he said, and began to dig furiously.

Despite repeated failures, hope always rises triumphant on treasure hunts, so Isaac got down on his knees to dig with his hands. "There!" he cried, and snatched out an octagonal coin with raised

Chinese letters around a square hole in the center. These *kepengs* were common, but the jinn had at last found them some money! They inspected the find, excitedly wondering whether they were standing upon real treasure. Ismail put the coin in his pocket. The boys dug for another hour, ending up with a wide, knee-deep hole, their spirits lagging when all the spade turned over was stinky muck. They soon recovered, flinging mud balls at each other, until Isaac realized that the sun was a reddish smudge close to the horizon.

"*Aduh,* look at the time. I got to get home before I get into trouble," he said.

Ismail glanced up at the setting sun. "*Iyallah,* if I miss *magrib* prayers, my father will be furious."

They began to run the mile back to town. Ismail outpaced a panting, overheated Isaac, who stopped for a moment to take off his muddy T-shirt. By the time Ismail reached the irrigation road by the first bridge, Isaac was still lumbering along the riverbed. Mosquitoes swarmed from the ponds and attacked him in clouds. He ran faster, flailing his T-shirt around his body. Ismail doubled over with laughter, slapping his knobby knees.

"You should have seen yourself," he said when Isaac climbed up out of the culvert. "You could be a circus clown."

"Funny," Isaac growled. Ismail slapped him on the back, a hard smack that stung. Isaac yelped. Ismail showed his palm, with a squished mosquito in the center of a crimson smear. "Wow," Ismail said in mock amazement, using the English exclamation before switching to Javanese, "your American blood is just as red as mine!"

✱

Isaac entered the compound by the secret gate. His stomach growled. He wondered what his chances were of talking his parents into going out to eat at the Hai Shin restaurant. The restaurant occupied the ground floor of an old trading warehouse down in the small riverside intestines of Wonobo. Two generations of Chinese Buddhist women ran the restaurant—three, if you included fifteen-year-old Meimei, who helped in the kitchen cooking her migrant grandmother's old Chinese recipes. Isaac drooled over images of frog's legs fried in garlic butter sauce and pork dumplings. The Hai Shin was the only place in Wonobo where the Americans could eat pork, since the mission forbade it anywhere on the hospital grounds out of respect for the Muslim patients.

Isaac scratched at the mosquito bites within reach. His mother had a radar sense for him, so he sneaked through the back garden of his house and into the outdoor laundry washroom for a quick rinse there. He'd just turned on the water tap to fill a bucket when the overhead fluorescent bulb hummed and flared into harsh light.

Behind him his mom said, "For heaven's sake, what did you get into?"

Isaac put on a smile and turned around. "Oh, hi, Mom. I was out playing with Ismail."

His mother's limp blond strands were pulled back and held in place by a fake tortoiseshell barrette, and the smudges under her soft blue eyes had deepened with another day's hard work. She sniffed. "That smells like river mud. Were you playing in the river?"

"No, not exactly—"

"Isaac, that river is filthy with disease. And what's this?" She grabbed his arm and looked at his upper shoulder. She turned him around and inspected his back. "You're covered with mosquito bites."

"There was a swarm, it wasn't even sunset—"

His mother overrode him. "Since we've been back, I've already seen five shantytown children die of malaria," she said in a low, dense voice that did not bode any good for Isaac. "That's why we have the rule that you stay away from the river."

"I know, but—"

"No buts. You shower out here; I'll get some clothes for you."

Fifteen minutes later Isaac, clean but still itchy, was being hauled away by his mother to the hospital clinic. They crossed the front lawn, big enough to be used for helicopter landings when high government dignitaries came to visit the hospital. Robert the Slobert stood on the porch of his house. His dad, Dr. Higgenbotham, was an oncologist, and his mother was the head nurse trainer. Slobert was thirteen years old, the closest in age to Isaac of all the school students, and the meanest.

"What's up, Dr. Williams?" he called out to Isaac's mother.

"Don't answer," Isaac muttered, but his mom replied that Isaac had been eaten alive by mosquitoes and that she was taking him to the clinic for some medicine.

Isaac kept his gaze on the ground. *Great, now Slobert's going to tease me about malaria and think of a stupid trick to pull on me.*

She added, "You boys remember to stay away from the river."

Slobert laughed and said, "Only Isaac ever goes to that stupid river."

Mr. Theophilus, on compound duty this evening, opened the grilled gate for them. They crossed Doctors' Alley. The narrow lane separated the hospital from the rest of the compound and dead-ended in a large empty lot slated for future hospital expansion. Mary took Isaac into the bright dispensary, its walls painted a canary yellow, the air rich with the smell of alcohol and antiseptic. She gave Isaac some chloroquine tablets and a cup of water. Isaac dutifully swallowed them without comment, although he knew that the bad malarial strains were chloroquine-resistant. She handed him another tablet. Lariam. The nuclear-bomb pill.

"Oh, Mom, please not that," Isaac begged. "That makes me sicker than a dog."

"Better sick for a night than dead forever," she said grimly. "Drink it down."

Isaac did. The Lariam started to erode his hunger with an ache that later would turn nauseous.

It happened quickly. By the time he got back to the house, he was gagging. His mom told him to keep it down, or he'd have to have another Lariam pill. She escorted him into his bedroom and helped him onto his bed. "Just stay still and think of something nice," she said.

The Lariam's radioactive fallout overwhelmed all thoughts, whether nice or not, and he groaned with misery. He finally couldn't take it anymore. He got up and raced to the bathroom, where he retched as quietly as he could. He didn't want his

Richard Lewis

mother to hear and make him take another pill. The nausea subsided to a tolerable level, and he crawled back to bed. His dad came in to check up on him, a dark, lanky shadow smelling of germicide detergent.

"How are you feeling?"

"Terrible. Lariam should be outlawed."

Graham Williams chuckled. "That's what you get for breaking the rules. We're going to have a little talk about that tomorrow."

"I didn't do anything *wrong* wrong—"

"We'll talk about it tomorrow. Your mother asked me to see if you want to eat something."

"Are you kidding?"

"Okay." His father moved to the door.

"Oh, Dad, wait."

Graham Williams paused. "Yes?"

Isaac closed his eyes, seeing again the cunningly made secret gate in the compound wall. If he got grounded, it might come in handy. "Never mind, it doesn't matter."

Sometime later that night he dreamed of a crow spiraling out of the sky, landing on the railing of his bedroom's small porch, such a realistic dream that he was certain he was awake. The crow hopped into the room, spread its wings . . . Isaac woke, really woke, in a sweat. He didn't fall asleep again for a long time.

Chapter 2

THE NEW SCHOOL YEAR started on Monday. During Opening Assembly, Isaac, along with fifty-five students and eight teachers, pledged his allegiance to the United States flag, a new one the size of a bed sheet that hung stiff as starch from its bronze eagle stanchion. The one teacher excused from pledging was the new Indonesian language and culture instructor, a Javanese man who spoke perfect BBC English, and from whose amber skin wafted English Leather cologne. The principal, Miss Augusta, asked the teacher to introduce himself. He said that his name was Mr. Suherman, that his father was a banker, that he'd grown up in London, and that he was a Muslim but was honored to be teaching in this Christian school.

After Assembly, Miss Augusta called Isaac into her tidy office and told him that since he'd already skipped two grades, they didn't want him to skip again, even though he could do high-school material. "You'll get ahead of your age group," she said, gazing at him with her left glass eye that saw all. She was the only black-skinned American Isaac knew, and he'd known her for as long as he could remember. Each year more of her crinkly hair turned gray. "So this year, we'll be assigning you special projects."

One of these projects was Esperanto, in one-on-one sessions with Mr. Suherman, as the language was one of the teacher's hobbies. Isaac, born and raised in Wonobo, Java, was already fluently trilingual in English, Indonesian, and Javanese. He didn't see why he should learn a new language, especially an artificial one, no matter what Mr. Suherman said about it being created in part to help bring the world together. But he did help Isaac with several complicated logarithmic problems that the math teacher Mr. Patter had given to Isaac ("The same type of problems occur in banking," Mr. Suherman said). Mr. Suherman was unfailingly courteous and polite, but when raucous Slobert threw spit wads during the first Indonesian culture lesson, one of two regular classes that Isaac attended with the seventh and eighth graders (the other being Bible study), Mr. Suherman's skin and voice seemed to shift as he softly scolded Slobert, revealing steel underneath the softness, the quiet but compelling authoritative aura that only the highest-born Javanese displayed. Slobert reddened but shut up.

The boarders ate lunch at the dorm, and the few day students ate bag lunches at picnic tables under the flame tree, but Isaac ate at home, meals prepared by the Williamses' housekeeper, Ruth, a Muslim widow who'd converted to Christianity. Each day that week as he trudged home for lunch, he detoured into the grove to have a look at the secret gate. He'd placed a small black thread in the crack; it remained in place, telling Isaac that whoever had made the gate was not using it.

On Saturday, after getting permission from his mother and

leaving properly through the hospital gates, Isaac went with Ismail to search for treasure in the cane fields. They came up empty-handed, although the excitement of spotting a large python squeezing through a culvert more than made up for that. When they said their good-byes in the late afternoon, Ismail reminded Isaac of the dangdut show at the village square the next day. No way Isaac would be able to get permission for that, but he said, "I'll be there," thinking excitedly that at last he had a real reason to use the secret gate.

That evening Isaac's mother came into his room to tuck him in. "Remember to take out what you need from here tomorrow morning," she said to Isaac as she kissed his forehead. "Reverend Biggs will be here early."

Reverend Biggs normally would have taken the guest bungalow, but it was currently occupied by a missionary from Kalimantan, hugely pregnant with twins refusing to be born. The reverend was going to be sleeping in Isaac's bedroom because it had a big bed. Isaac was moving into his sister's old room with its small four-poster, and he wasn't happy about it.

Reverend Biggs was pink and plump. His thick silver hair rested on his head like a helmet. It didn't move, not even when he got all wound up during his Sunday-morning sermon at the Maranatha Church of Wonobo. The thought of that head on his pillow unnerved Isaac.

The sonorous "amen" of the reverend's final benediction was still rolling toward the gates of heaven as Isaac quickly slipped out to the foyer. He halted in surprise. Out of the sanctuary's other side strode Mr. Suherman. He waved a greeting at Isaac, who blurted, "I thought you were a Muslim."

"I am, but that does not mean I cannot attend church," Mr. Suherman said. He bent close, humor rising in his clear black eyes, and said, "Are you praying with the others for my salvation?"

Actually, Isaac wasn't, even though he knew he should be. This was one of many things that had been bothering him at night as he tried to sleep. "All my prayers get used up for myself," Isaac said, surprised he would admit such a thing.

"Including a prayer for an A in Esperanto?" Mr. Suherman said, laughing. "Remember to study for the lesson tomorrow. *Adiau, mia bona studanto.*"

After Sunday lunch Isaac used the secret gate to sneak out of the compound to meet Ismail for the show in town. He stopped by Pak Heru's fruit stand for a slice of chilled melon. A soft-faced Javanese trying to cultivate a full beard and wearing a black turban and cream-colored robe stood behind the counter.

"Where's Pak Heru?" Isaac asked.

"He's moved to Surabaya. I own this shop now." The man gave Isaac that ultrapolite Javanese smile that said something was seriously wrong. Isaac saw too late the picture of Tuan Guru Haji Abdullah Abubakar hanging on the wall. The man said, "I know who you are. Who you all are. After three days guests and fish begin to stink. You Americans should leave Java. Let Muslim doctors treat the Muslim sick."

Isaac felt embarrassed for the man, that a Javanese would

descend to such discourtesy. He left the shop without a word. Something was indeed fishy. Wouldn't Pak Heru have told Isaac he was moving?

Isaac scurried down the avenue. As usual, the legless beggar slumped against the wall of the bus stop's security post, his eyes closed and his mouth moving sporadically as he mumbled in his sleep. His begging cup, out by the sidewalk, had toppled over. Isaac set it upright. He hesitated, thinking of the money in his pocket. But he didn't know how much he would need at the square.

And besides, he thought, with a flare of anger that surprised him, *let the Muslims take care of their own poor.*

He passed the cemetery and the Pertamina gasoline station and came to the town's chaotic bus terminal, perpetually screened by the black smoke of diesel exhaust fumes.

A trio of heavily made-up women in tight satin gowns stepped down from a grimy bus into Isaac's path. One of them waved her extraordinarily big fingers at him.

"What a cute bulé boy," the second said in a deep male voice, speaking Javanese and clearly not expecting Isaac to understand.

Oh, boy, Isaac thought. *Bencongs.*

The third *bencong,* the most petite and prettiest of the three, said, "I wonder if he's going to have blond hair all over when he's older."

"His balls are probably as blue as his eyes," the first bencong said. "And being an infidel, he's probably got an uncircumcised snake between them."

"At least my balls are not black and rotting like yours," Isaac said in fluent gutter Javanese.

The three bencongs stared at him and then burst into helpless laughter, falling into one another's arms. When their mirth subsided, the first one asked, "Where are you going?"

"To see the dangdut singers in the town square."

"Why, we're three of them!" the second bencong said. "Come along with us, we'll make sure you get a good seat." They waved Isaac into their midst and merrily made their way to the town plaza, several blocks away.

The grassy plaza was big enough for two soccer fields. Majestic mahogany trees lined three sides. On the treeless north side stood a large wooden stage shaded by a canvas awning. Twin stacks of loudspeakers backed a fleet of microphones. The drums looked like a gym set. Technicians checked the sound system. The one wearing a T-shirt printed with the stern visage of Tuan Guru Haji Abdullah Abubakar took the test mike and said in Indonesian, "The only good American is a dead American." He withdrew for a second and then put his mouth to the mike again to add, "But don't kill Eminem or Limp Bizkit." His friends on the stage laughed. Isaac, who'd never heard such a sentiment expressed publicly before, slowed his steps. He glanced around the rapidly filling square, an unease pricking him like a mosquito bite. At least fifty policemen in riot gear were filing out of the police station adjacent to the eastern side of the plaza and were assembling underneath the mahogany trees.

Maybe being here wasn't such a good idea.

"Don't worry," the petite bencong said. She—for she was too pretty for Isaac to think of as a man—knelt as far as her tight gown would allow and gave him a hug and a delicate kiss on the cheek. "That bastard is only a loudmouth; we'll keep you safe."

She took his hand and led him into the performers' tent, pitched on the windward side of the stage and cooled by the light breeze. Cloth screens sectioned the space into cubicles. Performers perched on stools in front of portable cosmetic stands and mirrors, touching up their makeup. The bencongs found their cubicle and put Isaac on a folding aluminum chair right next to the steps leading up to the stage. One flame-cheeked, kohl-eyed girl in black tights and a red tube top with a pin in her navel caught Isaac's gaze in her mirror and, after an initial flare of surprise at seeing a white boy, blew him a ruby-lipped kiss. His ears felt like they'd burst into flames.

From his seat, he had a good view of Wonobo's Grand Mosque on the other side of the wide avenue. Even though Isaac was a good Christian boy, he was proud that his town had the province's most beautiful mosque, so beautiful that *National Geographic* magazine had published a full-page photograph of it. The vast marble prayer hall could hold ten thousand worshippers. The central dome soared hundreds of feet into the air, thrusting a pure gold star and crescent insignia up to the clouds. A throng of several hundred men, most in Islamic robes or caftans, stood expectantly on the wide steps to the main entrance, ignoring the happenings on the square.

Ismail soon found him. "Can't miss your big blond head," he

said, giving that crooked grin. Over his tattered jeans he wore a bright new T-shirt printed with the picture of the Tuan Guru. Isaac frowned. Ismail laughed, plucking at the sleeve. "There's a stand at the corner selling them. You want one?"

"No," Isaac said.

Ismail drew closer and whispered, "I didn't actually buy it, you know. It was sort of lying discarded on the ground."

The fact that Ismail had shoplifted the T-shirt made Isaac feel better about the fact that he was wearing it. "That's stealing," he said with mock sternness. "You'll get your hands chopped off."

"Ah, that's just for crazy Muslims like the Taliban. Look at this." He tugged on a leather thong around his neck, which was strung through the hole in the Chinese coin they had found at the river. "Maybe we'll find one for you next time."

The band members took their places on the stage and warmed up with drumrolls and flute warbles and electric guitar twangs, now and again melding together for a few bars of the blood-itchy *dang dut dang dang dut* rhythm. The crowd on the plaza had thickened considerably. The teenage kids pressing toward the stage were held back by a phalanx of private security guards.

The MC, a portly man wearing a red bow tie and green suspenders, rattled through his opening speech. Isaac still couldn't figure out the purpose of this festivity—it wasn't a special holiday, and no political campaigning was going on. But so what?

The first performer, the girl in the black tights and red tube top, sang to a hot and spicy *dang dang dut* beat that set the air to quivering. Most of the crowd danced in place. This wasn't the ridiculous hopping and jerking that his sister Rachel loved to watch on MTV, but a slower-paced movement of shuffling feet, rotating buttocks and waist, undulating shoulders and arms, the hands occasionally high over head. The singer's movements were so languid as to be sultry, putting the crowd on slow boil. A lad old enough to sport a tiny mustache ducked underneath the security guards and jumped up on stage. The guards let him be, for this was part of a public dangdut show. The singer fluttered her eyelashes at the lad, and the two danced together as she sang.

The pretty bencong bent down to Isaac's ear. "You know what she's singing about?"

"No, not exactly, what?"

"Losing her virginity. You know anything about that?"

Isaac gave her a grossed-out look. She laughed and clapped him across the shoulders. "You will, you will. Oh, our turn."

The bencongs minced up on stage to roars of laughter. Their lyrics Isaac understood, about a man falling in love with a woman who was a man. The pretty bencong, mike in hand, stepped halfway down the stairs and extended her hand to Isaac, who went rigid in alarm. She wiggled her fingers. Ismail, laughing, pushed Isaac toward her. She clamped her hand around his wrist and dragged him onto the stage. The crowd momentarily hushed upon seeing a blond-haired, blue-eyed bulé boy on stage and then cheered in delighted surprise. Isaac's stage fright eased. Something strange began to happen to him. The infectious beat pouring out of the speakers vibrated along his spine and loosened

Richard Lewis

his muscles. He started to dance, really dance. The bencong's eyes widened, the band members grinned at him, and the crowd doubled its roaring, with cries of *"dangdut bulé, dangdut bulé."* Several photographers rushed forward to take his picture. When the song ended and Isaac descended from the stage, he was flush with a new, grand feeling. Who cared if he was in no grade, with no classroom friends, when he could have an *audience*?

"That was great," Ismail said, slapping him across the back. "I didn't know you could dance like that."

"I didn't either," Isaac said breathlessly.

Other performers took the stage. On the sidelines Isaac danced with Ismail. The tree shadows lengthened across the field. The crowd at the mosque across the boulevard had grown as well and began to stream down the white marble steps, a tight nucleus of men at the center. Isaac spotted Imam Ali at the front of this nucleus, and his feet stopped dancing. His inner glow turned into alarm as the robed men strode across the boulevard to the stage. But nobody else was perturbed. Many in the tent craned their heads to see the new arrivals.

The MC got up on stage. He cracked a joke and thanked the performers, giving time for the nucleus of men to gather at the bottom of the stage steps. Imam Ali stood on the first step. The MC grandiloquently said, with rising volume and inflection, as though he were announcing a Las Vegas boxing match, "And now, ladies and gentlemen, good Muslims all, the patron of this afternoon's entertainment, the Nahdlatul Umat Islam!"

Sporadic cheers. Imam Ali took the microphone and stuck his

beaky nose to it. He spoke Arabic words of greeting, his beady eyes sweeping the crowd.

Isaac was a good Javanese-American Christian boy who believed in signs and portents upon the earth and in the heavens, and so when a flock of crows wheeled out of the clotted sky and settled in the branches of the mahogany tree nearest the stage, his blood seemed to thicken. As Imam Ali talked the robed men on the steps moved forward to unfurl banners and set up chairs that had been hidden behind the speakers, leaving only three men behind as bodyguards for a stooped, tuft-bearded, turbaned man with bristling white eyebrows and tombstone cheeks.

Tuan Guru Haji Abdullah Abubakar.

The crows cawed raucously.

"Iyallah," Ismail muttered, "it's him!"

The Tuan Guru turned his head toward the tent. Isaac backed up into the shadows, his eardrums pounding with his thudding heartbeat. The Tuan Guru's attention slowly, inexorably settled upon Isaac. Despite the stooped back, there was no sense of infirmity in that body or on that face creased with age. His severe gaze burned. Isaac quickly looked down at the ground.

When he glanced up again, the Tuan Guru was climbing the steps as spry as a goat to Imam Ali's effusive introduction. Throughout the crowd there rose Nahdlatul Umat Islam posters stapled to sticks. Other signs as well, in Indonesian and English: AMERICA THE TERRORIST. ZIONISTS ARE THE CAUSE OF ALL DISASTERS. INDONESIA: MUSLIM STATE, SHARIAH LAW.

Imam Ali continued to speak, warming up the crowd for the

Tuan Guru. He orated with wild flaps of his arms and thrusts of his beaky nose. He spoke of unjust American government policies oppressing Muslims around the world, even here in Indonesia. He ratcheted up his voice and thundered, "We are a Muslim nation, yet here in Wonobo, in the heart of Muslim Java, there is an American Christian hospital run by American Christians trying to convert Javanese Muslims!"

Some people in the crowd shouted their angry agreement at this. Isaac's skin prickled. The Tuan Guru, seated upon a plush velvet armchair, once again swung his gaze to Isaac. Isaac wanted out, he wanted to become invisible, he wanted Scotty to beam him up. *This is not good. I should not have come here.* The Tuan Guru's thin lips moved—he was saying something to Isaac—a threat, a curse. Isaac's soul shriveled. The aide next to the Tuan Guru leaned toward the old man, listening to what he was saying, and then stood and whispered in Imam Ali's ear.

Isaac was so light-headed with fright that his thoughts came from another dimension. *Oh, boy, here it comes. Imam Ali is going to haul me up there, bring out a sword, and if I don't say the confession of faith and convert to Islam on the spot, he's going to whack my head off.*

But instead, Imam Ali broke off what he was saying and scowled down at his feet. He took a breath and changed the subject, moving to a denunciation of the Indonesian authorities for timidity and cowardice and corruption. Now the shouts of angry agreement rose from thousands of throats, solidifying into a roar.

Policemen in riot gear, reinforced by Red Beret special commando soldiers, raided the stage and shut down the speaker system. A detail of Red Berets respectfully escorted a calm Tuan Guru and the other men off the stage and back to the Grand Mosque, an orderly retreat in a general scene that grew increasingly chaotic. The angry crowd surged toward the stage. The cops shot rubber bullets at the front ranks, dropping four young men who writhed in agony on the ground. The crowd fell back. Other Red Beret troops fired their automatic rifles into the air. Tear-gas smoke exploded on the east side of the square, drifting downwind. People screamed and fled. Police whistles shrilled, sirens blared, cop cars squealed to a swinging stop, closing off all the roads. On the plaza's western flank a volley of rocks hurtled toward the policemen on stage.

"A riot, a riot," Ismail shouted. He grabbed Isaac's hand. Isaac, more bewildered than frightened, didn't resist and ran with Ismail behind the stage to the throng of rock throwers, mostly young men with a few of the robed men among them, exhorting and inciting. Ismail plucked a stone from one of the garden beds and was getting ready to chuck it when a troop of helmeted policemen waded into the stone throwers, cursing and flailing with rattan whips and batons. Photographers and video cameramen ducked and wove throughout the commotion, viewfinders to their eyes. A police officer crunched his baton on Ismail's head, and Ismail crumpled to his knees.

A pair of hands grabbed Isaac from behind and yanked him away from the one-sided fighting. Isaac yelped in fear and struggled. A familiar voice said in BBC English, "Calm down, it's me."

Isaac whirled around. Mr. Suherman stood before him, dressed in the same crisply ironed slacks and sport shirt that he often wore when teaching. "Come with me behind the police lines," he said. "You'll be okay."

"But Ismail," Isaac said, "I have to get Ismail."

Mr. Suherman clutched Isaac's wrist and dragged him between two army personnel carriers and around a caged transport van into the recessed sidewalk arches of the town's movie theater. Isaac stood beside a poster of Tom Cruise with a knife slash on his cheek.

"Let's wait here until things quiet down and we can get you home," Mr. Suherman said.

A square-faced police lieutenant whose name tag read NUGROHO stood by the open rear of the van, barking instructions into a walkie-talkie. He was stuffed into a crisp brown khaki uniform. He spotted Isaac on the sidewalk and strode over. "What you bulé boy doing here?" he snapped in English.

Isaac's mind went blank.

"It's okay, he's with me," Mr. Suherman said in Indonesian.

"And who are you?"

"I'm his language teacher."

"You stay right there," the officer ordered.

"That's what we're doing," Mr. Suherman said.

Cops marched a group of handcuffed rioters to the waiting van, most of them the excitable stone throwers. A photographer followed, sidling and crouching for shots. Among the detainees was a dazed Ismail, the back of his head oozing blood. The policemen shoved the men into the van, and one put a hand on Ismail to do the same. Without thinking, Isaac darted out onto the street and tapped the arm of the burly lieutenant, who spun around with a snarl of surprise.

"That's Ismail," Isaac said, pointing. "Ismail Trisno. I know him. He's my friend. Why are you taking him? He didn't do anything. He's just a boy." The Javanese words rushed together.

"Back, back!" the lieutenant shouted, pointing a rigid finger over Isaac's shoulder, his breath garlicky.

Isaac flinched but held his ground. "He's just a boy."

The lieutenant gritted his teeth and said, "He was throwing rocks, the little bastard."

"He didn't know what he was doing."

"We'll let the judges decide that." The lieutenant's knotted face relaxed some. "He'll be all right, my Javanese-speaking white boy. He'll probably be held a few hours to scare him. Now step back, please."

Isaac did so, shouting, "Hey, Ismail!"

Ismail, already seated in the van, turned around and stared through the wire with glazed eyes.

"I'll tell your parents what happened," Isaac yelled. "You'll be okay."

Ismail licked his lips but gave no other reaction. He must have taken a pretty good wallop.

Mr. Suherman said to Isaac in his adult voice, "This is why your State Department advises Americans in Indonesia to stay clear of crowds."

Richard Lewis

The photographer, young and keen, wearing a safari vest with lots of pockets and a baseball cap on backward, approached them, a notepad held in his hand. "What's your name?" he asked Isaac.

Mr. Suherman stepped forward. "Don't involve him."

"Now, brother—"

"Get away," Mr. Suherman said harshly. Isaac stared at Mr. Suherman. He'd never heard the teacher be this rude. He'd never seen Mr. Suherman look like this, either, his expression hard and unyielding. Almost scary. The photographer retreated.

In fifteen minutes the town square had cleared, and workers were dismantling the stage. Clumps of people ambled away on the sidewalks, talking and laughing excitedly. Traffic began to flow. Mr. Suherman hailed a number five bemo, which plied the hospital route.

"But I've got to go tell Ismail's parents," Isaac protested. "They don't have a phone."

"I'm taking you straight home," Mr. Suherman said.

"But I promised Ismail."

"I'll tell them." He pushed Isaac into the bemo, following close behind.

When Mr. Suherman and Isaac got out at the hospital entrance, Mr. Suherman paid the driver with coins in his pocket. He knelt on the sidewalk so that he was eye level with Isaac. He sighed and then smiled. "You're like a little raja, aren't you, wandering around Wonobo as though you ruled it." The smile faded. "But let me tell you something. These days it isn't as safe as it has been. You shouldn't be going out on your own anymore. Will you promise me that?"

Isaac scowled.

Mr. Suherman cocked his eyebrows. "If you don't promise me, I'm going in with you to see your parents. You don't want that, do you?"

Isaac shook his head.

"So promise me you won't go out on your own anymore."

"I promise."

"Good lad. In you go, then. Don't forget your Esperanto lesson."

Before the Williams family left for the Sunday-evening service, the phone rang. Isaac, sitting at the kitchen counter reading the Sunday edition of the *Jakarta Post,* picked up the extension beside him. "Hi, Williams household."

"This is Sheldon Summerton. Is Dr. Graham Williams in?"

Sheldon Summerton was the senior foreign service officer at the American consulate in Surabaya. The previous year, before Rachel left for the States and boarding school, the Williamses had attended the Fourth of July party at a Surabaya mansion, complete with hamburgers and hot dogs on a big green lawn by a big blue swimming pool. Sheldon Summerton had outrageously teased Rachel, attention that made her blush with delighted embarrassment and Mary Williams's face darken with displeasure. A short while later Isaac, carrying a tray of drinks, had tripped and stumbled into the consular officer, soaking him with various sorts of liquor and beer. It had been an accident, honest, but Sheldon Summerton was the sort of man who found accidents caused by babies, dogs, and boys both suspicious and intolerable.

Isaac said in his most unctuous voice, "An urgent skin problem, sir? Necrotizing fasciitis of the genitals?" He did not give Sheldon a chance to reply, but punched the numbers that transferred the call to his parents' bedroom.

A short while later, as the family left the house for church, Graham Williams asked, "Isaac, in your past wanderings around town have you heard anything about a Muslim organization called the—what was it—Nadul Umat Islam?"

Isaac pretended to think for a few steps while frantically trying to get his heart to beating again. "No," he said, "not really."

"They held a rally in the town square this afternoon that turned violent."

"Really? Gee."

"Some anti-American rhetoric. Screeching for heads—"

"Graham," Mary said.

Isaac asked, "But everything's okay now?" His worry wasn't so much for Wonobo's peace as it was for his own. Did his father know he'd been at the square?

"It seems to be." Graham smiled and rubbed Isaac's head. "In fact, it is. Let's forget about it, and enjoy the service."

The Maranatha Church of Wonobo was an A-frame structure of gleaming teak and glowing stained-glass windows, located a quarter mile east of the hospital gates, down a quiet lane lined with old, unproductive rubber trees. On the northern side of the lane driveways led to middle-class brick-and-tile houses. On the lane's other side a curbless verge dropped off into a ten-foot wide concrete irrigation ditch as dry as the Sahara and filling up with garbage. Churchgoers parked underneath the rubber trees and

crossed the ditch on a concrete footpath. The church itself was surrounded by a waist-high brick wall meant to keep out chickens
and dogs. Prayer and angels protected this house of the Lord from
more dangerous creatures.

Isaac, sitting in the back pew, sang the hymns while his
mind busily reviewed the crazy events on the town square. He
felt again the unsettling stare of the Tuan Guru. He glanced
uneasily out the windows into the night surrounding the church,
but all was calm and quiet. Not even a crow on the low wall. Was
Ismail okay? Was he back with his family? Isaac wasn't sure the
police lieutenant could be trusted. Everyone knew that once the
police had you, you could disappear. Isaac had made a promise to
tell Ismail's parents what had happened, and he intended to keep
it. Mr. Suherman had said he'd tell them, but he didn't know
where they lived, did he?

Reverend Biggs preached his sermon. Isaac was so drowsy, he
couldn't follow. His gaze fixated on the large copper cross hanging over the pulpit, and he had a fantasy of the cross falling and
bonking the reverend into silence. Ashamed of such a thought, he
switched his attention to the back of Mr. Patter's fine black head,
which bobbed up and down with regular and emphatic agreement
to the reverend's sermon, a motion that hypnotized Isaac into
chin-nodding sleep. A crow flew into his dream. He jerked awake
again to the sound of snickering from the opposite pew. Slobert
and some of the junior highers were giggling at him. Slobert had
a shirttail hanging out and he'd misbuttoned his shirt. How come
nobody ever picked on him?

Richard Lewis

As if on eerie cue, Isaac's mother, sitting next to his father, turned and gave him an odd, psychic sort of look. Isaac raised his eyebrows, as though to say, *What?* She smiled and returned her attention to Reverend Biggs.

Later that evening he lay sleepless on the mattress on the floor in Rachel's room underneath the screened window, staring at the half-moon, which was a baleful yellow. Why did the sky always hide the sun but let the moon appear?

The door opened. For a crazy tilted moment he thought it was Rachel, teleporting herself from the States to complain about him being in her bedroom, but it was his mother who spoke in the darkness. "Isaac? Isaac, honey?"

He stirred to let her know he was awake.

She felt his forehead. "Are you feeling okay?"

He nodded.

"But something is bothering you."

He couldn't tell her about Ismail being in jail, and he didn't want to tell her about his bad dreams. "No, not really."

"Don't you 'no, not really' me, young man. What is it?"

"Mom, is anything bad going to happen to us?" The words surprised him, coming out in a blurted rush.

There was just enough light for him to see the stillness settling on her face. Then a glint of teeth as her lips widened in a soft laugh. "I'd say that is a real big bother, not a 'no, not really' bother." She knelt beside him and took his hand. "No, honey, nothing bad is going to happen to us. We don't have to worry at all because God will take care of us. We'll be fine. Okay?" She touched his nose with her finger.

The Flame Tree

Isaac nodded. "Okay." And it was, at least for now, really okay. Nothing bad was going to happen to them, to any one of them, Ismail included.

He slept soundly, without once dreaming of crows.

Chapter Three

ISAAC, ALONE IN THE computer section of the library, fired up the fastest Compaq and clicked on his private encrypted folder. The other day, during a library period, Rhyan Strang had called his sister, Sairah, over to have a look at a picture he'd downloaded off the Internet. Isaac was doing some complicated algebra calculations at a back table. Sairah scowled and said, "Gross." That got Isaac's attention, but by the time he got to his feet to have a look himself Rhyan had cleared the screen. "Not something for little boys to see," he said.

But the Web guardian kept track of the sites that users visited. After the Strangs left, Isaac got the address and downloaded the picture. He stared at it, stunned, and then quickly saved it in his private folder.

He looked at it again now, a side shot of a man kneeling on a patch of dirt, genuflecting toward the front of an unpainted cinder-block church just visible on the left side of the picture. The superb resolution showed the ironed creases in his black trousers and the crispness of his white button-down shirt. His chocolate brown hands rested on the front of his thighs, and his head was bent. He could have been praying, except he wasn't.

He was being beheaded.

Standing immediately beyond him, facing the camera but looking down on the kneeling man, another man wearing baggy athletic shorts and a soiled T-shirt had just swung a long machete through the kneeling man's neck. The standing man's skin was a deep blue-black, glistening with perspiration. His thick arm muscles bulged with the power of the killing stroke.

This JPEG image had caught the precise moment when the blade of the machete, having sliced through skin, bone, arteries, veins, muscle, and gristle, was exiting the bottom of the kneeling man's throat.

The machete-wielding man was a Hutu, and the man he was killing was a Tutsi. Isaac vaguely recalled something about genocidal atrocities of which this picture was supposed to be proof. But it hardly looked like an atrocity at all. The Tutsi's hands were unbound, the bend of his neck was unforced—a man, possibly the pastor of the church, submitting without protest to a foreordained fate. On the Hutu's face was no murderous rage, merely the concentration of a man intent on doing his job as best he could.

The edge of the blade had been honed to such sharpness that the strong sun flashed along the metal like a line of silver. The Hutu had cut so precisely that the Tutsi's head still appeared attached to his body. Where the blade had entered was marked by only a little notch of flesh, with a thin line of blood.

The photo was accompanied by a Webmaster's notation: *Cool photo. Maybe a bit disappointing for you Gore Phreaks. You'd think with a little tape and a little glue, the guy'd be walking around again.*

On a wire stretching from a crooked pole by the church

hunched three crows, their beaks sharp enough to impale the eyes of a decapitated head.

Isaac thought of Imam Ali.

A few kids entered the computer section just then, startling Isaac. He quickly shut down the Compaq and headed over to the common sitting area of the library.

Rhyan Strang sat at the back corner table, reading an archaeological magazine that he had brought to school with him. David Duizen, another ninth grader who boarded, entered the library for study period, late as usual. He sat down next to Rhyan. "Hey, Rhyan, explain to me again the theory of evolution," he whispered loudly enough so the other kids could hear, an earnest, thirsty-for-knowledge expression on his ruddy face. "Is it the survival of the fittest, or is it the survival of the fattest?" He poked a finger into Rhyan's pudgy arm and grinned.

"Well, David," Rhyan said, turning a page of the magazine without looking up, "if Wonobo ran out of food, I'd survive longer than you would, that's for sure."

"No wonder, with all that extra padding you've got."

"Nope. I'd survive because I know how to live off roots and snakes and spiders and scorpions and cicadas and grubs. Grubs are pretty tasty if you like squishy things. You roast them up on a fire and the skin gets hard, but when you bite into them, the insides squirt out. They're very nutritious. You can live on grubs for a long time. Studies have been done—"

"All right, all right," David said. "Grubs, jeez."

Rhyan smiled and continued reading his magazine.

The lunch recess bell rang. Isaac ran home. Ruth had prepared a rice curry with a fiery hot *sambal*. She was just on her way out for her noon break. As she always did before she left the house, she unclasped the thin gold necklace and cross that she wore when working. She folded it in a handkerchief and stuffed the wad down into the bosom of her blouse. She took no chances with the increasingly abundant and brazen purse snatchers.

Isaac said, "Ibu Ruth, do you know anything about Tuan Guru Haji Abdullah Abubakar?"

She turned to face him, her eyes flared in surprise. Then they narrowed. "The Tuan Guru. Who doesn't? To him, you are an infidel. Either you convert and become a Muslim right there on the spot, or"—Ruth leaned closer and whispered—"or he'll cut your head off and put it on a pole for other infidels to see."

Isaac's mouth opened. Absent from Ruth's voice was the telltale tone of truth-stretching that adults used when saying scary things to kids. She patted Isaac's cheek with her free hand. "This isn't something for a boy like you to fret about. You're safe enough here." At that she left.

Typical grown-up, Isaac thought. *Get you all worried, and then tell you not to fret.*

Isaac loved curry and sambal, but he was in a hurry. He quickly fixed himself a sloppy peanut butter sandwich and raced out of the house, not bothering to clean up the mess he had left behind.

Rhyan and Sairah sat side by side at their usual table under the flame tree. Isaac sat down across from them. They stared at him without speaking. His courage nearly failed. He tried to think of something to say to break the ice. "I've been wondering why you are going to school here and not at the international one in Surabaya."

"It was our choice," Sairah said, civilly enough. "We would have had to board there. Surabaya would have been so boring. We enjoy working with our parents on their digs."

Surabaya was to Isaac the world's second most exciting city, the first being Manhattan, where his grandfather Butch Williams lived in a brownstone building. During the Williamses' recent vacation in the States, Isaac had visited his grandpa Butch as much as he could, partly because he enjoyed the stories the former secretary of state loved to tell, but mostly because Manhattan had lots and lots of people to make up for the eerie lack of them in Connecticut.

Around a mouthful of goopy bread, Isaac asked the question that he'd really sat down here to ask. "Is it true what you said about eating grubs and snakes and all that gross stuff?"

Rhyan took a bite of his tuna fish sandwich. "Gross?" he said. "A lot of it is delicious."

"Especially barbecued field rats," Sairah said.

"You're kidding," Isaac said. The way Sairah smiled at him, with those owlish eyes of hers looking quite carnivorous, he thought that perhaps she wasn't. "Hey, Rhyan, I've got something to show you."

"What's that, Isaac?"

"It's a secret."

"Then why do you want to show it to me, if it's a secret?"

"I mean, it's a secret thing that we're not supposed to know about. But if I show you, you have to teach me how to eat grubs."

Rhyan laughed, the first time that Isaac could remember hearing him laugh.

Isaac said, "It's a pretty cool secret."

Rhyan glanced at his sister.

"Let's humor the little genius," she said.

They quickly finished their lunch and slipped over to the tangerine trees, Isaac leading the way. The Strangs followed single file in the humid shade to the wall. Isaac pointed. "Somebody's made a secret gate," he said. He undid the latch and pushed the gate open an inch.

"Cool," Sairah said.

Rhyan moved in front of Isaac and opened the gate wide enough to stick his head through.

Isaac grabbed Rhyan's arm. "We shouldn't go out."

"Who made this?"

"I don't know."

"There's fresh oil and everything. Does your father know about this, Isaac?"

"Nobody knows about this except whoever made it and us."

Rhyan tugged his arm loose and stepped through the hole. His passage created a vortex that tugged Isaac along so that before he knew it, he, too, was beyond the wall and standing in the patch of scrawny bamboo. He wasn't breaking any rules; it just happened—one of those mysterious quantum events where you could find yourself anywhere in the universe. Sairah crowded up behind him.

"Are there any grubs here in the bamboo you could eat?" Isaac asked.

Rhyan, his nose wrinkled against the smell, laughed. "Sautéed in piss? You kidding?"

Isaac persisted. "But if you found one, how would you know if it was poisonous or not?"

Rhyan shrugged. "You bring along a sister to try it."

Sairah swung a fist at her brother.

"No, really," Isaac said.

"First rule, if you're allergic to shrimp or dust or chocolate, never eat any critter raw. Second rule, avoid any critter that is brilliantly colored. That's evolution's warning not to mess with them. Third rule, take a nibble and wait at least six hours to see what happens."

"Could you show me how to cook a grub sometime?"

"Nothing to it. Fire. Grub. Eat. If you're hungry enough, you won't be fussy, I tell you."

They filed back through the gate. Rhyan latched it shut. "I wonder if we should tell somebody about this," he said.

"No," Isaac said.

"Something isn't right about this, though. What if some Muslim fanatic leads his army through here?"

Isaac hadn't thought of that. He should have thought of that, he realized, as the stern visage of the Tuan Guru filled his mind. It was something to worry about, all right. "No," he said after a moment. "Don't tell."

Rhyan studied Isaac. "Okay," he said. "You're the one who sleeps here at night. Not us."

✳

The day's last class was Indonesian culture. The classroom's overhead fans sluggishly stirred the air around twelve wooden desks. These teak desks had been made years ago by Wonobo's finest cabinetmaker, now deceased and his business gone to plywood. They bore the markings inflicted on them by years of doodling students, the hieroglyphs of the American Academy of Wonobo, hearts and arrows and unknown initials, loops and figures. Isaac had left his own mark in the left rear desk, surreptitiously carved only last year, an all-seeing, almond-shaped eye.

When the class had settled in their seats, Mr. Suherman stood behind his desk. He held up a book. "Can anyone tell me what this is?"

"A Bible," Slobert said. "New International Version."

"That's right." He held up another book, with Arabic writing on the front. "Now, can anybody tell me what this is?"

Slobert frowned. The kids looked at one another. Isaac raised his hand. "It's a Qur'an. The Muslim Scriptures."

"That's correct. We Muslims revere the Qur'an as much as you Christians do your Bible."

"Yeah, but the Qur'an is wrong," Slobert said. He pronounced it "Core-ann."

Mr. Suherman arched his eyebrows. "Do you know what is in the Qur'an, Robert? Quote me a verse. Arabic is best, but an English translation is fine."

Slobert shifted uneasily. "Don't know any."

"Don't argue beliefs out of ignorance, Robert, for that surely leads to enmity."

Slobert colored, staring down at his hands.

Mr. Suherman said, "Indonesia is the world's largest Muslim nation. To understand its various cultures, most of which are Islamic, it is necessary to understand Islam, both the religion and the history of it. And the beginning of Islam is actually recorded in the Bible." He handed Slobert the Bible and asked him to read Genesis 16. Slobert reluctantly did so, the story of Sarah and Abraham, how Sarah had borne Abraham no children and so gave her maidservant Hagar to him to build a family. Hagar became pregnant, and Sarah grew jealous, despite the fact that this had been her plan. Hagar was afraid of Sarah, but God reassured her of His will. Hagar bore a son whom Abraham named Ishmael.

"And now Genesis 21," Mr. Suherman said. Slobert dutifully continued, reading aloud the story of how Sarah finally conceived and bore her own son, Isaac, when Abraham was one hundred years old. She then demanded that Abraham send away the slave woman Hagar and her fourteen-year-old son, Ishmael. Abraham did so. When Ishmael was near death in the desert, God heard Hagar's and Ishmael's cries and rescued them, making a promise.

"'Lift the boy up and take him by the hand, for I will make him into a great nation.'" Mr. Suherman repeated the verse that Slobert had read. "And that nation is, through the blessed prophet Muhammad, the great nation of Islam."

"Sheesh," Slobert muttered.

Mr. Suherman ignored him. For the rest of the period he presented the pre-Muhammad history of the Arab peoples, a bunch of idolatrous, feuding tribes.

Isaac listened with intense interest. Ishmael and Isaac. Ismail and Isak. Of course he'd been aware of the coincidence, but that was all it was. Coincidence. But now, jeez, it was like he and Ismail were the Bible story come to life!

Slobert, making a show of being bored, sprawled in his chair. He sneered at Isaac's absorbed attention. "Teacher's pet," he whispered.

When the bell rang, Mr. Suherman said, "Tomorrow, the birth and life of the blessed prophet Muhammad."

Isaac lingered to ask Mr. Suherman if he'd gone to see Ismail's parents. Isaac hadn't had the chance to ask earlier during his Esperanto lesson, for his teacher had been summoned out of the room by Miss Augusta to help her plan next semester's curriculum. Mr. Suherman told Isaac now that not only had he visited the Trisnos, but Ismail was already back home.

Isaac skipped out into the hallway, hugely relieved. Slobert, lounging beyond the doors, said to the others, "Are we in an Islam class now? Maybe Miss Augusta should know about this."

Isaac said, "Hey, Slob, Mr. Suherman is right, we really shouldn't be ignorant. After all, we live in a Muslim country."

"Who's ignorant?" Slobert shot back. "Who's stupid enough to play down by the river at sunset with his good Mussie friend and get all bit up by malarial Mussie mosquitoes? Hey, maybe instead of getting malaria, you'll come down with a good case of Islam."

After school that afternoon Isaac's parents summoned him to the study at the house. His father, face like granite, held out the front page of the day's *Jakarta Post*. Isaac grew slightly faint because on

Richard Lewis

the front page was a photograph of him with his head tilted sideways, chin thrust upward, a scowl on his face, exchanging glares with the square-faced police lieutenant. He glanced away, at the short gray safe in the corner of the room, wishing he were inside it.

His mom said, "I thought we had an understanding, Isaac. Can you tell me what that understanding is?"

Isaac lifted his gaze from the safe and looked out the window, as if trying to find the answer written down somewhere. The light from the lowering afternoon sun, instead of softening and turning golden, was merely coagulating. Despite the air-conditioning, it was clammy hot in the study. The silence lengthened. Isaac puffed out his cheeks, let them deflate, and said, "I have to ask permission before I leave the compound."

"And did you ask permission yesterday?"

"But you and Dad weren't here, you were at the hospital."

"Isaac."

Isaac muttered something.

"What was that?" his mom said.

Isaac muttered more distinctly, "It's sometimes better to ask forgiveness than permission."

Mary bit the sides of her cheeks. Graham took a deep breath and said, "That sort of attitude got your grandfather Williams fired by the president. Remember, you are a PKO boy. Polite, kind, obedient. You made us a promise, and we expected you to stick to it, not break your word. You could have been seriously hurt in that riot."

Isaac studied his dirty sneakers.

Graham said, "The 'O' in 'PKO,' let's work on that."

Mary said, "You are grounded starting immediately; you are not allowed outside the compound by yourself at any time. Is that clear?"

Isaac nodded penitently. A heavier punishment could have been meted out.

From her large canvas tote bag, Mary produced a Reebok shoe box. A pair of red-trimmed Reeboks. "Those old ones are irredeemably filthy," she said.

Isaac's eyes widened. "Wow, cool. Thanks, Mom."

When his parents left, he put on his new Reeboks and trotted around the study, admiring how they molded to his feet.

The clank and sputter of an uncooperative lawn mower filtered through the study's window. Isaac stopped and looked out. Tanto squatted in the shade of the gardening shed at the far corner of the compound, trying to start the machine.

Isaac raced to the front door of the house, stood there for several seconds working up his courage, and then opened the door and strolled with hands in his pockets toward the shed. He squatted in front of Tanto, watching him disassemble the carburetor with practiced ease. Tanto ignored his audience. An unfiltered clove cigarette popped and crackled in his mouth. Smoke twirled up around his broad nose and over the thick protruding ridges of his eyebrows. The ash on the cigarette grew longer. He finally took a deep drag that put enough weight on the ash to break it. He let the smoke dribble out of his mouth and nose as he fastened his gaze on Isaac, the pupils of his eyes as flat and impenetrable as lead disks. "Why have you been staring at me?" He spoke in Javanese.

"I haven't been staring at you," Isaac said. "I've been watching you fix the mower."

"This is interesting, is it? Maybe you want to be a mechanic when you grow up."

"Mas Tanto, can I ask you something?"

Tanto did not answer. He took another drag.

Isaac said, "I've been seeing pictures of an old man in a white turban around town. His name is Tuan Guru Haji Abdullah Abubakar. Do you know anything about him?"

Tanto put the burning cigarette butt underneath his bare right heel and squished. "His father was Bugis, and his mother Madurese, but he is the slave of Allah."

Isaac's heart turned into a vacuum, sucking all blood from his limbs. The Bugis had long been feared as bloodthirsty pirates. During the colonial era, many a Western mother had warned her naughty child, "Stop that, or the Bugis man will get you."

Tanto said, in Indonesian, as though reciting a memorized passage, "Soon we will see the day when justice reigns in this unjust land, when the evil corrupters who steal from the poor to fatten their purses finally face the wrath of Allah, when infidels who mock the name of Allah and the Blessed Prophet meet their fate." Memorized or not, Tanto sounded as though he meant it.

The empty feeling in Isaac's chest expanded into his throat, pressing against his vocal cords. He coughed, clearing his throat so that he could ask, in a small voice, "Is the Tuan Guru Haji going to kill all the infidels?"

Tanto's eyebrows rose to meet the flat trim of his crew cut.

"The Tuan Guru is an honorable man, with the honor of a true slave of Allah. Why do you ask this question?"

This wasn't, Isaac noted, an answer. "Because that is what somebody told me," he said in a smaller voice yet.

"That woman who works for you." Tanto spat on the ground. "She is nothing, she has turned away from Allah, and He will answer her." He ran his tongue around his teeth and then slapped his knee as he laughed. "And you believe this, from an apostate worm lower than a *kafir*? You are afraid that because you are a kafir the Tuan Guru will kill you?"

Well, yes, Isaac thought, but he said nothing.

"*Hai,* little Isak, it is true that you are an infidel, but it is also true that not everyone can be a Muslim. In a world that is not paradise, there must be at least a handful of infidels allowed to exist. Hmm?" He patted Isaac on the back, his calloused hands rough against Isaac's neck. A small smile played across his lips and then disappeared. "But let me tell you, little Isak, that there are good infidels and bad infidels. Which are you?"

"What's a good infidel?"

"A good infidel is one who accepts Islamic rule and pays the proper taxes."

"And a bad infidel?"

"An infidel who deliberately tries to poison Islam, who tries to turn Muslims from the straight path. Against these infidels the Tuan Guru Haji has declared jihad."

"So is he going to kill all the bad infidels? How will he know the difference?"

"*Ma sha'allah!* Why do you speak of killing? There are many ways of jihad. I have said, the Tuan Guru Haji is an honorable man." Tanto smiled again. "He has a human side, you know; he is a great fan of the bull races and even has a small stable of his own racing bulls. He races them, but he doesn't gamble, because gambling is a sin. Now, I'm tired of talking and I have this bastard of a machine to bring to life."

"Thank you, Mas Tanto."

Tanto did not reply. He lowered his head to the mower and began inspecting the fuel lines.

Isaac returned to the school library to start his book report on *The Lord of the Flies*. The room was empty except for Miss Jane, the new American teacher from Georgia. Despite her contact lenses, she was the only person Isaac knew who could trip over smoke. Isaac spread the *Jakarta Post* on a table. On the third page was a smaller picture of him on stage, showing him in a polished Javanese dancer's pose, which actually sort of pleased him. Fortunately, the pretty bencong didn't look like a bencong at all. He read the article about the Nahdlatul Umat Islam, a new and somewhat secretive Muslim organization, whose "enigmatic leader refuses all requests for interviews." The Nahdlatul Umat Islam, the article said, was an unusual exception to the constant, virulently anti-American militant stance of most of the fundamentalist Indonesian Islamic groups in that it was mainly concerned with internal rather than external politics, with its principal aim of establishing *shariah* law within the country. An unnamed State

Department official was quoted as saying that, unlike several of the other groups, there was no evidence that the Nahdlatul Umat Islam had any links with any Middle Eastern terrorist organizations.

Is that so? Imam Ali sure sounded anti-American enough to me.

From behind him, Miss Jane said, "How does it feel to be famous?"

Isaac returned the paper to its place. "I'm not sure I like the idea of a whole bunch of people I don't know reading about me."

"Tomorrow they'll forget all about you."

"Hope you're right."

He turned on the computer at his usual stall and opened the word processing program to start writing his book report. He thought for a minute before typing, *It is said that the beast of the book is the evil within man, but that's not entirely correct. There are beasts without as well . . .*

His fingers slowed. The back of his hair prickled. He sensed a presence in the dim shadows of the book stacks. "Miss Jane?" he said, turning around. But she wasn't there.

A figure leaped out from behind a stack. "Arrrrrggghhhh!"

Isaac yelped, jumping backward.

Slobert roared with laughter, his jowls quivering. "That was great! Should have seen your face."

"Very funny," Isaac said.

"Hey, how about dancing for us sometime?" Slobert struck a silly pose.

"Very, very funny."

"Maybe when you grow up, you're gonna be one of those

queer ballet dancers or something. A Mussie queer ballet dancer."

"They're called Muslims."

"Feeling any malaria yet?"

Isaac saved his work and shut down the computer. "Get real, Slobert."

Slobert's face reddened. He clenched his thick fists and shouted, "I *am* real. You're the one who's not real, slumming around with that Mussie boy instead of us American guys, too smart for us, nose-in-the-air teacher's pet." He snorted. "And a mama's boy, too."

Isaac jumped to his feet and headed for the door. *Stupid Slobert, a nothing beast of a boy.*

But there were greater beasts, of that Isaac was sure.

Chapter Four

ON TUESDAY MORNINGS, Isaac's special project was to continue with last year's assignment of helping in the hospital laboratory. Although he wasn't anything more than a glorified dish washer, it was still an important job, making sure all of the dirty labware was meticulously sterilized and put away spotless. The best thing about the assignment, though, was that the hospital's morgue was next door to the lab. Isaac wasn't morbid or anything, but he was a curious boy, and Mas Gatot, the morgue attendant, had occasionally let him have peeks at corpses. The thing that struck Isaac was how utterly still they were—forget this nonsense about dead people looking as though they were asleep. They looked, well, dead.

This Tuesday, since it was Spiritual Emphasis Week, Isaac went to the lab earlier than usual. After washing the beakers, he crept around the gray metal cabinet and out a door in the back of the lab. The hospital corridor beyond was empty. To Isaac's left was a cargo elevator and to his right, at the corridor's farthest end, a portcullis gate.

The gate was open. Beyond, in a sparkling patch of garden, rosebushes in seemingly perpetual bloom triumphed against the outdoor heat, casting off a powerful scent. Mas Gatot was curved over one of the bushes, his full attention taken up by a bud. He was a Muslim whom other Muslims considered a mystic.

Mas Gatot looked up at Isaac's approach. Isaac could not recall a time when he had not known the morgue attendant. Mas Gatot was a part of his life like the flame tree was, old but never aging. He had pinched cheeks and oversized dentures that looked suspiciously like those ready-made choppers available at Mr. Muhammad Ali's dental office. They gave his face a puckered expression.

"Hi, Mas Gatot," Isaac said. "What do you have today?"

"A new hybrid," Mas Gatot said, smiling around his big teeth. The size of his dentures seemed to promise thick, moist lisping, but his speech was always dry and precise.

"I mean—"

Mas Gatot chuckled. "I know what you mean. One: a man gored by a bull, stomach ripped open."

"*Aiyah,*" Isaac groaned.

"And two," Mas Gatot said, "a beheaded man, with his feet and arms cut off for good measure. A black magician, I am told. My assistant is in the process of sewing him together so I can say the prayers for the dead."

Isaac gaped. "A *beheaded* man?"

Mas Gatot sighed, shaking his head. "He was probably innocent. What is our world coming to?"

Isaac wasn't listening. He was already pushing through the morgue's heavy ironwood doors, metal sheeted across the middle for slamming gurneys.

The decapitated torso, its genitals covered with a cloth, lay on a stainless-steel autopsy table in the middle of the room. To Isaac's continual disappointment, autopsies were rarely done, since Muslims considered them to be desecration. Mas Gatot used the table to ritually wash Muslim bodies prior to burial. Mas Gatot's nephew, who resembled his uncle except that he was younger with a smaller set of natural teeth, was attaching the black magician's right hand, stitching rapidly, digging deep with the large needle, making tight loops with the heavy nylon. The head was a lump underneath another cloth, placed just above the severed neck.

A gurney with a sheet-covered form was shoved up against the refrigeration units. Despite the heavy-duty fan in the ceiling that sucked air out of the room and the liberal use of disinfectant, there always lingered the sour green smell of death and decay. On the right-hand wall hung a blackboard. Two pieces of chalk lay in the board's tray, rusty brown on their fat end, the color coming from bloody hands.

The assistant hummed a dangdut song, the one the bencongs had sung. Isaac frowned at him, wondering if he'd been at the square on Sunday. Mas Gatot's nephew had been working here for a few months, without official hospital wages. Isaac still didn't know his name. The assistant, accustomed to Isaac's presence, ignored him. He briefly admired his handiwork on the hand before plucking the cloth off the severed head.

Isaac stepped back with a gasp. Adi the tofu maker stared lifelessly at him through half-opened eyes. Isaac started to slump.

Mas Gatot caught him and sat him down in the single chair underneath the blackboard.

"Deep breaths, take deep breaths," he said. Isaac slowly recovered. Mas Gatot said, "You've seen lots of dead bodies. I guess this man you knew."

"Adi the tofu maker. Lives on Ismail's street."

"It's always harder when you know the person," Mas Gatot said sympathetically. They sat there until his nephew had the head sewn back on. "Well, the Nahdlatul Umat Islam people took him apart, and now he's together again." Mas Gatot stood at the foot of the table and closed his eyes, lifting hands with palms upright. He intoned in Arabic words that Isaac knew by heart from hearing so often, "In the name of Allah. To Allah we belong, and to Him is our return."

His nephew handed him latex gloves, which he put on. He took the hose and washed the body. Next, he took three dazzling white cotton cloths from the supply cabinet and began wrapping the body. When he was finished, the body looked like a mummy packaged in a white candy twist. He turned this mummy over on its right side and stood once more at the foot of the table. He glanced at Isaac, who got up from the chair and stood behind Mas Gatot out of respect. Mas Gatot lifted his head, closed his eyes, and cried out in a loud voice, *"Allahu akbar!"* His lips moved in a silent and private prayer. He repeated the cry and his private prayer three times. He smiled at Isaac and said, *"As-salamu alaikum wa rahmat ullahi."* The peace and mercy of Allah be upon you.

Isaac replied solemnly, *"Alaikum as-salam."*

Mas Gatot and his nephew transferred Adi's sheeted corpse to an empty gurney. They hoisted the sheeted corpse from the other gurney onto the stainless-steel table. The nephew said he was stepping out for a smoke.

Mas Gatot pulled off the sheet. Isaac stared down at a dark-skinned body, still clothed in bloodied shirt and shorts, with the curly black hair and sharp features of an eastern islander.

"This one was a Christian," Mas Gatot said.

"How do you know?" Isaac asked.

Mas Gatot lifted up a shirtsleeve, exposing the bicep's tattoo of a cross intertwined with the words *Yesus Kristus*. Isaac refrained from mentioning the fine theological point that the name of Jesus tattooed on the flesh does not save the soul.

Mas Gatot used scissors to cut off the shirt, revealing a gory tear in the abdomen. He shoved a pair of long narrow forceps into the wound and poked around. He answered Isaac's slightly horrified and unasked question. "Standard procedure. Always check holes. You never know, you might find a broken-off knife blade or a live swamp eel. The other year in Surabaya a corpse was booby-trapped with a grenade. Well, nothing in this one."

When he was done washing the body, he said, "Would you say a prayer for this Christian, young Isak?"

The unexpected request startled Isaac. "Me? But I'm not a pastor or an elder or anything, I'm only a kid."

Mas Gatot looked surprised. "Christian children are not allowed to pray for the dead?"

"No, we're allowed . . . ," Isaac said, and was quiet for a moment, before he added, "and so I will."

Richard Lewis

He clasped his hands at his waist, closed his eyes, and prayed in English, "Dear God, I don't know who this is, but if he is a believer, then welcome him to heaven; and if he is not, then . . .". Here Isaac faltered, because if the dead man hadn't been a Christian, then his soul was destined for only one other place. He ended with the phrase he had heard pastors use before, realizing for the first time how diplomatic it was: "And if he is not, then have mercy on his soul. Amen."

Mas Gatot said, "I need to smell my roses."

Isaac went out into the tiny rose garden with him and had a cleansing whiff himself. They sat down on the wooden bench there. Isaac said, "I wonder if Adi was alive when they beheaded him."

Mas Gatot said, "Oh, yes" with such certainty that Isaac started. "You saw it?"

"No, no, I didn't see it. There are ways to tell. I guess the hands and feet were cut off afterward, though." Mas Gatot rubbed his nose.

Isaac shuffled his new Reeboks on the ground and then asked, "Do you think the Nahdlatul Umat Islam is going to behead any more people?"

Mas Gatot smiled and said, "Such as hybrid little boys who are neither American nor Javanese? Don't you worry about them. You are sweet-smelling unto Allah. As the Holy Qur'an says, Almighty Allah made men into different tribes so that we would learn how to cooperate, instead of how to fight and kill one another."

A sense of reassurance stole into Isaac's heart, like a fresh sun rising into a clear sky. *Ismail is okay, and what I'm going to tell him is that God made us different so that we can be friends. And then we'll go to the mall and buy a couple of those Magnum chocolate-covered ice-cream bars.*

Once more he used the secret gate. He had to. This wasn't a matter of breaking rules. It was a matter of moral principle, which far outweighed any promises he might have made to his parents.

He ran across the street and down Hayam Wuruk Avenue, dodging pedestrians, afraid that at any moment he would feel a heavy hand fall upon his shoulder and hear a stern voice ordering him to march straight to his father's office.

None of those hands did fall, but another one snaked out from the fruit shop entrance and grabbed him, swinging him around to a stop. Udin, the creep who used to work at Ah Kiat's store until he'd been fired the previous week. Now all he did was hang out at the mosque. He said, "Isak, what's the rush?"

"Let me go," Isaac said, trying to pull away.

Behind Udin the new turbaned proprietor was grinning. The poster of the Tuan Guru observed all. An old woman in long dress and white scarf was in the shop, her back turned to Isaac, counting her change from a purchase of oranges. She turned around at the commotion. It was Ibu Hajjah Wida, who snapped at Udin, "Let the boy go."

Udin did. "Just having some fun," he said.

Isaac didn't wait to hear what else Ibu Hajjah Wida had to say. He sped up again, running past the legless beggar at the bus station's security post. Then, ten steps beyond, what Mas Gatot had said slammed down on his brain and put the brakes on his feet. If God made different tribes so people would learn to cooperate, then God allowed beggars to exist so people would learn charity.

Reluctantly, thinking of the ice cream he was now forgoing, he put his two 5,000-rupiah notes in the cup.

The legless beggar stirred. "Water," he whispered, a cracked tongue flickering out of parched lips. He extended a trembling hand. "Water."

Isaac stared. The poor fellow was literally dying of thirst. Isaac grabbed the rupiah notes and ran back to the fruit shop. Ibu Hajjah Wida was not there, but neither was Udin. He marched in and told the surprised proprietor he'd like as many bottles of the Aqua mineral water there on the shelf as 10,000 rupiah would buy.

The proprietor, recovering from his surprise, laughed. "I don't sell anything to Americans, and I don't sell anything to Christians. And as for American Christians—" He drew a line across his throat.

Isaac backed up a step, but he persisted. "It's not for me. It's for the legless beggar down the way; he's dying of thirst."

The proprietor said, "Get out of here."

"But he's a Muslim!"

The proprietor's face darkened menacingly. "Don't you tell me of Muslims. If it is Allah Almighty's will for him to die of thirst, he will die of thirst. Now go!"

Isaac spluttered, "You're mean and stupid and . . . and . . . not even a Javanese!"

The man cried out in rage. From behind the counter, he picked up a machete and smashed the flip-top counter open to rush at Isaac, who flew out of the shop on wings of fright. He dashed up the sidewalk toward the hospital, looking over his shoulder. The proprietor stood in front of the shop, brandishing the machete.

Isaac kept running until he reached Ah Kiat's store, where he bought three large bottles of Aqua. He returned to the beggar, using the other side of the road to pass in front of the fruit shop. Isaac started to open one of the bottles, but the beggar grabbed it out of his hand. He couldn't get his shaky fingers to open the plastic pull tab of the bottle cap. Isaac tried to take the bottle to open it for him, but the beggar snarled at him, whipping the bottle away, holding it close to his body. He put the cap in his mouth and bit it off. He guzzled the water, which gurgled down his throat. When half of the bottle was gone, the beggar paused, groaning, his eyes closed in rapture.

Isaac put down the other bottles and left. He looked up at the murky sky and thought he glimpsed the blue of heaven, and a cool refreshing breeze seemed to blow upon his sweaty skin.

Ismail went to school only in the mornings. He'd be home by now. At the Trisno house men in sarongs and black *peci* caps thronged the living room and veranda. What was going on? Isaac opened the latch of the gate without announcing himself, as he usually did, but this time his entry was more cautious. From within the house, the television blared. Isaac caught a glimpse on the screen of the impassioned orator, a tall Arabic man wearing a turban and

Richard Lewis

robe. He had a crooked face and a long beard. The men on the veranda craned their necks to see. At places they cheered, yelling, "*Hidup* Osama! *Hantam* Amerika!"

One man spotted Isaac, and his excited face instantly hardened, eyes as cold as frozen coal. He said something, and the others turned around to stare at Isaac. Somebody muted the television. The silence and the collective chill of their gaze halted Isaac, as though an invisible avalanche of hostility had entombed him.

The men by the door made way for Ismail's father. Bapak Trisno should have been at work. His expression was no warmer than the others'. Isaac's heart plummeted into his shoes, but he still bowed and said, "*Al-salamu alaikum.*"

Bapak Trisno did not make the customary reply of *alaikum as-salam.* Isaac wanted to flee. He forced himself to say, "I came to see Ismail."

Bapak Trisno still made no response. His face was unyielding. Little butterfly wings of panic began to flutter in Isaac's stomach. Had Lieutenant Nugroho lied? Had Ismail disappeared while in police custody? He said, his words running together with nervousness, "I saw Ismail on Sunday, the police had him, and I came down here because I wanted to see if Ismail was okay."

Bapak Trisno stood to the side, motioning someone forward. Into view stepped Ismail, a smaller version of his father, wearing an identically patterned sarong, a black peci, and his Tuan Guru T-shirt, laundered of its Sunday blood.

Isaac felt a smile bubble up onto his face, which withered as it dawned on him that Ismail didn't look happy to see him. His father bent and whispered into his son's ear, nudging him on the back. Ismail stiffly walked down the porch steps and past Isaac without a word. He opened the gate and stood to the side, his hand on the latch. It was an unmistakable order for Isaac to leave.

Isaac walked toward him. "Ismail?" he said softly. "Ismail, what's going on? Did something happen at the police station?"

"No."

"So what's wrong? I know I made a promise to tell your parents, but I couldn't get away to see them. I really tried, truly I did." Isaac was speaking as fast as he could, aware of the heavy silence on the porch behind him.

Ismail cut him off. "My father was fired from the sugar mill yesterday, along with half the workforce. Without warning. Against the law. The big bosses think they are above the law, but they are wrong. They'll see." He looked at Isaac, really looked at Isaac, as if seeing Isaac for the first time in all the years they had known each other. Isaac became conscious of himself—not of his big bones or blond hair or blue eyes, but of the expensive and well-tailored school clothes he was wearing, which were not the cheap clothes he wore out to play. For a second Ismail's gaze lingered with naked longing on Isaac's new Reeboks.

Ismail switched from intimate Javanese to formal Indonesian. "You American bulés will see too. Now it is best that you leave us, please."

Isaac, bewildered, walked out the gate. This situation was fraught with complexities beyond his depth, but he seized on the one thing that was solid enough to anchor his thoughts on. He turned around. "Are we still friends?" he asked, in Indonesian.

"Maybe, maybe later," Ismail said, softening. He switched to Javanese to say, "Please, Isak, don't come around here." A pause, then a lifting of brow. "Unless you want to become a Muslim. If you become a Muslim, we could be good friends all the time."

Ismail was serious. He said this as if it were an obvious solution to a problem. "That's not possible," Isaac said. "You know I'm a Christian."

"No, it's easy. All you have to do is say the *shahadah* in front of two Muslims, and then you are a Muslim yourself." Ismail took a breath. *"Ashhadu anna la illaha illa allah wa ashhadu anna muhammadan rasul allah,"* he intoned, the lilt of prayer creeping into his voice. "Can you say that, Isak? It's easy." His eyes lit up with the familiar Ismail current. "You can say it right now, my father and another man can be witnesses, and then we can be best friends again. Right away. Right now."

"Ismail—"

"Look, you don't have to be a *strict* Muslim," Ismail whispered furtively. "You don't have to tell your parents or anything. You can even still go to church and all that. Please, Isak?"

And God help him, for a moment Isaac was tempted. After all, he couldn't lose his best friend. He simply couldn't. Wouldn't God value true friendship over a faked confession of faith? How could anyone lose his salvation over that?

Ismail added, "Of course, I think you'd have to be circumcised by a cleric, but that's probably the only ritual you'd have to observe."

Perhaps that was what brought Isaac to his senses. "I can't, Ismail. I wish I could, I really do, but I can't." The words were wrenched out of him like teeth being pulled without an anesthetic.

Pain flared through Ismail's eager eyes, and then they dulled. "Better you go, then," he said, reverting to Indonesian. "And better you don't come back." He shut the gate and turned around and walked back to the house without another glance.

The men on the veranda were still coldly watching Isaac. He waited for Ismail to turn around, to give him one last sign of friendship, but Ismail disappeared into the house.

Isaac wheeled and ran. He was stunned into a blank, emotionless state, not feeling a thing, knowing only that he had now to get back to the compound without getting caught. He had turned the corner at the Friendship Store when, down the street, he noticed that the tips of the bamboo in front of the secret gate were quivering and shaking. Out of the bamboo popped his father, in his white clinic coat, looking around him with the confusion of someone who has found himself in another universe.

Just then, a group of hospital visitors descended from a bemo. Isaac used them as cover to pass through the hospital gates.

A few moments later he slinked around his house. A somber-looking group of men and one boy—Graham Williams; the hospital business manager, Mr. Ali; the chief of security, Mr. Theophilus; and Rhyan Strang—were gathered by the wall, watching as a work crew finished chopping down the hibiscus hedge to more clearly reveal the secret gate.

Two security guards, Frengky and Petrus, burly Ambonese

with the size and carriage of heavyweight boxers, stood with Tanto between them as though he were a felon. His red-veined eyes were the only ones to notice Isaac.

Graham Williams said grimly, "A wall is only as secure as its weakest gate. Thank you, Rhyan. You'd best head to school now."

"Yes, sir," Rhyan said.

Isaac waited for Rhyan on the school side of the hedge. "You told," he said as soon as Rhyan came through the wicket gate. Isaac's eyes pricked. This minor betrayal penetrated his numbness over Ismail's greater one. "You said you wouldn't and you told."

"This isn't some Peter Pan fairy tale with enchanted gates for kids to play with," Rhyan said. "This is serious business. Your dad had to know and right away. Period. End of fairy tale. I didn't tell him it was you who showed me, though." He sped up on his long teenage legs, leaving Isaac behind.

A chain saw began to buzz with an earsplitting whine, startling Isaac. He looked up. Standing on a branch up in the flame tree was a worker in overalls, wearing earmuffs and a safety belt, holding the chain saw. He put the whirring blade to the lowest branch over the wall. Wood chips began to fly.

"No!" Isaac screamed, and kept screaming as he ran for the tree. He scampered up the trunk and swung on the branch where the oblivious worker stood, chain saw biting deep into the wood in front of him. Isaac grabbed the man's safety rope. Tugged off balance, the worker fell from the branch with a cry, but the harness jerked him to a safe stop above the ground. The jar dislodged his earmuffs. The chain saw automatically cut off, clattering to the ground.

Isaac was still shouting in a mixed-up jumble of English, Indonesian, and Javanese, screaming at the worker not to touch the tree, not to dare touch the tree. Blood flooded back into the worker's pale brown face, turning his skin dark chocolate. He yelled back at Isaac as he dangled on the rope, cursing him in an unknown dialect.

Mr. Theophilus and Graham Williams raced to the tree. "What happened, what happened?" Graham said to Isaac, his upturned face an oval of consternation.

"He was cutting the tree down," Isaac said, trembling. He held tightly to the trunk to keep from falling. "He was cutting the tree down!"

The worker began to climb back up the rope, hand over hand. "Your fool son pushed me off the branch," he said to Graham. "He could have killed me."

Graham exclaimed, "Isaac, for heaven's sake. Isaac, get down here, please."

Isaac did so, not to obey his father, but to get to the chain saw and stomp all over it, break it, smash it. His heart banged away in his chest, feeling as if it were about to break loose. His dad grabbed him. "What the heck's the matter?"

"He was cutting down the tree," Isaac babbled.

The worker hauled himself up to the branch. Mr. Theophilus picked up the chain saw and handed it to him. Isaac lunged. His father clamped his hands down tight and said, "Isaac, he's *not* cutting down the tree. He's only trimming those branches over the wall. So nobody can use them to climb over. Are you listening? Do you hear me? What the heck is the matter with you? If you don't calm down right now, I'm taking you to the ER."

Isaac stopped struggling, aware of faces around the auditorium window, watching the commotion. The little kids were practicing a play. To his utter embarrassment, he began to sob. His dad knelt and pulled him to his chest, patting the back of his head, saying, "Hush now, hush."

Isaac struggled and gulped and finally got his weeping under control. He unresistingly let his father lead him by the hand back to their house and sit him down on the living-room sofa. "Now, what's the matter?"

Isaac sniffled and rubbed his nose. "Nothing."

"Nothing my ass." His dad made an intercom call. A minute later Mary Williams swept through the front door.

"What's happened?" she asked.

Graham raised his hands. "I don't know. Isaac threw this fit." He briefly told her what had happened, clearly perplexed and worried. "The guy was only cutting the branches. That's all, only cutting branches, and Isaac went crazy. He won't talk to me."

Mary sat down beside Isaac and put her arm around him. "You want to tell me about it?"

Isaac, staring at his new Reeboks, now dirty from the cemetery and scruffed a bit from scrambling up the flame tree, shook his head. "No."

She studied him. She said, "It's not about the flame tree at all, is it?"

She waited for an answer. He took a deep, quavering breath and shook his head. "No."

"It might help to talk about it."

"I can't . . . it's . . . I'll be all right."

"You certainly weren't all right a few minutes ago," Graham said.

"I feel like such a stupid idiot."

Mary squeezed his shoulders. "Honey—"

"There's nothing for you to worry about. Honest." He took another, stronger breath and stood. "I'm way late for class."

After school Isaac climbed the tree to his perch. Even though these branches had not been harmed, the mutilation below made him feel uncomfortably exposed. He looked out of the corner of his eye at the Al-Furqon Mosque across from the compound. To his relief, Imam Ali was not in sight.

What had the gate been there for? Nobody would know now what Tanto had been planning. The word had already gotten out that Mr. Ali, the business manager, had fired him.

A great yellow haze rose from the earth, the vapory heaves of a land being tortured under an oven sky. The edges of rooftops a mere hundred yards away were smudged and blurred.

Isaac suddenly realized how ominous the whole idea of a secret gate in the wall really was. He really should have told his dad about it straightaway, instead of seeking reassurance from Tanto that a sour-faced old Muslim cleric in a turban wasn't going to go around beheading infidels. How stupid he'd been;

when Tanto had patted him on the back, right there where his neck joined his shoulders, he'd probably been calculating the size of blade needed, the force of the strike that would be required.

Below and across the street Imam Ali stepped out of the mosque's prayer room. He slipped into his sandals, lifting the hem of his dun-colored robe to do so. He crossed the dusty yard and stood on the sidewalk, looking toward the hospital gates. He stared at them for a long time, taking in the workers placing barbed wire on top of the compound's wall, before sweeping his gaze along the wall to the bamboo stand. There his attention lingered, before moving on the few yards to the flame tree. His gaze rose along the stumps of the cut branches and higher yet until he was looking straight at Isaac. Under his beaked nose his thin lips spread into a curve sharp as a scimitar's blade. He put his hands together in front of his chest and bowed in a salaam. He straightened, now smiling fully, as though his Lord had granted him a pleasing vision of Isaac's fate. He strolled down the street toward the Friendship Store.

Isaac watched him until he turned the corner. He relaxed for a second, then stiffened again, sensing something stir beyond his left peripheral vision. He turned his head. A shriek stuck in his clogged throat. A large crow was perched on a nearby branch, close enough that Isaac could see the individual feathers of its glossy, folded wings. The crow stared without fear at Isaac, contemplating his blue eyes as though they were trophies to be plucked. Isaac shouted again and flapped his left arm. The bird at once flew away above his head, the powerful beat of its wings causing a draft of air that stirred his hair.

During Spiritual Emphasis Week, Tuesday evening was Singspiration night, a favorite service of the local Christians. The church was packed, all seats taken. Even Ruth and her son, Jon, were present, Jon still looking sluggish from the flu. He had on a JCPenny shirt that Isaac had outgrown two years ago. Ruth wore her finest blue dress, the one with the beads, which glittered with reflected light. She had on a thick gold necklace Isaac hadn't seen before and new dangling earrings that she touched from time to time.

Isaac sat on a spare stool in the engineering balcony, where Herdi, the technician, sometimes allowed him to sit during mid-week services. His mother strode into view below him, with two guests, May and her daughter, Meimei, from the Hai Shin restaurant. They sat down in the pew that Graham had reserved for them.

From up here, Isaac could see every head in the main sanctuary, although not the overflow crowd in the back. There were at least three hundred people present. For Wonobo this was an extraordinary turnout. Isaac figured that every Christian in the area was in attendance tonight.

The younger dorm children were grouped in one block behind the Williamses, with dorm parents Aunt Janice and Uncle Jimmy keeping an eye on them. The older dorm kids sat together in their own group halfway down the right side of the church.

There was no formal opening. The song leader moved along from chorus to chorus without a break, as Miss Jane adeptly kept up on the organ, and soon all the congregation was loudly singing along. The Batak lawyer sang the loudest.

But even a Singspiration needs a short homily. The song leader nodded his head at Reverend Biggs, sitting in the front row. He rose and made his way to the pulpit, Pastor Cornelius following behind him to do the translation into Indonesian of Reverend Biggs's talk. Both wore informal short-sleeved batik shirts. The congregation quieted to expectant silence.

Reverend Biggs did not speak immediately, swinging his gaze across the congregation. The hush deepened.

Reverend Biggs opened his mouth and thundered, "Who are you?"

The congregation shifted in startled surprise. But the reverend was not talking to them—he was addressing somebody in the back of the church whom Isaac couldn't see. A lot of somebodies, with harsh male voices, making quite a commotion, accompanied by gasps and rapid scraping of chairs as though people were trying to get out of the way.

Heads in the congregation whipped around. More gasps of shock bubbled up to the ceiling fans.

Ruth sounded the loudest and most panicked alarm. Her face blanched. Her trembling hands flew to her neck to take off her necklace.

Too late.

Tanto darted into view below Isaac and grabbed her forearm.

He carried a scythe, the tip of which hovered at her neck. He was dressed in a sarong, a Nahdlatul Umat Islam T-shirt, and a black peci cap.

Other men streamed down the aisles. They were all dressed like Tanto. They carried iron bars, wooden clubs, and scythes. The worshippers on the aisle ends of the pews shrank inward, away from the armed intruders.

Ruth shrilled, "No, this is mine. I worked hard for this—"

Tanto shouted, "Shut up, you apostate bitch." He and Ruth fought over her jewelry. She was fierce and sharp-clawed in her effort to keep her gold, but Tanto overpowered her and shoved her down onto the pew. He yanked the chain off her neck and was no more careful with the earrings. Isaac noticed a drip of blood on her left lobe.

"You thief!" Ruth shrieked. "You pig!"

Tanto knocked her on the head with the scythe's handle. "I should use the other end and slit your throat," he said. "One day I will. Your day of death will come, you apostate dog."

Ruth began weeping. "My gold, my gold, give me back my gold."

Except for Ruth's sobbing, the congregation had fallen into a stunned, disbelieving silence. Reverend Biggs found his voice. He roared again, "In the name of Lord God Almighty, who are you to disturb the gathering of His people?"

Pastor Cornelius leaned forward to the microphone and asked more quietly in Indonesian, "Who are you? What is the meaning of this?"

Tanto jumped up onto the podium and shouted in Indonesian into the pastor's face, "Who are we? We are the Muslims, the rightful citizens of Wonobo." He turned and said to the congregation, "We are not rioters. We are not looters. We are not arsonists. We are not murderers. We are the citizens of Wonobo. And we are hungry, our land stolen from us, the sweat of our labor buying us nothing except cassava roots to eat." He pointed, gesturing from left to right. "You are not Muslims. You have no right to live in the territory that belongs to Allah's people. You deserve death by the sword, but Allah is merciful. You can live here if you pay *jizyah,* the tax of the infidels, to the Tuan Guru. This is why we are here. We are here to collect the tax that is long overdue."

Isaac scanned each intruder's face and blew relieved air when he did not see Imam Ali. He did see scruffy Udin lurking in the back.

"This is a holy sanctuary," Reverend Biggs said in English, striding forward toward Tanto. "You are desecrating the house of the Lord."

Tanto raised his scythe. Cornelius rushed forward and stepped between the two men. He whispered urgently to Reverend Biggs. The reverend closed his eyes and began to pray, his lips moving.

Tanto said, "We are not here to hurt anyone, but we will if you resist. We are here to collect the tax."

The men in the aisles held open black plastic garbage bags. The Batak lawyer shot to his feet. "This is illegal! This is extortion! You have a greater duty to Allah to obey the laws of this country and—"

One of the intruders jabbed the sharpened end of his wooden stave into the lawyer's neck. He used the tip to guide the man back down into his seat.

Meimei cowered between Mary Williams and her mother. Mary had a protective arm over the girl. The other Chinese Christians, knowing that if anyone were to be singled out for harsh treatment it would be one of them, were deathly silent and pallid.

Udin stepped closer to Mary Williams's pew and leered at Meimei. Mary seemed to swell. She rose off the pew, her eyes ablaze in such aroused warning that Udin backed off.

From behind Isaac came the *click-click-click* of a rotary phone being dialed. He had forgotten about the telephone up here. Herdi whispered for the police.

Graham Williams stood up and addressed Tanto in level, measured words. "And how will this tax you propose to collect be spent? How will it be accounted for?"

"Shut up," Tanto said.

Gideon Wira not only bounced to his feet, but stepped out into the aisle, his round face red with anger. "How dare you talk to Dr. Williams like that! Don't you know what he and the hospital physicians and staff have done for you? Don't you realize the sacrifices they have made for the poor and needy of Wonobo and all of this province? Isn't that more than enough tax? In whose name do you speak, anyway? You do not represent Wonobo, we are as much citizens of Wonobo as you!"

A murmur rose from members of the congregation. Tanto

reacted instantly. "You Chinese *kafir*," he said, jumping down and striding toward Gideon. "The Tuan Guru has no place in his kingdom for usurers of shaitan such as you." He swung his scythe by the handle, the blade slicing horizontally through the air.

Isaac, watching with wide mouth and even wider eyes from the narrow balcony, thought that he was going to witness a decapitation right here in the house of the Lord. Gideon's head would topple off his body, a great gout of blood spraying from his neck in all directions as the torso stumbled about, hands jerking in lifeless motion.

Gideon calmly held up a hand, and the metal blade of Tanto's scythe stopped and quivered in the air. Gideon raised his voice and paraphrased Jesus' words in his own unique style: "Don't keep yourself treasures on earth, worthless rust and thieves to steal them, but put them in heaven, safe they are there, where your treasure is where your heart is."

Then he began singing.

He sang loud and clear the lyrics of a familiar hymn: "Rejoice in the Lord always." As he sang he tugged off his gold Rolex and pulled out his wallet, which he handed over to Tanto, who took them with surprise, almost suspicion. Gideon continued to sing. "Rejoice in the Lord always, and again I say rejoice."

The raiders looked at one another bemusedly, some even nervously.

Gideon sang even more enthusiastically, pumping his arms like a choir director. His wife, Ruby, took off her watch, earrings, and necklace and donated them to Tanto as well.

The Batak lawyer took up the chorus, and then several others joined in. Within moments, the whole church was singing and rejoicing and gladly handing over their watches, their jewelry, their purses and wallets. The rafters of the church vibrated with the booming voices. "Rejoice! Rejoice! And again I say rejoice."

The gold wedding bands of all the married congregants were freely given. The bag man had gotten to the schoolkids, and they were behaving as if this were a lark, singing songs to the Lord and giving alms to the poor. Dave Duizen stripped off his round black sports Seiko and told the guy, who probably had never gone swimming in his life, "Waterproof down to a thousand meters, man." Slobert handed over not only his Nintendo Game Boy, but also a spare game cartridge from his other front pocket.

This was the most unlikely, the most joyous, the most glorious tithe that this house of the Lord had ever given.

Tanto stood at the front, frowning with more than a touch of confusion at all these people singing and happily handing over their valuables.

Behind Isaac somebody said, "I want your shoes."

Isaac turned. Ismail stood at the top of the stairs to the balcony.

"I want your shoes," Ismail said again, pointing down at Isaac's new Reeboks. He stared at Isaac with eyes so alien and hostile that it was as though the Ismail whom Isaac had known, with whom he had flown kites and stalked the cane fields and hunted for treasure, was someone else, that this person in front of him was an imposter who at any moment was going to pull the skin off his head and reveal the green creature underneath.

Isaac unlaced his Reeboks and took them off. Ismail snatched them from his hands and darted back down the stairs.

The robbers left swiftly, bags slung over their shoulders. Isaac pressed his face against the small window in the wall. Figures flittered across the footbridge and down the street, among them a boy wearing white Reeboks with red trim that flashed away into the darkness.

The police arrived fifteen minutes later. Aunt Janice and Uncle Jimmy escorted the children back to the dorm, but at the request of Lieutenant Nugroho, the other adults stayed to give statements. Ruth needed no prompting. Upon spotting the first policeman, she began screeching out Tanto's name and his address and other salient and less salient and some outright insulting facts about him. She demanded that the police lock up Tanto for life for stealing her jewelry and to take off his balls for threatening to take off her head. This she said in Javanese, so it was only Isaac among the expatriates who understood.

Mary Williams told him to go home. Once at the house Isaac lay on his back on the living-room sofa, his arm draped over his eyes. A lethargy had soaked into his muscles and an apathy into his spirit. He'd walked home barefoot, and while the soles of his feet were Javanese and tough enough to take the rough asphalt, each step was like Ismail spitting into his face.

Who am I? What am I?

The phone rang. Isaac let it ring, but it wouldn't quit. "All right, all right," he shouted. He snatched up the phone. "What?" he barked.

A click of a long-distance connection, and then a clipped voice said, "Hello, Isaac, can you hear me?"

The shock of hearing this voice in this house made him exclaim, "Grandpa, is that you?"

"I need to speak to your father."

Isaac's shock expanded. His grandfather and father had not spoken to each other for years. "You want to speak to *Dad*?"

"Immediately. His cell phone is not on, and neither is your mother's."

Isaac heard in the background of his grandfather's voice screams and shouts and frantic voices at runaway speeds that he recognized as CNN talking heads reporting on breaking news. "That's because they're at church. They don't take them to church. What's going on, Grandpa?"

"You'll find out soon enough. Go. Get. Your. Father."

Isaac was now astonished and not a little afraid. This wasn't Grandpa's voice; this was the voice of Butch Williams, former secretary of state, a forbidding glacier of a man. "He's still at the church. There was a raid by some Muslim fanatics—"

"*What?*"

"Yeah, these guys came in with sickles and poles—"

"Isaac, do whatever you can to get hold of your father immediately, and have him call me at once on my secure line. At once, do you hear? I cannot overly stress how urgent this is."

"Yes, sir."

"I'll phone back every ten minutes." His grandfather hung up.

Isaac turned on the television and clicked to CNN. What he saw was at first bewildering. Then the shock struck like a body slam, the most awful, terrible, fascinating thing being the people who jumped to escape the fire, kicking and flailing, falling one hundred stories. The remote fell from his hands. He ran as fast as he could on his bare feet back to the church. The police were still taking statements. His father was talking to Lieutenant Nugroho out in the church foyer. Isaac was screaming even before he crossed the footbridge, "Dad, Dad, terrorists attacked the World Trade Center. They flew planes right into the World Trade Center and the towers collapsed and twenty thousand people are dead!"

Chapter Five

THE PHONE IN THE house rang constantly that night. Isaac listened in using the upstairs cordless. The conversation between his dad and Grandpa Butch was a terse one about Muslim militants and personal safety that ended up with Graham Williams shouting, "Where is safe? Where? New York, even Connecticut, is no safer now than Wonobo is. I don't care what intelligence information you have. We're not leaving."

The celebration at the Al-Furqon Mosque started around midnight. The speakers blasted festive Arabic music, interspersed with cries of *"Allahu akbar! Allahu akbar!"* The celebrants danced and clapped and shouted with a glee that needed no amplification.

Isaac wondered if Ismail was right now dancing in his stolen Reeboks, chanting *"Allahu akbar,"* his lively face all bright and sparkly.

Reverend Biggs paced the living room, his countenance shining with an impotent fury. He clenched his fist and shook it at the unseen mosque across the street. "What kind of monsters are they to cheer such an insane crime? Murder done in the name of Islam, murder celebrated by Muslims." He stopped pacing, faced the direction of the mosque, put his right hand on his heart, and sang, "Mine eyes have seen the glory of the coming of the Lord, He is trampling out the vintage where the grapes of wrath are stored . . ."

Graham Williams made a phone call to Lieutenant Nugroho. A few minutes later the power on the other side of the street went out, streetlamps blinking to darkness and speakers falling silent.

"World's changed," Graham said. "This is one of those moments. History divided. A before, an after."

Isaac tried to understand, but he just didn't get it. The whole thing was terrible. But why was everyone taking it so hard? Terrible things happened all the time. When he woke up on Wednesday morning, life for him wasn't a whole lot different than it had been Tuesday, except he was short one friend and a pair of Reeboks and had a headache.

After a breakfast of cereal that he ate alone, Isaac trudged across the back lawn to school. He stepped through the hedge and halted in astonishment. Overnight the whole crown of the flame tree had bloomed a bright crimson red. Isaac stared, squeezed his eyes shut, stared again. After having watched those airplanes crashing into the WTC towers and exploding in fireballs, the sight of the tree unseasonably—unnaturally—in blossom was more than disquieting. He told himself that it was yesterday's branch cutting that had catalyzed the blooming. The tree was protesting the circumcision of its foreskin branches.

He climbed the tree, barely having the energy to reach his perch. In the glassy morning swelter the mosque was quiet. Five lads in Nahdlatul Umat Islam T-shirts were sprawled asleep on the mosque veranda, possibly drunk, considering the several unlabeled green bottles strewn in the dirt. Two policemen with first private stripes on their starchy brown uniforms stood in front of the mosque's fence, hot and bored.

The entrance to the hospital looked like a transplanted flower shop. Dozens of wreaths with varying expressions of grief and condolences for the Americans' tragedy were stacked beside the gate and under the hospital sign and were beginning to spread down the sidewalk. Some hung from the new barbed wire up on top of the wall.

A public bemo pulled over to a stop just beyond the hospital gates. An old man with a white haji's cap wobbled out of the vehicle, helped by two attentive young women, perhaps his granddaughters, wearing *jilbabs* and full-sleeved, black dresses. One of the women carried a small bouquet of common flowers wrapped in newspaper and a small, hand-inked sign on a stick that said simply in Indonesian, WE GRIEVE WITH YOU. They guided the old haji onto the sidewalk. He took the bouquet, and with one of the young women holding on to his arm, he painfully bent to place the wreath and the sign in front of the others. He struggled erect and, shaking off the woman's hand, lifted his own, palms up, in the gesture of Muslim prayer, while the two women respectfully bowed their heads. One wiped away tears from her cheeks. The old man finished his prayer and returned to the waiting bemo.

A special assembly was called for first period. The auditorium was more crowded than Isaac ever remembered, with many of the hospital's staff attending. Occasional sniffles broke the deep silence, as hushed as at any funeral service. The first and second graders were agog with wide-eyed wonder.

Ibu Hajjah Yanti from the hospital laboratory and Mr. Suherman were among the last to arrive, shortly after Isaac. Ibu Yanti spotted Isaac standing at the back. She went over to him and gave him a hug, kissing him on both cheeks, the starched forehead fold of her jilbab scraping across his nose. "I'm so sorry, so sorry," she said. Tears gathered in the corner of her eyes. "So terrible." All the seats were taken, but in the back row Mr. Patter stood and offered his to Ibu Yanti, who blinked away her tears and smiled gratefully before sitting down.

Mr. Suherman walked forward to offer his condolences to Graham Williams and Miss Augusta before returning to stand beside Isaac at the back.

Reverend Biggs rose from the front row and faced the audience. His jaw lifted resolutely, his shoulders broadened, his voice deepened. "We are on a crusade against those terrorists who slaughter innocent people and their supporters who celebrate murder. We are in a holy war against the evil forces of fear and darkness that come in the name of Islam."

Slobert yelled from his middle-row seat, "America should bomb them."

Ibu Yanti abruptly stood and left the auditorium. Her arctic passage attracted scant attention. Mr. Suherman regarded Reverend Biggs with a mild astonishment.

Graham Williams stood up from his chair. The dark circles under his eyes looked as though they'd dug all the way into his cheekbones. "I'd like to amend that a little, Brother Maynard. We all know that most Muslims are good Muslims. Each one of us here has good Muslim friends in Wonobo. This is not the time to back away in suspicion. Condemnation. If anything, this is the time to be deepening our friendships. Affirming our common humanity. Sharing our sorrow. Together seeking justice."

Most nodded in agreement, including Mr. Suherman. Reverend Biggs's silvered head was not one of them. Isaac noticed brimstone burning under his skin. Without further song or speech, he asked Miss Augusta to close the devotional with a prayer for the victims of the terrorist attacks and their families. Mr. Suherman lifted his hands with open palms upward, staring down at a spot on the green cement floor beyond his polished shoes. His lips moved silently.

After the devotional, Dr. Azakian, the hospital's psychiatrist, remained behind in the auditorium with the junior high students. Miss Augusta told Isaac to join them. Dr. Azakian pulled one of the folding chairs to the foot of the stage and told everyone to gather in a semicircle. Isaac sat in the outermost arc of students.

Dr. Azakian wore a long-sleeved powder blue silk shirt and a bow tie printed with tiny Komodo dragons. He sat on his chair with his right leg crossed over his left, his slim hands draped over his round little belly. He had soft brown eyes that drooped at the corners and rarely blinked. They fastened themselves on other eyes in a poultice of attention that drew out of people more than what they had intended to reveal.

So it was with the students. The discussion circled like a slowly forming whirlpool, centering itself closer and closer on the awful

Richard Lewis

images of people jumping to their deaths. The tragedy as a whole, from the planes crashing to the buildings coming down, had been broadcast as a generic sort of disaster. The falling people had made it horribly human.

"The guy was doing a swan dive with his head down and his arms back like this," Slobert said, standing up to illustrate. "I mean, can you imagine standing there on the edge and the fire coming closer and closer? I don't think—" There Slobert stopped, blinking rapidly, breathing harshly. "We oughta nuke 'em," he said.

Isaac wondered what Ismail had thought when he saw the man coming down like a delta-winged fighter plane.

"Isaac? What do you think?"

Isaac was startled. Dr. Azakian had fastened his poultice eyes upon him.

"Yeah, Isaac, what do you think?" Slobert said. "You're the one who loves these Mussies."

Dr. Azakian said softly, "Robert, that's enough. Isaac?"

Isaac started to shake his head and then stopped and sat up straight. "The other day somebody wanted me to convert to Islam. And, of course, I can't become a Muslim. So if I don't want to convert to Islam, then why should I want Muslims to convert to Christianity?"

All the other kids stared at Isaac with varying expressions of shock. Slobert, his eyes and mouth gashes on his plump face, hissed, "Mussie lover."

Dr. Azakian said, "Robert, one more 'Mussie' and you are

seeing Miss Augusta." His gentle gaze and voice didn't change on the outside, but Slobert sullenly ducked his head. Dr. Azakian turned his attention again to Isaac. "Tell me exactly why you can't become a Muslim."

Isaac, already regretting that he'd spoken up, said shortly, "Because I'm a Christian."

"You mean you believe in Jesus Christ."

Isaac nodded.

Dr. Azakian leaned back in his chair with a little shrug. "I don't see why that would stop you from becoming a Muslim if you wanted to. I don't see why you can't believe in Muhammad at the same time you believe in Jesus Christ."

The kids, Slobert included, now gaped at Dr. Azakian. He raised his eyebrows and said, "Why are you all so surprised? You should know that true Christianity isn't really a matter of beliefs. A lot of people believe in Jesus Christ, and it doesn't do them a damn bit of good." His use of the mild oath was deliberate, a titillating shock. He paused, looking at each child, ending with Isaac. "You see, Isaac, it's *faith* in Jesus Christ that makes the difference. If you have *faith* in a living Christ, then, yes, I agree, it's not possible to become a Muslim. Do you have faith in Christ, Isaac?"

"Yeah, Isaac," Slobert said. "Do you?"

Isaac said stubbornly, "But you haven't answered my question. Why can't we let Muslims be Muslims?"

Dr. Azakian said, "But we do. We preach the gospel to the kingdoms because Jesus himself has commanded us to, but we don't force people to listen. We don't save souls. The Holy Spirit does. God is almighty, omniscient; He calls whom He wills."

Typical adult hand waving, Isaac thought, but he didn't say anything more.

When Isaac went home for lunch, Ruth still hadn't shown up. His mom was in the study, crouched in front of the open safe, going through the family's passports and documents.

Isaac didn't have to ask what she was doing. The Williamses had been through this once before, several years ago when Suharto the Strongman had been toppled from power by widespread riots. The U.S. embassy had advised Americans to be ready to leave the country at a moment's notice and to make sure such things as exit permits were up-to-date. Mary Williams had pretty much laughed off the embassy's warning then, but she clearly wasn't doing so now.

Isaac grew alarmed. "But Dad told Grandpa we're staying," he said.

"That's just your father's automatic feather ruffle," his mom said. "He never agrees with your grandpa on anything, you know that."

Isaac didn't say anything.

His mom looked up at him. Her smile died. "Isaac, honey, your safety comes first. Even if we stay, we might put you in boarding school. Now, you want me to fix you some lunch?"

Boarding school? The thought made his stomach all sour, but he dutifully ate half a toasted cheese sandwich, one of his mom's hurried doctor specials. "Where's Ruth?" he asked.

"Don't know." His mom put down her own uneaten sandwich, staring out to an inner horizon. "I should stop by her place."

"She's probably out tracking down Tanto to get back her jewelry," Isaac said. "That seems to be all she cares about."

His mother shot him a look. "She's received several death threats over the past few months for apostatizing. She carries a burden that we don't."

During his seventh-period Esperanto lesson Isaac asked Mr. Suherman whether Muslims really did put backsliders to the sword. He was sitting beside Mr. Suherman, behind the teacher's desk, the Esperanto lesson spread out before them. Mr. Suherman rotated in his swivel chair and stared out the window for such a long time that Isaac worried he'd unforgivably insulted his favorite teacher. But when Mr. Suherman at last swung back around, his smile was warm, his gaze gentle. "Even after growing up here, running around town with your Muslim friends, you can still ask me that question?"

Isaac said, "I haven't thought about Islam as a religion until the last few days."

"After yesterday I daresay that's going to be true of the whole Western world," Mr. Suherman said. He leaned forward, curiosity in his eyes. "What do you think about the terrorist attacks in America?"

Isaac opened his mouth to say what everyone else was saying—they were horrible, terrible, insane. But instead he said, in a small voice, "That's far away from here. What's worse is my best friend

Ismail telling me we can't be friends anymore because he's a Muslim and I'm a Christian."

Saying those words was like lancing a festering heartsickness. Isaac found himself blurting out the whole story, all the way to Ismail taking the Reeboks, telling this Muslim teacher what he had not told his Christian elders or his parents. Mr. Suherman listened without interruption, his sympathy a pressure to Isaac's pain, squeezing the core of it to the surface.

"And now my parents are thinking of sending me away to a boarding school," Isaac said as he stared down at the desk, his voice cracking. Tears came, but this time he did not fight them. It was okay to weep in front of Mr. Suherman.

Mr. Suherman let him cry and, when the tears subsided to sniffles, reached out an arm and hugged Isaac close to his side. He murmured, *"Patro nia, kiu estas en la cxielo, Via nomo estu sanktigita. Veno Via regio, plenumigxu Via volo, kiel en la cxielo, tiel ankaux sur la tero."* He released Isaac with a smile and said, "You know what that is? That's the beginning of the Lord's Prayer in Esperanto. I'm a Muslim, but I, too, pray that God's will be done on earth as it is in heaven." He plucked a couple tissues from the box on the desk and held them out.

Isaac wiped his face and blew his nose. He settled down to his Esperanto lesson, not knowing why God would have used a Muslim to make him feel better, but quietly grateful for it nonetheless.

Chapter Six

THE NEXT MORNING, ISAAC woke up with another headache. He took a Panadol. His mother told him to stay in bed because she wanted to do a blood test later, just in case malaria was rearing its head. Lieutenant Nugroho was downstairs at the breakfast table, along with a policewoman and Reverend Biggs, discussing the raid on the church with the Williamses. Isaac listened through the bedroom's open door.

"Aside from the ringleader, your former gardener, Tanto, no one recognized any other of the men," the lieutenant said. He was speaking Indonesian, as were Mary and Graham.

Graham Williams said, "They were from the Nahdlatul Umat Islam." He'd learned to the say the name right. As a matter of fact, Isaac reflected, everybody in the compound was saying the name right. "Why don't you question them? Bring in that Tuan Guru fellow of theirs for some questioning."

The lieutenant did not reply.

Graham said, "You a sympathizer?"

"I'm no follower of the Tuan Guru Haji."

"Then why not question him?"

"That would be difficult," the lieutenant said.

"Okay, let's try for something less difficult. The mosque

across the street is harassing us with its speakers. Overly loud. We are a hospital, you realize. Patients need rest and quiet. Something must be done."

The lieutenant said, "The Imam of the Masjid Al-Furqon is one of the Tuan Guru Haji's important deputies and—"

"Then bring him in for questioning."

The lieutenant ignored that. "Do you know what *kunut nazilah* means? It is an Islamic concept, a type of jihad against enemies who threaten Islam."

Reverend Biggs, who knew no Indonesian and had been silent until then because of the language barrier, said, "Jihad," spitting out the word.

The lieutenant said, in labored English, "Not WTC, no jihad, that terror of bad men. Not good men."

"The president says 'crusade,' and the Muslim world shouts in outrage," the reverend said, "but this bin Laden monster cries 'jihad,' and the Muslim world keeps silent. No wonder Islam breeds terrorists."

Graham said sharply, "Maynard, be quiet. The last thing we need right now is such inflammatory rhetoric."

The lieutenant said calmly, "It okay, many stupid people everywhere."

Isaac smiled, wishing he could see the reverend's reaction. The lieutenant continued, in Indonesian, "That attack is not jihad, that is evil. *Kunut nazilah* is a different jihad, a jihad of prayer against you."

"But we're a hospital," Mary protested. "We're doctors treating the poor and the sick."

"To the Nahdlatul Umat Islam, you are trying to seduce Muslims from the true way of Islam by your doctoring."

Mary said, "We have never hidden the fact that we are Christians. We try to show the love of Christ to everyone. Everyone receives the same care and compassion."

"Speaking as a Muslim, I have no quarrel with that or with you," the lieutenant said. "Wonobo needs your hospital. Now, speaking as a police officer investigating a crime, let me ask a few more questions." He did so, filling in a few blank spots about the gang of robbers.

Mary said, "That boy took our son's new shoes, you know."

"Yes?" the lieutenant said. Paper rustled. "That was not mentioned on the list of stolen items. And where is your son?"

"Upstairs," Graham said. "A bit sick."

"I'd like to see him."

"Isaac, would you come down here, please?" his father called out.

Isaac trudged down the stairs. He knew what was coming. The lieutenant was going to ask him about Ismail. No matter that Ismail wasn't his friend anymore, he couldn't tell on him. That wouldn't be right. He sat down next to his father, opposite the lieutenant. Reverend Biggs sat on the living-room sofa, watching CNN with the volume turned down.

The lieutenant's uniform was as tight and crisp as ever, but his eyes were red with tiredness. The creases in his cheeks had deepened. "Would you please tell me what happened Tuesday night?"

Isaac did, with strategic omissions.

The lieutenant said, "So you don't know this boy."

"No, sir."

The lieutenant said, "I bet you get around town, the cane fields a lot. I used to play in the fields when I was a boy. I bet you have a lot of local friends your age. In fact, didn't I meet one last Sunday? A local boy who likes to throw stones?"

Isaac stared out the living-room window. The slash of sky visible above the top of the compound wall was sickly brown, oozing hazy patches of yellow pus.

"Do you know the boy?" Graham asked.

"You don't want to tell on him, do you?" Mary said.

Isaac shook his head, left, right, left.

Graham said, "I don't think the police are after your friend. They want the bad men because they broke the law, in a vicious manner. If we let that be, don't care about it, we might as well let everything fall apart. Into lawlessness."

Before and after. Ismail had chosen the side of the Lord of the Crows. It wasn't Isaac's fault.

"Ismail," Isaac said. "Ismail Trisno." He gave the lieutenant Ismail's address. He kept his gaze on the table. Tears pricked. *I'm not going to cry. Ismail chose, not me.*

The policewoman wrote down the information in a notepad.

Isaac looked up at the lieutenant and said, "His father had his land stolen, and then he was fired from the sugar mill."

The lieutenant said, "Life's hard for everybody." He and his assistant stood. He paused and then said, "My condolences again for the New York tragedy. That is not Islam."

Isaac meandered over to the living-room window and gazed out at the pustular sky. No crows in sight.

The telephone rang. Graham looked at it with a heavy tired blink and then rose to get it with a disarticulated sigh. "Hello, Sheldon. I'd say good morning, but it isn't. Yours must be hectic as all—excuse me? You're on your way here? Okay. I'll be waiting."

A half hour later Isaac got out of bed again. He put on his old, dirty sneakers and went out to inspect the flame tree. Yesterday's crimson bloom had spread and strengthened. In past years this annual blossoming always cheered Isaac, not because of any mystical symbolic meaning about life, but because it normally marked the changing of Wonobo's season from dry to wet. The first rains of the easterly monsoon were to Isaac what the first snowfall of the winter was to his New England cousins.

Isaac felt too weak to climb the tree. He wandered across Doctors' Alley to the hospital. The gray-black tarmac had a squishy feel to it, softened by the day's heat. The rest of his body was cold. His head felt bigger than his skull capacity. Thoughts kept expanding in front of him, and he could never quite catch up with them. A work crew was fortifying the walls around the empty plot of land upon which Doctors' Alley dead-ended.

Hospital Street was not its usual weekday-morning bedlam of traffic. The sidewalks were empty, as were most of the outpatient clinic's green waiting benches. Isaac sat down on one of the shaded ones. He had a clear view of the hospital gates, open to Hayam Wuruk Avenue. The emergency room was directly inside the gates, off to the right.

A group of neighborhood men walked through the entrance,

carrying the legless beggar's wheeled trolley, the legless beggar slumped upon it. One of the men carrying the trolley was the nasty fruit merchant. A male nurse rushed out the doors. "No hurry, he's dead," the fruit merchant said.

A female intern joined the nurse. After a minute of probing and checking she declared the beggar to be dead. "Take him to the morgue," she instructed the nurse. "And make sure Mas Gatot reports it the police."

"Mas Gatot isn't working today," the nurse said, "just his nephew. He doesn't have authority to do anything official."

"Then keep him on ice until tomorrow," the intern said.

The male nurse, with the fruit merchant's help, transferred the beggar to a gurney. The nurse wheeled the gurney down Doctors' Alley, heading for the portcullis gate at the back of the empty lot. The beggar's last ride.

Isaac didn't have much spare emotion to feel anything for the legless beggar, except a brief pity mixed with a vague gladness that at least the poor guy hadn't died thirsty.

A minute later there appeared on Hayam Wuruk Avenue a dark blue four-door Ford with white diplomatic corps license plates, blaring its horn, gunning past an intercity bus on the wrong side, timing the gap with split-second precision. The Ford careened around a couple motorbikes and roared up the emergency ramp, squealing to a stop. The windshield was shattered into a spiderweb of cracks. The fragments on the driver's side had been punched out from the inside, leaving a jagged hole, through which Isaac saw the lean-jawed visage of Sheldon Summerton, aviator sunglasses accentuating his chiseled cheekbones and smooth forehead, a signet ring with ruby twinkling on the hand clutching the driving wheel.

The Ford's back door opened, and a plump Indonesian wearing a blue chauffeur's uniform emerged. His face was pale and waxy. He promptly bent over and threw up. He wiped his mouth with the back of his hand and raised his head heavenward and gave heartfelt praises to Allah that he was no longer moving and was still in one piece.

Sheldon opened his door and got out. Not a hair of his lemon-streaked hair was out of place, despite the wind that must have been whistling through the hole in the windshield. From the front passenger's side emerged another white man, who brushed off the lapels of his dark blue blazer and straightened his blue patterned tie. Isaac wondered if the guy was in his right mind. Anybody else in this heat would be taking the jacket off and loosening the tie, not tidying himself up as though going into a meeting. But the man appeared impervious to the sweltering humidity.

The chauffeur, recovered from his bout of fear and car sickness, opened the trunk of the Ford and retrieved what looked like a gray laptop computer complete with a built-in carrying handle, which he handed to the consular officer. The two white men headed for the hospital entrance.

Isaac knew he should go to school, to his algebra tutorial with Mr. Patter, but math held no interest for once. And he didn't want to return to the house. So there was only one thing left to do.

He climbed the flame tree in a trancelike state, seeing again

Richard Lewis

all those people jumping off the World Trade Center. The branch he put his hand to dipped alarmingly. He had, without realizing it, climbed higher than he had ever before, where the branches were thinner and bending under his weight.

He stopped. He was sweating profusely. His sweat chilled when he saw that the crow was back, with a friend, both close enough to be touched. Were crows territorial? Isaac had no idea, but the birds hunched forward with fearless menace. Isaac was looking for a way down when they exploded into flight. He automatically ducked his head, thinking they were going to dive-bomb him, but instead they flew across the street and settled on the roof of the mosque.

Were crows and other furtive creatures feeding on the dead in Manhattan?

Worshippers were gathering early at the Al-Furqon Mosque, both men and women, the women segregated from the men by a fabric screen. Down at the corner Mr. "Ah Choo" kept popping in and out of his shop. He peered about at the empty street. He pondered the hospital gates and squinted down the road at the mosque. He scratched his chin and wiped his nose. He barked an order, and a shop boy began sliding wooden planks in their slots across the storefront, leaving only a small gap for customers.

From this new height, Isaac could see over the roof of his house. He saw his father, Sheldon Summerton, and the other man walking across Doctors' Alley. Sheldon was still carrying his odd-looking laptop. Isaac's immediate impulse was to get back to school before his father spotted him, but he had trouble figuring out a way down from this new and unnerving perch. He stopped fidgeting as he heard his father's voice rising from below.

"Very cunningly done," Graham said.

The three men stood at the section of wall where the secret gate had been. The unknown man took off his jacket and hung it on a branch. With a swooshing thrill, Isaac saw that the jacket was only camouflage for a handgun in a shoulder holster, held snug up to the armpit by the narrow black straps.

The man jumped and grabbed the top of the wall, hoisting himself up by the flat of his hands, avoiding the barbed wire's coils. He peered down the length of the wall, first to his right and then to his left. He scanned the street and studied the mosque. He pushed himself off the wall and nimbly landed back on the ground. He put on his jacket and strode under the tangerine tree to the school grounds. Graham and Sheldon followed.

"What about the rest of the perimeter?" the man said.

Graham said, "Excuse me?"

"Were there more 'secret gates,' breaches intentional or otherwise, in the perimeter?"

Graham Williams massaged his forehead. "Truth to tell, I don't know. We didn't check."

The man turned his gaze toward Graham, who lifted his hands. "Mea culpa. An oversight. Particularly in view of recent happenings. But I'm a physician. My suspicions are mainly of a medical nature."

Without a word, the man began an inspection of the wall surrounding the school and boardinghouse. He moved along the wall's perimeter, sweeping his eyes up and down. He inspected the grass verge next to the wall, at times bending over to put his nose to where the wall's foundation emerged from the earth.

Graham stared after him, frowning. "Is it legal for him to be carrying a weapon like that?" he asked Sheldon.

"A gray area," Sheldon said. "Joe had to fire a round off outside Wonobo to clear a mob that came out of nowhere. You saw the car's windshield. One of their rocks did that."

The two men sauntered back across the schoolyard and sat down at one of the tables underneath the flame tree, facing each other, the laptop between them.

"What's he do?" Graham asked.

"He's State DS, Bureau of Diplomatic Security. Perimeters and securing of such are among the things he does."

Graham was silent for a moment. "What's going on here?" he said. "I don't think I have the full picture."

Sheldon said, "I must say you look as ragged as an Arizona arroyo. Do you ever take any vacations?"

Graham said, "Vacations? I'm a permanent part of the Wonobo landscape, as ragged as I may be."

"You may be taking a vacation sooner than you think," Sheldon said. He glanced at the slim watch on his wrist. "Frankly, it strikes me as ironic that if you had stuck to your vaunted family tradition, you'd probably be way up the chain of command by now and bossing my bosses around. Instead, you're an overworked and underpaid missionary doctor in some hick Javanese town. You and Mary could at least be doing some greater good in a medical institution that has a more global impact. You're a Yalie, for God's sake. The Big Picture—Nobels, Pulitzers—that's the sort of thing the Yale admissions committee has in mind when it deigns to accept freshmen."

"Mary and I are in the hick town of Wonobo precisely for God's sake," Graham said. "Ever heard of William Borden of Yale? No? Famous missionary. Famous in missionary circles, that is. He heard the call of Christ. Just like Mary and me. And the call of Christ," Graham added wryly, "is a more consequential thing than the siren song of, say, the diplomatic corps. My father could never figure that one out. I don't expect you to."

"Your pop still hasn't figured it out," Sheldon said. "My old man attended one of those A.F.S.O. luncheons in Georgetown and saw his old partner in crime, your pop. Asked about you, and Bully Williams growled that since you would be getting your just rewards in heaven, there was no need to have you in his earthly will." He added, somewhat apologetically, "The sort of bon mot that my old man loves to pass around, you know him."

Bully Williams. Another name for Isaac's grandfather, that aloof and imperious old man who autocratically reigned from a palatial three-story brownstone as though he were the Last Emperor of Manhattan.

Joe was inspecting a motorbike, the only vehicle in the school's small parking lot just outside the unlocked gates. He bent over and peered at the engine, his hands on his knees. He poked the seat. Isaac couldn't figure it out. A Honda Tiger was a pretty neat motorbike, but it wasn't a Harley Hog or anything.

Graham said, "Sheldon, let's cut to the chase. If you're not going to fill me in here, fair enough. Okay? But I have a more than full schedule this morning."

Sheldon glanced at his watch again. He patted the laptop on the table. "This is a secure transmission unit. Encrypts and decodes messages, using a built-in antenna for direct satellite uplink. Part of my job description is, quote, 'the protection and welfare of U.S. citizens living in Indonesia,' unquote. And right now the protection and welfare of U.S. citizens in Wonobo is a very big blip on the Foggy Bottom radar. And I'm point man on the spot, so to speak."

"Why is it that I don't like the sound of that?"

Sheldon looked at his watch again. "In half an hour I am to cable an update to Washington about the Wonobo Situation. It already has an official title. The 'Wonobo Situation.' Do you know who termed it the Wonobo Situation?"

"You?"

"Nope. Not Atkins, either—he's the Jakarta DCM—nor the ambassador, nor any of the directors, the bureau chiefs, the nineteen assistant secretaries of state, the five undersecretaries. Nope, it was the secretary of state himself who named this the Wonobo Situation. All the clamor for his attention after Tuesday's terrorist attack, and he still finds time to cast his gaze halfway around the world to a small town in Java."

"A little raid on a church in a third-world town gets the secretary's attention? I find that hard to believe."

"Graham, a lot of back-road third-world places are getting his attention. Haven't you heard of Osama bin Laden?"

"Anybody who didn't know before certainly knows now."

"Osama bin Laden has operatives in over twenty-five countries. Including—perhaps especially including—Indonesia, the world's largest Muslim nation, its borders porous as a sieve, its law agencies . . . well, in this country you can hide an elephant in a haystack. Bin Laden's fellows are in Aceh, Irian, Maluku, Sulawesi. In Java, too. More specifically, right here in Wonobo, where we have not only an American mission hospital with a big sign out in public view that announces the Immanuel Hospital of the Union of American Baptists, but more than that, even better than a hospital or a church or even an embassy, we have a whole bunch of beautiful young American schoolkids in a lovely American-style schoolhouse, an absolutely gorgeous target for a truck bomb. The secretary and the president are keen to prevent the Wonobo Situation from turning into the 'Wonobo Tragedy.'"

A long, thoughtful silence followed, one that included Isaac's thoughts forty feet overhead. Joe hadn't been admiring the motorbike, he'd been inspecting it for a bike bomb. Isaac scanned the street again with more urgency, craned his head to scan the vehicles parked around the hospital. He did not see any that should not be there.

"Is there any hard intelligence to go along with these, uh, grandiose suspicions?" Graham asked.

Sheldon tilted his head sideways, as if deciding whether to say something. "I'll tell you this. Need to know, eyes only, all that, so you hear this and then forget it, forget that you forgot it. Tuan

Guru Haji Abdullah Abubakar, chief of the Nahdlatul Umat Islam. The CIA's been keeping a quiet eye on him."

Sheldon opened the secure transmission unit, clicked some buttons. "There's also additional intelligence that some of bin Laden's heavies are in the area. Affiliated with the Nahdlatul Umat Islam. I mean truly nasty people. We got old file photos of a couple. Let me download them. It'll take only a minute. Now, regarding your staff, double check all IDs and bona fides immediately. Every one of them, even your most trusted employee."

A silence. Then, "That would cause a lot of unnecessary hurt. Loss of face."

"Graham, look yonder. A school full of innocent children." Graham did not reply. Sheldon said, "By the way, Joe is truly from the Bureau of Diplomatic Security, but he is not your ordinary security officer. Last night he was in Pakistan. Today he is in Wonobo. Figure it out."

Over at the school Joe was on his stomach, in a push-up pose, peering at the crawl space underneath the auditorium floorboards. His tie lapped the brown grass. The auditorium window above him flung open. Miss Augusta stuck out her head. Her shiny gray hair was luminescent against her ebony skin. She said in her teacher's voice, "Who are you? Why are you skulking around the school?"

Joe cranked his neck until he was looking upward at her from his horizontal position. After a second of eye contact he pushed himself up into a standing position with the abrupt speed of a jack-in-the-box.

"It's all right, Augusta," Graham yelled from across the yard. "I'll explain later. Let him continue poking around."

"Graham!" Miss Augusta exclaimed. "What are you—what is going on? Is this the architect for the elementary addition? I thought we were going to use a local firm instead of—"

"I'll explain later," Graham repeated. "Not to worry."

Miss Augusta considered this. "All right, then," she said. She looked down at Joe. "Remember that the volume of space school-children require is inversely proportional to their age. Think big and then double the size."

"Yes, ma'am," Joe said.

Miss Augusta withdrew and shut the window.

Graham Williams ran both his hands through his hair. He said to Sheldon, "What you have told me sounds—I mean, if we are a terrorist target, why haven't they attacked before now?"

"Jesus, Graham. What sort of logic is that? People in Pearl Harbor could have said the same thing on December sixth. Listen carefully now: A certain United States naval asset is steaming straight toward Java, with certain flexible mission capabilities, a full complement of marines on board. Its helicopters will be in round-trip reach of here within twenty-four hours. Our little Javanese town of Wonobo is a big bright coordinate on all sorts of situation maps and navigational computers."

Graham said, "Why marines and helicopters? If we need to evacuate, why not a couple big buses and a police escort to the Surabaya airport? Doesn't make sense."

Sheldon drummed his fingers on the table. "All right, more

hear-and-forget information. We also have intelligence reports that the Nahdlatul Umat Islam and other militant groups have been pouring into the area since the WTC attacks. I told you we were assaulted on the way in. Stupid of me to use a car with diplomatic plates. This could turn into a major crisis."

The two men fell silent, each one wrapped up in his own troubled thoughts as they watched Joe disappear around the corner of the boardinghouse.

Sheldon spoke up and said, "If the secretary orders an evacuation, I trust there will be no argument."

"Of course not. The safety of those kids is one of my major concerns too. I happen to have one of my own in that building."

Well, actually, not quite, Isaac thought. He was getting tired up there in the tree. The branch underneath his buttocks dug into his flesh. His headache had returned.

More worshippers arrived at the mosque. Someone began reading from the Qur'an in a singsong voice—a woman, reciting into a microphone from her side of the curtain. Isaac squinted through the side window at the thin face, framed by a stern white jilbab. It was Ruth. The recognition was a punch to Isaac's brain.

Joe appeared on the other side of the building and strode up to the table. "I need to check the resident side of the compound, but what we have here is lousy perimeter security, especially that school gate. But nothing at the moment seems to be suspicious. Except there is a blond-headed boy up in the tree above you." He said this without looking up.

Isaac closed his eyes, as though that would make him invisible.

His father shouted, "Isaac! What are you doing up there?"

Isaac glanced down, composing surprise on his face and in his words. "Oh, hi, Dad. There's this pretty neat nest up here."

"Let the nest be and get down," his father ordered.

Isaac started to move, but a wave of dizziness froze his muscles. He was high up. How had he managed to get up this high? He still didn't see an easy route back down to the thicker, safer branches.

"Isaac!" his father shouted again.

"I can't, I'm stuck!"

Joe began climbing the tree with the surefootedness of a cat. "Hold on, don't panic, we'll get you down." A moment later he was standing on the branch five feet below Isaac with the aplomb of an acrobat. He held out his left hand. "Can you grab this?"

Isaac took a deep breath and stretched out his right hand. It came to within a foot of Joe's. Those twelve inches were to Isaac as wide a chasm as the Grand Canyon gorge.

Joe moved to a higher part of the branch and closed some of the gap but not enough.

"All right, then, this is what we'll do," Joe said. "See how you're sitting there? If you turn and lean out in one motion, I can get hold of your hand."

"I'll fall." He was whimpering. He sounded like a coward. He was ashamed of that, but he couldn't help it.

"No, you won't fall. Lean out and turn, and I can get your hand and swing you down here next to me. I promise. Don't even think about, just do it. Come on, just do it."

That voice held such competent authority that Isaac acted

without thinking, doing what Joe said. Joe's fingers closed around his wrist. He did not give Isaac a chance to freeze up but tugged hard. Isaac had a giddying sensation of falling, a microsecond of gravity's pull, and then he was safe on the larger branch, tucked up against Joe's body. A hard object pressed against his back. Joe's gun.

A minute later they were on the ground. Isaac's legs were shaky. His dad, standing beside him, said, "You're as white as a sheet. What were you doing up there?"

"Just climbing. I kept going up to see that nest; I didn't mean to get that high." Sheldon Summerton stared at him with a hard look. "Hey, Mr. Summerton. What are you doing here?"

Sheldon laughed. His teeth flashed between his square jaw and his chiseled cheekbones. "Perfect," he said. "Absolutely outstanding. You'd be right at home in Washington, Isaac, a master of the three rules of success there. You know what they are? Admit nothing, deny everything, make counteraccusations. You're Bully Williams's grandson, all right." He chuckled again, but his humor melted as quickly as an ice cube in a Wonobo drink.

Isaac let his gaze drift down to Sheldon's odd laptop. Its screen pixelating away with the downloaded old file photograph of the bin Laden heavy. *Bam.* Another blow to his head. His knees sagged for a moment before he caught himself. He pointed to the screen, at the image of a smiling man with bright black eyes standing in a dusty, mountainous land, carrying an AK-47, and said in a voice that he initially had a hard time finding, "Mr. Suherman. That's Mr. Suherman."

Chapter Seven

THE BLOOD DRAINED FROM Graham Williams's face. He sprinted for the school's emergency bell on the entrance portico, shouting, "Everybody out!" In his panic he forgot that the cover flipped upward instead of sideways. He pounded futilely with his fist.

Joe calmly asked Isaac, "Who's Mr. Suherman?"

"One of the teachers," Isaac said, and told him where his classroom was.

Joe loped to the double doors, pausing to raise the alarm's cover and pull the handle.

Bells clanged, sirens whooped.

Joe stuck his right hand inside his jacket and withdrew his gun. Holding it discreetly against the back of his thigh, he slipped into the building as the first group of kids marched through the double doors, their calm, rapid response a result of Miss Augusta's rigorous fire drills. Isaac glided in right behind Joe, keeping a careful distance from the man but moving with him against the outward stream of students. No one noticed Isaac. Joe went straight to Mr. Suherman's classroom. Its door was closed, as the fire drill protocol said it should be. Joe pressed himself against the wall and reached for the door handle.

Just like in the movies, Isaac thought.

As if on cue, the alarms cut off. Isaac, refusing to believe that Mr. Suherman was a terrorist, wanted to shout out a warning. He might have done so if his mouth hadn't been so dry.

Joe swung into and through the door's widening gap, extending the gun as he did so. No shots rang out. Isaac stuck his head around the doorjamb. Except for Joe, the room was empty. The window to the west garden was open. Joe holstered his gun, spotting Isaac in the process. He showed neither surprise nor anger. He pointed to the window. "Get out and join the others. There might be a bomb somewhere."

Isaac obeyed. The usual gathering spot for fire drills was underneath the flame tree, but no one was anywhere in sight. Where was everybody?

Mary Williams, still in green operating scrubs, blood splattered on the blouse, raced through the gate in the hedge. "Isaac, run! There could be a bomb!"

I know *that, silly*—then Isaac abruptly realized he was the silly one. Bombs meant shrapnel. Isaac ran. When he reached her, she put her left arm around his shoulder, running with him, keeping herself between him and the school building.

Nothing blew up.

The other students had gathered on the large front lawn of the residence portion of the compound, standing in their appointed rows, the teachers flanking them on the sides. Some of the kids spotted Isaac and yelled, "There he is!" Several of the students broke rank.

"Back into place!" Miss Augusta snapped. "This is *not* a drill. Everybody sit down."

Isaac sat down in his place behind Slobert, while his mother entered their house. Mr. Theophilus paced on the lawn with a walkie-talkie plastered to the side of his face, giving orders and listening to reports, directing a search of the residences and gardens around them.

Dave Duizen said to Sairah Strang, loud enough for everyone to hear, "There must have been a bomb threat." A minor tumult swept through the seated children. Miss Augusta told everyone to calm down, there was no need to panic, although it seemed to Isaac that it was excitement rather than fear that was causing all the bright eyes and animated whispering.

Yesterday Mr. Suherman had prayed for Isaac in Esperanto, a language of global unity. Now he was a terrorist. It didn't make sense.

Slobert swung his big rear end around on the grass and said to Isaac, chomping on chewing gum, "Where were you? Having a yakkity-yak with Suey Herman about how great Islam is and how Mussies are kind, peaceful, loving people?"

Isaac smiled at him and said in highly impolite Javanese, "You look like a big fat cow chewing its cud, and you stink like one too."

Slobert's mouth stilled. "What'd you say?"

Isaac gave him a pressed-lip smile and looked away.

Slobert grabbed his forearm. "You talk to me, you talk in English, you Mussie-loving Judas. What did you say?"

Isaac tried to jerk his arm away. Slobert tightened his grip, his fingernails digging into Isaac's skin. "Let go," Isaac said.

"Tell me what you said."

Isaac said, in the rudest gutter Javanese he knew, "If your fondest dreams came true, you'd be wallowing in dogshit."

Slobert's jaw stopped in mid-chew. His big nostrils flared. He lunged at Isaac, getting him in a vicious headlock. Isaac had learned from experience that the best way to minimize the pain was to abjectly surrender. This time he didn't. This time he fought back. An anger as red and unnatural as the flame tree's flowers blossomed within him. His last coherent thought was one of minor amazement: *So this is what it's like when a polite Javanese can't take it anymore and goes amok.* Then fury swamped that thought, and he punched and kicked and bit without restraint, not realizing that Slobert had let go and was trying to get away from him, screaming at him to stop. Isaac was dimly aware of fingers grasping his ear and twisting. The pain finally brought him back to his senses.

Miss Augusta stood over him, her good eye and her glass eye both angry and shocked. "What on earth's gotten into you?"

The other kids were frozen in place, staring. The only noise was Slobert's whimpering as he held a hand to his left eye.

"He started it," Isaac said, getting to his feet, breathing hard, the red fury still in him.

Slobert stood as well, shaking his head. "I did not. No way. He started it." His muffled voice quavered. "He called me names, he cursed me in Javanese." Slobert began to cry. He said to Isaac, the words catching on his sobs, "You're not a real American. You shouldn't be in this school. You should be going to some Javanese Mussie school, you love them so much."

"That's enough, Robert," Miss Augusta said.

From behind them, Mary Williams said, "I'll take care of Isaac. He needs to come with me for a blood test."

Slobert spat, "I hope you really do get malaria and *die*."

Mary stepped forward and slapped Slobert hard enough to leave a red print on his cheek. "That's a wicked thing to say, Robert Higgenbotham." She said to Miss Augusta, "Have one of the ER doctors take a look at Robert's eye. Isaac, you come with me." She took Isaac's hand and pulled him along after her. He nearly lost his balance and had to trot to keep up. She swept across the alley and crashed through the clinic's outer doors. She let go of him only when they reached the air-conditioned White Room, equipped with a dozen examining stations, now empty. She sat him on one of the beds, the brown plastic pad crackling underneath him. She assessed him first with her mother's eye, not saying a word as she searched deep into his own eyes, checking his inner well-being and not looking too happy about what she saw, and then she scanned his body with her doctor's eye.

"We'll have a talk about what happened later," she said. "Nurse Retno will take the blood sample. Malarial symptoms would present around now if the meds didn't take, so I'd like to be sure. When she's done, you go straight to your bed and stay there, you hear me?"

Isaac nodded dumbly.

She strode away, the heels of her sandals slapping against the tile floor. Isaac waited for Nurse Retno, minutes passing in a rubbery manner.

He'd never been in a fight before. The adrenaline surge had inflated everything inside of him, and now that his anger was gone, he felt hollow, lost and small within himself.

Nurse Retno finally appeared. She made him undress and put on a green gown. Isaac protested that he was only here to get some blood taken. "Full checkup," she said, "your mother's orders." She first tended to his battle wounds; both elbows were bloodily scraped, and a scratch on his arm was oozing blood. She clucked, but not over him. "That nice Mr. Suherman," she said. "Who could have ever thought he was a terrorist?"

I can't believe it either. But he realized he hadn't known much at all about Mr. Suherman, nothing about his family, where he was from, even where he lived in town. Isaac had told Mr. Suherman everything about Ismail, had cried freely in front of him without embarrassment. But now the embarrassment roared in at double strength. *He was probably laughing at me.* Isaac recalled the way the teacher had leaned forward to ask what Isaac had thought of the terrorist attacks. What Isaac had taken to be sympathetic curiosity had no doubt been glittering exultation. For the first time in his life Isaac felt like a true fool.

Nurse Retno left, saying she'd be back in a moment.

What about the hospital? Isaac wondered. *Is anyone checking the hospital for bombs?* He got off the pad and crossed the room to the door. He craned his head and looked out the door's inset window to the hospital's main hall. Everything looked normal to him—if anything, the few people he saw seemed more lethargic than usual, except for Mas Gatot's nephew, who was trotting to the main exit doors.

Other memories slipped into his mind. The legless beggar. The male nurse saying that Mas Gatot was not working. That was ridiculous, for Mas Gatot practically lived in the morgue. Isaac pushed open the door to run after Mas Gatot's nephew to ask about his uncle when another memory clanged into place: the nasty fruit shop owner's odd solicitousness toward the dead beggar whom he'd earlier mocked. And then another memory: Sheldon telling his dad to do complete ID checks on everybody. Gatot's nephew hadn't been hired by the hospital, had he? Yet another memory presented itself as crisply as a dynamite stick's crackling fuse: Mas Gatot probing a death wound with a pair of forceps and commenting that corpses were known to be booby-trapped.

Isaac ran as fast as he could, the tails of his hospital gown flapping behind him, exposing his naked rear end to the bemused nurses and patients he left in his wake. He skidded around a left-turn corner and then a right-hand one and raced down a short ramp by the cargo elevator into a bright corridor.

The portcullis gate at the far end was open, but he didn't see Mas Gatot. He banged through the morgue's double doors. The sole occupant within was the legless beggar's corpse, lying upon a gurney placed directly underneath the overhead fan that spun with the roar of a mini-tornado, sucking air out of the room. Two dark green glass bottles, corked shut and bound together with surgical tape, had been laid on the beggar's abdomen. One held a granular substance and the other a liquid. Isaac's mind flipped through chemical equations: Acid plus potassium cyanide equals cyanide gas, ready to be sucked up through the ventilation duct. Or maybe the bottles held a mix for a gas even more deadly. All that was needed was something to simultaneously break them—a small bomb in the beggar's stomach would do.

Isaac hit the switch on the wall by the doors, and the fan grumbled to a stop. He held his breath and picked up the bottles. He carefully gripped them with both hands as he walked across the room and gingerly placed them underneath the stainless-steel autopsy table. He grabbed the gurney's foot bar and shoved the gurney through the double doors. The beggar's corpse quivered and bounced as Isaac ran the gurney down the corridor, through the portcullis, and out onto the empty lot. The shaking popped the corpse's eyelids open, and it seemed to Isaac as though the dead beggar were staring at him. With a cry, he gave the gurney one last shove. Its wheels rattled over the empty lot's hard dirt. He raced back into the building. He'd just cleared the portcullis when the air behind him whomped and a huge blow smacked him from behind, throwing him forward onto the corridor floor.

After a vacant stretch of time he got to his knees and looked behind him. Through a clearing cloud of smoke and dust emerged a twisted, mangled gurney, two of its wheeled legs splayed high into the air. The cloud parted some more, revealing on the ground all that was left of the beggar: his head, a bloody hole for one eye, the other half-lidded eye staring off into the distance. Isaac shrieked and scrabbled backward. The heel of his hand flicked something soft and round. He glanced down at several rose petals. In their midst was the beggar's missing eye, big as a golf ball, the yellow, red-streaked cornea with its black iris staring right up at Isaac. His vision shrink-wrapped around the gruesome object and then blinked out altogether as he fainted.

Chapter Eight

WHEN ISAAC CAME TO, he found himself on the mattress in his sister's room, staring blankly at a yellow sky beyond a window.

His mother bent over him. "How's my hero boy?"

Isaac looked down at himself. He was wearing his own clothes. He'd been in a hospital gown, hadn't he, getting a checkup? "How did I get here?"

"By a stretcher," Mary said. "And a knockout shot. You were quite agitated."

He sat up. "There was a bomb in the beggar's corpse."

"My *foolish* hero boy," Mary said. Her smile faltered. "Dear God, Isaac, I tremble to think how close—" She gave him a long, fierce hug. "You should have called one of the guards. But if you'd done that, maybe there wouldn't have been time to—"

"There were a couple bottles on the beggar's stomach."

Mary nodded, her lips pressed grimly together. She glanced up at the bedroom doorway. Joe stood there. He came in and squatted beside Isaac. "Those bottles were the real danger," he said. "The bomb was a small one as bombs go. But the bottles didn't break, thanks to you. And you are not to tell anyone of them. No one. We don't want mass panic."

Isaac said, "Mas Gatot's nephew—"

"The police already nabbed him," Mary said.

"Mr. Suherman?" Isaac asked.

"Nobody knows." Joe was not wearing his jacket. His shoulder holster was empty. He noticed Isaac looking at it. He said wryly, "Your mother made me put it away in the safe."

Mary Williams was once a card-carrying member of the National Rifle Association. That changed the day when, as an intern in an ER rotation, she had dealt with the aftermath of an accidental shooting involving three young children. She'd burned her card and for a while wrote incendiary letters to the NRA.

Isaac grabbed his mom's arm. "Ruth. She's become a Muslim again."

Mary nodded, a pained sadness on her face. "I know, I've heard. Literally. She's been on the mosque speaker telling us infidels about it."

Isaac drifted off again. Some time later—long or short, he had no idea—the school bell rang in the distance, rousing him. He was aware of tense voices downstairs.

"Continuing intelligence confirms a strengthening blockade around Wonobo by militant Islamic groups," Joe said. "Vehicles are being stopped and searched for Americans."

"When do those helicopters get in range?" Graham asked.

"Sometime tomorrow around noon," Sheldon said. "I'm expecting an update in an hour."

Miss Augusta said, "I don't see why we can't get the children out before then. A bus convoy with an army escort."

A brief silence, and then Sheldon said, "There is some question of factions within the East Java Brawijaya Command and the loyalty of some of the troops to their own officers."

Isaac recalled the way the Red Berets had respectfully ushered the Tuan Guru off the square when the rioting broke out.

"Why doesn't the embassy raise a big stink, then?" Mary asked. "Why isn't the morgue bomb on the news? Why are we keeping that hush-hush? That would put pressure on the Indonesian government to assure our safety."

Another silence. "Operational reasons," Joe said.

"What on earth do you mean?" Mary said. Then, in a suspicious voice, "Are you implying you *want* us to be a target? Maybe to flush out the bin Laden terrorists?"

Sheldon said, "Everyone will be out of harm's way this time tomorrow. Now, let me go over the ground rules for the evacuation."

He droned on and was sharply interrupted by Graham. "Wait a sec," Graham said. "I thought we were only evacuating the children and school staff."

"Everybody, including doctors. I thought that was clear."

"You didn't make that clear at all," Graham said.

"Did I make myself clear to you, Reverend?"

Reverend Biggs cleared his throat. "Yes, very clear."

"The evacuation is for all U.S. citizens without exception," Sheldon said. "That's the instruction from the secretary of state himself. Mandatory and nonnegotiable."

"Don't be ridiculous," Mary said. "You can't order us to leave. We're a private mission foundation. You have no authority here."

"Order you? An appeal to your common sense should be more than sufficient. Your lives are truly at risk here."

"Evacuate the children, yes. But we doctors have been called here, we have chosen to be here, and we're going to stay here. We know the risks and accept them."

"I'm the hospital director," Graham said. "Not a dictator. I can't make my colleagues leave. Not against their will."

"We can't—we won't—abandon our patients and our people," Mary said.

"You are not abandoning anyone," Sheldon said. "It is a temporary evacuation until the situation stabilizes."

"If we get on those helicopters, our people will think we are running away. Which is exactly what we would be doing. And besides, does our leaving also remove this threat of terrorist bombs?" Mary changed her voice and manner as though speaking to someone else: "'I'm sorry, Dr. Priyono, we're leaving here in this awful hurry because there's a chance the hospital might get blown up by a terrorist bomb, but you hang in there, be strong, be brave, our prayers will be with you, God is with you.' Ha! I'm not leaving."

"You don't want to be with your son when he gets on that helicopter?" Sheldon asked, with surprise. "It's going to be a stressful time for him. What comes first? Your child or your career?"

"That's a low blow, Sheldon," Mary said grimly. "You be careful. My work here in Wonobo is not a career. It's a calling. I. Am. Not. Leaving."

A shiver started on the nape of Isaac's neck and coursed down his ribs. He knew that tone of voice. As his father often said, the

Richard Lewis

only thing on earth more stubborn than a two-headed mule is a Connecticut Yankee with her heels dug in. His mom was staying, and if she stayed, his dad would stay, and then Isaac would be alone and far away.

Reverend Biggs cleared his throat again. "You are not a solo effort, Mary. None of us are. We are a team with a hierarchy of authority. I spent nearly an hour on the phone earlier discussing the situation here in Wonobo with President Saxton and the other members of the board, and it is our unanimous decision to evacuate all—*all*—of our expatriate mission staff for the time being. It is the prudent thing to do. We do not want unnecessary heroics, and we do not want martyrs just for martyrdom's sake."

"I want to see these orders, Sheldon," Mary said. "I want to see something in writing from the secretary of state himself ordering this—what did you say?—mandatory and nonnegotiable evacuation. I stay until I see that in writing."

"There is no way I am going to agree to such a ridiculous demand."

"Sheldon, I have the funny feeling that you are engaging here in the art of diplomacy called letting others have it your way. I think your main purpose is to look good and come out smelling like a rose and gather what credit you can at others' expense."

Sheldon sighed, a contemptuous sound. He said, his voice thrown in a different direction, "I don't need this on top of everything else, Graham. She's your wife, you deal with her, will you? Remind her of that biblical instruction of wives submitting to their husbands."

Isaac's stomach soared in a weightless loop. *Oh, boy.* He scrabbled to the front of the stairs to witness the forthcoming explosion. His mother's temper compressed to critical mass, her cheeks paling to alabaster, her blue eyes turning violet. The quiet that fell had a numinous quality, the silence of the moment before God breaks His bowl of wrath. Sheldon must have sensed something terribly awry, the moist pinkness of his gums showing as he opened his mouth, his pupils widening in the nanosecond of realization that a catastrophe of meteoric proportions was about to engulf him.

It was in that nanosecond that a muted warble came from somewhere around Sheldon's midsection. He grabbed at the cell phone at his waist with the desperate relief of a man offered rescue by blind luck from being quarkified and scattered throughout the universe. He answered "Summerton," and at once stiffened. "Mr. Ambassador, sir." He listened for a half minute. After he clicked off, he said, "The Nahdlatul Umat Islam, in solidarity with the Taliban regime in Afghanistan, has declared jihad against all Americans in Java."

"Jihad means many things," Graham said. "Not necessarily war. The Javanese are a gracious people. Not hostile."

"Is that so? The ambassador just told me that in Mojokerto the decapitated head of an American businessman was tossed into a hotel lobby. It was wrapped up in a Nahdlatul Umat Islam banner."

Incredibly, that evening the adults decided to have an Evacuation Eve party out on the large front lawn of the compound. Three library tables had been placed on the grass, under the glare of fluorescent lights rigged on bamboo poles. All the households and the dorm had donated the entire contents of their fridges and larders to the buffet spread upon the tables. It was the potluck of potlucks.

Isaac sat in a chair by the toolshed, watching everybody. The scream of the dorm children playing Red Rover made his headache worse. Slobert sat on the steps of his house, giving Isaac the stink-eye. Isaac ignored him.

Graham Williams yelled that Reverend Biggs was going to be saying grace. When everyone was quiet, the reverend prayed, "Lord God Almighty, Yahweh and Jehovah, the God of Moses and of the Israelites, the God who led His chosen people out of Egypt and to the Promised Land, who comforted and succored them, who provided them with sweet water when tongues were swollen with thirst, who provided sweet manna when bellies were shrunken with hunger, who lit up their way when all was dark, Lord God Almighty, we your children here in Wonobo are also gathered on the eve of an exodus. Yet unlike the Israelites' departure from a land they loathed, we leave a place we love, we leave friends and neighbors, we leave a life's work, not knowing where you shall lead us in the days and weeks to come. Yet do we trust in your grace and in your love and know that you will provide in the days to come for all our wants and all our worries. You will dry our tears and you will comfort our hearts and you will soothe the strains of separation, for you are the Lord God Almighty who makes straight the crooked paths and who will lead us back once more, when we shall know the place we left and know it joyously, as home. Amen."

The skin on the back of Isaac's neck tingled. He didn't like Reverend Biggs, but this prayer had the power of a prophecy. No, it *was* a prophecy: "We shall know the place we left and know it joyously, as home." Isaac took back all the unkind things he'd thought about the reverend.

"Ladies and gentlemen, boys and girls, the food is served," Beth Patter called out. "Children, you line up on this side."

Isaac picked at his food and then threw his paper plate in the trash bin. He slipped through the night shadows to the flame tree. He felt weak, but he had to keep an eye on things. He worked his way up the familiar, smooth-barked passage. With that alien red color hidden by the night, the tree under his hands and feet was a living creature, possessing a warm-blooded interior. Isaac was a symbiont, a tree ant. If this tree were to die, he would also perish, for there was no other flame tree in the whole world to which he could flee for refuge.

Wonobo was calm, its evening lights murky blobs in the haze. Ismail was somewhere out there beyond the curve of luminescence. As the Lord of the Crows might fly, Ismail was close by. But not to Isaac, whose world had shrunk these last few days, from the cane fields and streets of Wonobo to within these compound walls, and it was shrinking even still and tomorrow would be a space of lawn and then not even that as the helicopter lifted. The chasm between him and his former friend, already unbridgeable, was rapidly becoming immeasurable.

Richard Lewis

Chapter Nine

ARLY FRIDAY MORNING, AFTER a tense and silent break-fast, Isaac went into his bedroom to pack. Reverend Biggs had already vacated his room. Isaac pulled out shorts and shirts and underwear from his closet. He surveyed the familiar clutter: the books, the games, the empty bottles of his chemistry set and a broken plastic microscope, the posters, the knee-high scribblings and scratchings on the walls that repainting could not completely hide.

He should be sad, desperate, but he felt no emotion of leave-taking. He felt nothing except a general malaise in his bones and the hollows of his heart. Was malaria starting to stir? In all the confusion it seemed that nobody had gotten around to his blood test. He had a brief shower, hoping that would make him feel better. It didn't. As he put on his underwear, a sudden dizziness sat him down on the bed.

He thought he could hear, like a susurration of blood, the murmured prayers of tens of thousands of Wonobo Muslims preparing to go to mosque for Friday congregational prayers. *O Allah, make light in my heart, and make light in my tongue. O Allah make light in my ear, and make light in my eye. Make light behind me, and light before me, and make light above me and make light beneath me. O Allah, bestow upon me light.*

Was Ismail praying? Would he proudly wear his new Reeboks to mosque, to take off before entering?

Isaac put on a pair of light cotton shorts and a blue chambray shirt and slipped sockless into a pair of old Hush Puppies split along the sides. He closed his suitcase and hauled it down the stairs and out to the lawn. Reverend Biggs, ticking names off a clipboard, said, "There you are. I was wondering where you'd got to. You're in group three with your parents."

"Who else?"

"That's it."

"You mean we get a helicopter all to ourselves?"

The reverend winked at him. "That's the way the cookie crumbles. Lucky you, huh?"

The boarding students were being sequestered in the dorm until it was time to march them out to the arriving choppers, but most of the other evacuees were gathered on the Higginbothams' and Patters' residence porches.

The consulate Ford was parked on the lawn, near the toolshed, bundled up with canvas straps with a big loop on top for a hook. Not only the American people of Wonobo were being evacuated, but also American cars. Sheldon Summerton was going to fly away on the fourth and last chopper, with his Ford slung underneath it. Maybe he was going to ride in the limo through the Java sky and be dropped off on a Surabaya highway near the consulate, where, with a wave of his hand and a tootle of his horn, he'd be off to do new derring-do.

Sheldon made an appearance on the Higginbothams' porch.

"Announcement, everybody. Helicopters arriving thirteen hundred hours. Reverend Biggs says we're still missing Dr. Azakian. He's not in the hospital."

There was a collective shrug. "Can't expect psychiatrists to keep track of time," Beth Patter said, "not when their official hour is forty-five minutes long."

"I think he went back to his town apartment," Dr. Higgenbotham said. "Some sort of closure thing."

Sheldon looked at his watch. "I'll give him another psychiatric hour before we send out the troops."

The evacuees waited. All was quiet—to Isaac, almost eerily so. Even the Al-Furqon Mosque speakers had fallen silent as the muezzin meditated for the last final moments before the noon call to prayer.

The first cry of his *azan* cleaved the air like a sword strike, a rending that continued out to the horizons as other mosques broadcast their summons to prayer.

Joe slipped out of the compound to be with the hospital security guards by the hospital gates. The assigned policemen were nowhere to be seen. The hospital garage and workshop staff had worked overtime to provide each guard with a stout shield made of plywood. They had no proper riot helmets, so as a substitute they donned motorcycle helmets with pull-down face-shields.

The characteristic whine of a Volkswagen engine at full rpm's grew loud. It was Dr. Azakian, hurtling up Hayam Wuruk Avenue in the VW Bug that he normally drove as sedately as a horse cart. The guards rushed to open the barrier for him. The

VW squealed to a halt in the alley. He trotted through the gate into the compound, the fastest Isaac had ever seen him move, a Gladstone bag in one hand and a Nikon camera in the other. Around his neck was a piece of cord on which dangled a card with his name.

"Where have you been?" Sheldon barked at him.

Dr. Azakian said breathlessly, his unflappable manner finally flapped for once, "I went to get my bag. I meant to be back earlier. I apologize for the delay, but it was quite unavoidable. There's a mob downtown ransacking the Citra Mall. Had a tricky time out-maneuvering them. Cars turned over and burning on the streets. One shop already going up in flames. I couldn't get through and tried a detour. A thick-necked goon saw me and led some rioters after me with gasoline bombs. I was blocked in and thought I'd had it. I got out this camera and an old conference badge and convinced them I was a journalist. Spoke with a French accent. I got them to pose for pictures they think are going be in foreign papers tomorrow, and then they cleared the way for me." He grinned. An eager light danced around in his brown eyes. "A Frenchman indeed! May the Lord forgive me for my little lie. Freud and Jung! I've never been in such a close call."

The other adults listened with growing consternation. They kept looking at the northern horizon. Sure enough, Miss Augusta, with her all-seeing glass eye, said, "There's black smoke, see it?"

Miss Jane said, "Dear God, please hurry up with the heli-copters."

Sheldon Summerton also had the same request, but not of

God. He got on his cell phone. "What's the status on the choppers? Can we hurry this up in any way?"

The service at the Al-Furqon Mosque seemed shorter than usual. The mosque emptied quickly, the congregation moving out onto the street. Some began unfurling and parading banners; the tops of some of them were visible over the compound wall. A few voices, none of which Isaac recognized, began chanting for American dogs to leave Java.

Sheldon yelled, "Everybody, get in your assigned groups. And for Christ—heaven's sake, would somebody—you, Dave, okay—run over to the dorm and tell the supervisors to get the kids out here."

Isaac followed Dave as if to help but veered off and climbed the flame tree. He didn't have the strength to make it to his usual lookout post. His breath came painfully short and his heart pounded. He stopped high enough to see over the wall.

The mob on Hospital Street was already several hundred people strong, and more were filtering in from the back alleys. Most were young males in battle uniforms of jeans and T-shirts and green headbands, many carrying staves and knives. A fair number of older adults, dressed in their conservative mosque cloths of sarong and blouse, seemed to be bemused by this turn of events. Pak Harianto, the barber, looked around him with alarm at his more agitated brethren. Sprinkled here and there were a dozen women still wearing their full white dresses and veils. The crowd gathered at the corner of Hospital Street and Hayam Wuruk Avenue. The front ranks of young males shouted their anti-American slogans.

But with their primary target bristling with hostile self-defenses, they soon turned to a secondary one. A few of the excitable lads began tossing stones at the second-floor window of the Friendship Store. "Open up!" they shouted. "We're thirsty and we want some drinks. We'll pay for them. Hey, listen, you Chinese dog, you're supposed to open for business hours. Why, are we not good enough for you? We said we will pay. Open up!"

Pak Harianto cried out, "Let him be."

The lads gave him the Javanese jeer, the long, high-pitched "Hiieeeee."

"He is our neighbor, and the Holy Qur'an says—"

A muscular man in a Nahdlatul Umat Islam T-shirt shouted, "What do you know of the Holy Qur'an? You still worship the spirits of your kris blades and seek magic charms from the *dukun santets*."

Pak Harianto stiffened. "I am as true a Muslim as you arrogant Nahdlatul Umat Islam windbags."

The Nahdlatul Umat Islam man raised an angry fist as though to strike the tiny barber. The mob was on the verge of splintering and disintegrating, for there were others who agreed with the barber and would have come to his defense.

A woman darted forward to pound on the shop's thick wooden shutters with a small fist. She shouted, "Open up, you bloodsucking thief. It's time for us to take back the milk you've stolen from our babies' mouths."

Isaac's jaw dropped. *Hey, that's Ruth.*

The other women followed her example, banging on the shutters and screeching.

The barber's protestations were overwhelmed, and he was shoved to the side. The young males and quite a few of their elders picked up pieces of crumbled sidewalk pavement and heaved them at the two-story building. The rocks did little harm. The shop had little exposed glass to break, except for the neon bulb over the shop sign, which shattered with a tinkling noise. A couple of the boys climbed on others' shoulders to claw at the sign with their hands.

Across the street the hospital guards stood in a tense phalanx, uncertain whether to intervene. Joe huddled together with Theophilus, who stepped forward and bellowed for the crowd to disperse, that this was a hospital area and the patients were not to be disturbed for the sake of their health.

This warning only served to rile the youths, who pranced and jeered. The more impetuous ones advanced a few steps across the tarmac and began throwing chunks of sidewalk at the guards.

At that Mr. Theophilus gestured for his guards to uncoil a hospital fire hose attached to a portable gasoline pump that suctioned a fifty-five-gallon drum. They fired up the pump and turned a crank. The hose spurt a powerful stream of liquid that Isaac at first assumed was water. It wasn't. Joe had cooked up a large tankload of something foul and sticky from the store of hospital chemicals and, by the smell that reached even Isaac, from the septic tanks as well. The liquid drenched many of the young men and sent them reeling back, retching and coughing. Many vomited. Some of the liquid splattered on the women, and they ran away yipping in disgust.

The gang of snarling youths regrouped. They began tearing up the sidewalk and chucked whole bricks at the security guards. Joe ordered a second volley of different ammunition. Three of the security guards pulled back slingshots made out of surgical hose and shot large test tubes. The test tubes broke on the pavement and hissed in white incandescent flares. Reddish orange smoke billowed. The young men began coughing, rubbing their eyes, scratching their skin. They scurried back in retreat.

"Wow," Isaac murmured, reminding himself to get the recipe.

The guards' actions bought a reprieve for the Friendship Store. Isaac did not descend the tree. He kept looking for helicopters. There'd be time to get down for the third one.

In the distance billows of smoke and gouts of flame erupted into the air, moving closer and closer to the hospital.

The remnants of the Hospital Street mob cocked their heads and ears. Two of the excitable lads ventured back to the corner of Hayam Wuruk Avenue to peer down the lifeless road.

A minute later the first vanguard of the town mob streamed into view on Hayam Wuruk Avenue, two dozen swaggering youths with ragged bandannas around their heads. They carried iron rods, sharpened bamboo stakes, antennas torn off cars. Some brandished fresh gleaming machetes taken from looted hardware shops. Many wore sunglasses with price tags still attached. One boy had a cassette stereo, partially wrapped in plastic, on his shoulders. With a bizarre sort of appropriateness, its speakers blared a Carpenters song about being on top of the world.

They marched forward in eager quickstep. From the back

rushed two lads with lit Molotov cocktails. The security guard sharpshooters took aim with their slingshots and got both boys with ball bearings as they were cocking their arms. The lit bottles fell to the ground, one bursting and spreading into a pool of fire. The two lads raced away to escape the flames.

The fire hose brigade also let loose with their foul liquid.

This first wave of attackers retreated and milled about in confusion.

Thirty seconds later the main force of the mob arrived. Hundreds of men of all ages swirled up the avenue. Some carried posters and banners, but this was no longer an orchestration of the Nahdlatul Umat Islam. The mob was beyond the control of any human agency.

One kid in a pair of new Reeboks too large for him hoisted a cardboard poster that showed a childishly sketched scene of a big-nosed, yellow-haired head on a spike, severed neck dripping blood, a crude scimitar in the background. Underneath this the slogan read: DEATH BY THE SWORD FOR UNREPENTANT INFIDELS.

Isaac blinked and blinked again, but this little vignette was not erasable. The kid was Ismail, wearing Isaac's oversized Reeboks, and the torsoless head was a gruesome rendition of Isaac's own.

The helicopters arrived just as the security guards were down to their last line of defense, firing off surgical gloves filled with supersticky rat glue. A number of the rioters were already stuck to the pavement, Ismail included. He finally had to pry himself out of the stolen Reeboks, leaving the shoes glued to the asphalt.

Sheldon yelled, "Get in place, everybody, we're on a count-down now."

Isaac got into his assigned place on the lawn. From the sky came a whirring. The first helicopter was on its landing glide, the whomping of its blades growing more visceral as it angled toward the big white "H" painted on the lawn. The helicopter became very big very quickly. A long boom jetted out of its nose. Stubby pods extended from underneath large square windows. A funny-looking tail rotor tilted off the vertical.

It blasted a hurricane at the ground.

When the helicopter was still six feet in the air, seven marines in combat gear jumped from its rear door, rolling on the grass to break their fall. Three raced to the alley gate, while another three darted to the northern wall, in time to face two of the rioters who had been hoisted over by the hands and shoulders of their com-rades outside. Upon seeing marines in full battle dress charging down on them, they lifted their hands in panicky surrender. They were swiftly and professionally trussed by two of the marines while the other jumped up with athletic vigor and used his rifle butt to smash two pairs of hands appearing at the top of the wall. Howls of pain rose from the other side.

The seventh marine was an officer. Sheldon ran up to the marine officer in a half crouch and shouted under the din of the chopper engines, "Boy, am I damn glad to see you. Cutting it pretty close there, I say."

The officer nodded. "First load up," he bellowed.

The schoolkids scurried out to the helicopter in two lines, supervised by Uncle Jimmy, Aunt Janice, and Miss Augusta. These three adults also boarded with them. The helmeted crew chief of the chopper got them seated and secured and then turned his attention to their luggage, which Sheldon, Joe, and the marine officer were passing on hand to hand. The officer made an "okay" sign with his fingers to the crew chief. The rear ramp lifted off the ground, like a jaw closing shut. The helicopter's blades sped up, and the metal body underneath them lifted off the ground in a mind-numbing noise that diminished quickly as the chopper flew off.

The quiet was deafening.

At the gate the faces of the rioters reappeared. A hail of stones came in over the compound wall. So did a Molotov cocktail in a Coca-Cola bottle. It did not break. One of the marines picked it up and made quick eye contact with the marine beside him. The second man grinned and nodded. The first marine tossed the bottle high in the air over the wall. The second marine tracked it with his rifle. As it began its descent he let off a burst that smashed the bottle. Flaming gas spewed onto the rioters below. The howls were even louder.

Graham Williams went over to Reverend Biggs and spoke to him, putting his mouth close to the reverend's ear. The reverend listened intently. When Graham was done speaking, the reverend said straightforwardly and with increasing volume over the noise of the second helicopter that was approaching, "You've made a hard choice. I was hoping you would buck against orders, even if they were my orders."

"The mission board might see it differently," Graham said, also increasing his volume.

"I'll back you the whole way. And when I get back home, I am going on a mission to the people of God about the persecution of Christians here. I am fired up, brother, I am truly fired up." The reverend was shouting at the end to be heard.

The second helicopter fell on its column of wind. Group two—all the rest of the adults, except for Graham and Mary Williams, Sheldon Summerton, and Joe—boarded. Loaded and with the ramp closed, the helicopter took off as though a giant's hand had jerked it upward. The third one descended at once, with the fourth circling overhead. Sheldon Summerton was already approaching Graham, yelling at him to get his family on board. A new salvo of Molotov cocktails, these properly made, arced into the compound, two of which landed on the garage roof, the instant flaring of flames biting deep. The marines let off more warning salvos.

Graham squatted and put his hand on Isaac's shoulder. "I have something to tell you. Your mother and I are not going. We're staying to be with the people here in the hospital, to try to keep them safe. This is not easy, but this is what God has told us to do. We won't be separated for long. I'm sure of that. You'll be just fine and we'll be just fine. Okay? We love you very much, so be brave and get on the helicopter without any fuss."

He hugged Isaac. He smelled as he always did, of stale coffee and aftershave. The skin on his cheek was as tough as a boot sole.

Mary escorted Isaac out to the helicopter. Her face was drawn and tense, her lower lip caught in a cruel bite between her teeth.

At the gangway she knelt and faced Isaac, one hand on her head to keep the wind from whipping her hair around. She took a breath and closed her eyes. When she opened them, they were moist and streaked with pain. She hugged Isaac hard and kissed him and then gave his hand to the crew chief, who pulled him on board with a swift, strong tug. The crew chief strapped him down on a surprisingly soft seat in the middle of the chopper. In front of them a gunner stood by a pair of machine guns that hung from some sort of swivel on the ceiling, and beyond him were the pilot and copilot. The crew chief placed headphones on Isaac's ears. The throbbing clamor of the engines and the blades quieted to a dull whisper. Isaac stared out the open rear doorway at his parents. Mary had rejoined her husband on the sidelines. Sheldon was gesturing at them. Graham shook his head in that deliberate, reasoned way of his. Isaac could almost read his lips. He was saying something like, *This is how it is, we're staying*. He smiled at his wife and took her arm in his.

The marine officer held up his palm in a wait sign to the helicopter pilot and then went over to the Williamses. He gestured toward the waiting helicopter. Mary spoke to him. The officer turned and gave the pilot a thumbs-up.

A volley of stones came over the wall. Half the garage roof was on fire. The consulate chauffeur dashed frantically back and forth around the Ford, ready to catch any bomb before it landed on the vehicle. Automatic rifles chattered.

Several men in khaki uniform appeared at the gate—

Lieutenant Nugroho and six of his cops. Graham caught his wife's eye and jerked his chin toward the policemen. Mary shook her head and pointed out to the helicopter. She wanted to make sure her son got off okay.

The crew chief fiddled with controls by the door. He was trying to shut the ramp, but after lifting only a foot it stuck and would not raise any farther. Isaac could see him talking rapidly into his helmet mouthpiece, communicating with the pilot. The marine officer made hurry-up-and-get-away motions.

The pilot made his decision. The ground outside the rear door suddenly pulled away, as though it were the solid earth that was dropping out from under the helicopter rather than the helicopter rising from it. The ramp remained as it was, a tongue sticking out into the sky. Graham put his arm around Mary. Through the open ramp way, Isaac saw them waving. Mary shouted something. Isaac continued staring at the dwindling image of his parents.

The helicopter did not ascend as rapidly as the others had. The pilot and crew chief were still trying to get the ramp unstuck. For a moment the craft lowered slightly as the pilot made some quick touches to the instrument panel. Through the large round window beside him, Isaac saw the fourth helicopter on the ground, with Joe rigging up the hoist lines for the Ford. The marines had retreated backward from the walls toward the helicopter. Isaac craned his head and peered out the open ramp way. The rioters had placed debris over the lake of rat glue. The hospital guards were now reinforced by a platoon of the lieutenant's loyal policemen. Several of the community leaders had joined the guards as well, Pak Harianto among them. Tanto stood between that final rank of defenders and the rioters. He had his back to the hospital, his arms spread, and he was shouting at the rioters. Was he further enticing them or now trying to calm them down?

A movement at the alley gate caught Isaac's attention. Lieutenant Nugroho, his gun drawn and ready, escorted Mary and Graham Williams into the hospital building.

Chapter Ten

THE HELICOPTER FLEW SANDWICHED in the lifeless space between a dying sky and a burning city. Hayam Wuruk Avenue was in flames. Through the window Isaac saw a car burning beside a pump at the Pertamina gasoline station. The helicopter flew over the car. The pilot must not have realized what was below, for it seemed to Isaac to be a stupid thing to do, considering there were underground bunkers of gasoline that could blow up at any second. He'd no sooner framed the thought when a tremendous explosion whooshed up from the ground, shaking the helicopter with bone-jarring jolts. The first jolt threw the unstrapped crew chief out the open ramp way. One moment he was there, the next he was not. Isaac yelled in stunned alarm, but nobody heard him. The helicopter leveled out, but not for long. A car door fell onto the ramp way. Then something else whacked into the whirling helicopter blades. The helicopter cavorted in wild circles and roller-coaster arcs. The ground below spun in and out of Isaac's view as gravity tugged this way and that.

His hands, with a calm intelligence of their own, removed his headphones and opened the buckle of his strap. As he stood the helicopter rose sharply, and he tumbled toward the rear. The chopper stabilized in a horizontal position for a second, and Isaac found himself at the edge of the ramp way. The chopper was still falling, though. The Buddhist temple on top of Wonobo's only riverside cliff flashed past. The helicopter was a second from crashing into the Brantas River when it started one last crazy swoop upward. For half a second it remained still, moving neither up nor down, teetering on the cusp of gravity.

Without making any conscious decision to do so, Isaac jumped. He didn't know how high off the ground he was. His stomach shot up into his throat. He fell into a back eddy of the Brantas, soft and muddy, which gently broke his fall. Isaac scrambled to his feet in time to see the helicopter falling onto the sandstone boulders of the riverbank. The stuck ramp sheared off, flattening a clutch of abandoned outhouses made of rusty iron sheeting. Isaac instinctively covered his ears, but instead of a deafening explosion, there was only a momentary crunching and grinding. A black rubber bag fell out of the helicopter's torn side, a self-sealable fuel bladder that worked as it was designed to. The busted tail pylon stuck vertically into the air over the crushed outhouses.

Screams and shouts swirled down the cliff. Isaac glanced up. Rioters brandishing spears and knives streamed down steps worn over the centuries into the sandstone face. Leading the pack was a teenager with coarse hair sprouting from a pimply chin. Udin.

Isaac waded toward the middle of the river. He struggled in the waist-deep brown water, the mucky bottom sucking at his shoes. He sobbed, beyond wit or reason, fleeing only on instinct. At last he made it to the far bank and scrabbled on feet and hands up the steep bank to the wall of sugarcane. He plunged into the field, the sharp leaves cutting the skin of his exposed arms. He ran until he could run no farther. He collapsed facedown between the thick cane stems. Each breath was an agony.

The sound of a helicopter beat into his consciousness. He flung himself over on his back. The cane was a good ten feet high, the stems swollen and purple, the last crop on the last of the river's juices, but there were gaps in the green-and-yellow ceiling. Isaac saw a dark blue Ford falling through the air, its four wheels parallel to the ground. Over the unseen helicopter's noise, he heard the car hit river mud with a thwacking splat.

The fourth helicopter had jettisoned its cargo in order to make a fast landing.

Isaac once more plunged through the cane to get back to the river. Heavy gunfire rattled, the sound seeming to come from everywhere. He became disoriented, and when he finally shot out into the open on the riverbank, he saw the helicopter lifting off the far side, already having rescued the living and the dead from the downed chopper. The gunner kept firing rounds to keep at bay hundreds of agitated men swarming down the cliff.

The helicopter moved backward at an elevation of twenty feet, its nose angled downward toward the crippled ship, as though it were giving a last salute to its fallen comrade. But all the pilot was doing was giving himself some firing room. The left armament pod erupted with a tremendous whoosh, and a pin-straight trail of white smoke zoomed toward the downed helicopter, the rocket moving too fast to see. The wreckage exploded in a tremendous roaring fireball.

The helicopter rose from its hover into fast-forward motion. Isaac belatedly began to jump, screaming and waving his hands. Nobody on the helicopter noticed him. It was soon a speck in the distance.

But several of the men on the cliff spotted Isaac, pointing and shouting. Isaac fled back into the sugarcane.

The earlier life-and-death panic that had fueled his frantic fleeing subsided to a more controllable fright. What he needed to do was to get back to the hospital. He moved more carefully between the cane stalks to avoid a telltale waggling of their tops. When he came to an open cart path, he looked in each direction before crossing. He saw no one. He moved on without stopping. The longer he walked, the slower time passed, until he seemed to be locked forever into the present moment called "now." His damp underwear chafed. After a while he stopped making his way through the cane but used instead the easier cart paths, walking out in the open. The concern of being spotted had drifted off his mental horizon. The entire world of his senses collapsed to that of his muddy, torn Hush Puppies appearing and disappearing in his downcast view.

Nausea struck. He doubled over and heaved, bringing up slimy bile. His teeth chattered against a sudden chill. A powerful headache gnawed the inside of his head and chewed on the back of his eyeballs. He recognized his symptoms. His red blood cells were beginning to rupture, releasing millions of malaria protozoa to wreak havoc on his body.

He came to an elevated, potholed tarmac road and a weedy

railroad track. The ditch fed a large iron pipe running underneath the road and track. Across the road was a traditional farmer's stilt house, surrounded on three sides by palms and a bamboo fence. On the far side of that house was a grander one of brick and glass.

The malarial attack gathered force. Isaac crawled into the iron pipe, like a wounded animal, not caring what creepy-crawlies were in there. He shook and shivered. The cloying air in the pipe became cold and thin. He crept to the opening at the far end, attracted to the light there and its promise of warmth. He collapsed, his teeth and bones rattling. The light at first had no heat to it. Then, as though a boiler switch had been turned on, it became hot and steamy. The light, even though hazy and indirect, squeezed his eyeballs in a vise.

Dear Lord, please help me.

But the ramparts of heaven were shut, and Jesus did not come to His child. Isaac realized that Reverend Biggs's prophecy of returning safely home was not meant for him.

His fever at last undermined his consciousness, collapsing it into a black hole, rimmed at the top with the faintest glimmer of light. At some point that light began to flicker, and Isaac thought, *I'm going to die.* But the flickering was not an internal arrhythmia of vision. Actual objects were moving around him. On him, too. Something dug into his chest with sharp claws. He jerked. A sharp, tearing pain flared in his left cheek. It hurt enough to bring him to a shallow level of consciousness again. He found himself staring into the bright eyes of a crow inches away from his face. The crow had taken a stab at his left eye and had missed because of his movement. More crows crowded around the lip of the culvert opening.

He shrieked and batted the crow away from him. It tumbled over the others. He kicked and flailed at them. They took wing with strident caws.

A voice from outside exclaimed, "I told you something is in there."

Two heads popped into sight at the end of the tunnel, silhouetted against the fading sunlight. Young Javanese teenagers. One let out a whoop. "Here he is! Right here! The bulé kid!"

Isaac did not have the strength to move.

More heads appeared, including Udin's. A cigarette dangled from his lips. He cleared the boys from the end of the pipe and stuck his head and shoulders inside. He got his hands around Isaac's feet and pulled. Isaac didn't have the strength to resist. More rough hands got hold of him and yanked him out of the pipe. They bundled him onto the road. Two boys had to hold his arms to keep him upright. He sagged in place, with his eyes closed.

"Is he alive?" somebody said.

"We'll see," Udin said. A fist landed in Isaac's stomach. He doubled over, groaning. "He's alive."

Isaac burrowed back into his fever, retreating from these teenagers. They stripped off his clothes and complained about his empty pockets. "Where's your money, bulé? Where did you hide it? Up your ass? Let's have a look." They ripped off his underwear and howled with laughter when they saw his penis.

Udin said, "A true infidel. Look at that thing. An uncircumcised worm in its blanket."

"Hey, I know, we can circumcise him ourselves," someone said, and tugged hard on his foreskin. This threat was enough for Isaac to finally open his eyes. The eager, shining, laughing faces surrounding him swayed and spun and melted into one another. He begged, "Please don't, I'm sick."

A few heads jerked back. "Hieee, he speaks Javanese!"

"Of course he does, but let's see if he can scream in Javanese," Udin said. He took a deep drag on his cigarette, drawing the glowing ember down to the butt. Holding the butt between his forefinger and thumb, he brought it down toward Isaac's groin.

"What are you boys doing? Here now, get away from him." A thin man with a farmer's splayed feet pushed away the outer ring of teenagers. The boys holding Isaac's arms let go, and Isaac crumpled to the road's gritty surface. Udin flicked away his cigarette butt and winked down at him.

The man said, "Why is he naked? You boys would tease a monkey to death."

A second farmer appeared in front of Isaac. The first bent over Isaac, touching his forehead and neck with calloused hands. "He's burning up," the man said.

One of the kids said, "He's the bulé boy from the hospital who ran away from the helicopter crash."

The second farmer said, "It's going to be trouble if anybody finds him here. Just put some clothes on him and toss him out on the highway somewhere. Let someone else deal with him."

"No, we'll let the Tuan Guru's people decide what to do with him."

The men helped Isaac to his feet and into his clothes. They tugged at him to get him walking, but his steps were so wobbly that they picked him up by his arms and legs. Udin carried Isaac's right arm and purposefully twisted it until Isaac yelped in pain. They carried him across the road and into the brick-and-glass house. The lowering sun's rays reflected blindly off the window-panes. He was taken into a storage closet of some kind just inside the back door. The air smelled of dust, turpentine, and rust. The only light came from the cracks in the shuttered window. One of the men kicked aside empty tin cans to make room for a straw mat that one of them brought in. They dumped Isaac on this mat and dropped his dirty shoes at his feet.

Isaac was left in the dark to the ministrations of his malaria. The cycle peaked, and his fever broke in another flood of sweat.

He felt around the door. It had no handle, and he could not shove it open.

Without warning, his bowels spasmed. He barely had enough time to place an empty, oily burlap bag as far back into a corner as he could to squat over to do his business. He had eaten so little over the last few days that what came out were little round pellets, small but concentrated in odor, which enveloped him and numbed his nose with the stench.

A tinkle of chimes sounded from the front door. Feet trudged up the corridor outside Isaac's little cell to answer and then came thudding back in a run. A boy shouted in a strangled stage whisper: "Father, it's the police. They are at the front door."

Isaac began shouting. "Hey, hey, I'm—"

The door to the cell flung open. Udin clasped his hand around Isaac's mouth and hooked his elbow around his neck. He half lifted Isaac off the ground, nearly breaking his neck. "Shut up if you want to stay alive," he whispered into Isaac's ear. He suddenly sniffed. "Allah, it stinks in here."

The *bapak* of the house opened the front door. "Yes?" he said guardedly.

"I'm looking for a twelve-year-old white boy. A report came into the station that he was seen near here." Lieutenant Nugroho's gruff voice galvanized Isaac, who squirmed and jerked in Udin's arms. He got the fleshy bit of Udin's finger between his front teeth and bit hard. Udin inhaled with pain and, with his free hand, whacked Isaac on the side of the head hard enough that Isaac saw red spots.

"Ah, the boy who ran away from the helicopter crash. I'm sorry for that. We want all the Americans gone without any complications."

"We want you flushed away like turds," Udin whispered. "By Allah, you stink, little boy. You're a turd that wouldn't go down the hole. This whole room stinks."

"He isn't here."

Isaac could hear the lieutenant's sigh. "I know this boy. He's only an innocent kid."

"Is he a Christian?"

"Naturally."

"Then he is not so innocent. The way and the truth of

Islam have been plainly there for him to see."

"You speak like a *kiai,* in fact like the Tuan Guru, whose portrait I see there. The boy is harmless, then. Is that better? A boy is a boy, no matter what race or religion. How would you feel if your son were lost in a strange land of Christians?"

"Officer, I have nothing against this boy. I wish him no harm. I only wish him and all Americans gone from here. It truly is unfortunate that the helicopter crashed."

"This is going to turn into a major diplomatic row, and the sooner the boy is turned over to the Americans, the better for all of us, including the Tuan Guru Haji Abdullah Abubakar."

The *bapak* said, his words stiff with frost, "The Tuan Guru is not afraid of Americans. If they are so mighty and powerful, why did their tall towers come crashing down? Why did one of their helicopters fall out of the sky? Allah is mightier than any power on earth, and Allah is on our side."

"Yes, Allah is mightier than all of us, mightier than the looters who thieved in his name with the cry of *Allahu akbar,* mightier than we faithful believers, mightier even than Tuan Guru Haji Abdullah Abubakar; and the Tuan Guru himself would be the first to tell you that," Lieutenant Nugroho said. Nothing more was said for a few seconds, and then the police officer said, "Thank you for your time. Please contact us if you have any further information about the boy. Remember that the hands closest to the fire are in the greatest danger of being burned."

"That is true," the *bapak* said.

The door closed.

Udin carefully let go of Isaac. Isaac spun around and shoved. Udin went tumbling backward, his arm and side landing on top of the burlap bag Isaac had used for a toilet. He was puzzled by the substance sticking to his skin. He took a quick suspicious sniff and then rocketed to his feet. He screamed, calling Isaac all kinds of obscene names. He got Isaac by his hair and the nape of his neck and forced his face down into the burlap bag.

Isaac fought back, but Udin in his fury was too strong.

"Hey, hey, here now, stop that," the *bapak* said, pulling Udin away from Isaac.

Isaac got to his knees, spitting and gagging and crying.

"He's worse than a dog," Udin panted. "Even dogs get trained not to shit in the house."

"Where else could I go?" Isaac wailed. He said to the bapak, "Please let me go. I'm sick, I have malaria, please let me go."

"By God," another man growled. "Are you keeping a boy or a pig in here?"

Isaac stared at the feet in the doorway—thick horny feet in sandals, the feet of a gardener who likes working barefoot so he can feel the earth under his soles. The stout legs were encased in trousers and the broad shoulders in a batik shirt. Isaac had never seen Tanto so dressed up before. Even his peci cap was a dark blue velvet that shone in the dim light of the corridor's single bulb. He returned Isaac's stare with a wrinkle-nosed frown of distaste.

Isaac stood. "Hello, Mas Tanto," he said.

"Shut up," Tanto said tonelessly but meaning it. "Don't speak unless it's to answer a question."

Udin and Tanto marched Isaac up a narrow stairway to a tiled bathroom with a cement cistern of water. A naked lightbulb dangled on a wire, shedding yellow light.

"Get him some clean clothes," Tanto ordered Udin. "And not rags. Something halfway decent. And a towel."

Tanto told Isaac to undress. Isaac complied reluctantly, recalling how the others had reacted to his uncircumcised penis. All Tanto said was, "You'll have to have that taken care of if you are going to be a Muslim."

"I don't want to become a—"

"Shut up. Use lots of soap. You stink."

Isaac stared at the water in the cistern. His thirst suddenly became overwhelming. The water looked clean enough, but he didn't care if it was loaded with enough bacteria to light up a thousand petri dishes. He dunked a plastic dipper and drank greedily. Tanto said, "Stop, you're going to blow up."

His thirst slaked, Isaac poured water over himself. He shivered and kept shivering, not from malarial fever, but because the fever had burned through so much of his insulating fat that the water seemed to be as cold as the Arctic Ocean.

Tanto said, "What is wrong with you?"

"I have malaria. Mas Tanto, my parents, are they—"

"Shut up."

"Are they okay?"

"*Shut up.*" It wasn't quite a roar, but the menace was loud and certain.

Isaac shut up. He soaped his skin and his hair. He cleaned the wound on his cheek as best he could. Udin brought back a hand towel and a Javanese high school uniform. Isaac rubbed himself dry and put on the blue shorts and the white short-sleeved shirt. The clothes were a size too big and smelled of mothballs.

Tanto blindfolded Isaac with the wet towel. "One word out of you and I will stuff another towel down your throat," he threatened.

They led Isaac out of the house and into the back of what he guessed was a box van. An engine started, and the vehicle drove off with enough wobble and bounce that Isaac had to brace himself against the front wall of the box.

Isaac lifted the bottom of his blindfold. It was pitch-black. He crawled to the rear of the box and tried the door for formality's sake. It was locked, as he knew it would be.

Isaac tried to trace the van's route in his mind, but it was hopeless. The vehicle rolled along the flatlands for a while and then turned up into the hills. Isaac grew nauseous from an interminable series of swaying curves that bounced him around. The ride seemed endless. At last the vehicle stopped. The driver shut off the engine. There was the sound of a key in a lock, and then the rear door opened. The bottom of Isaac's blindfold was still lifted and tucked into the top. Night had fully fallen. There were enough scattered lights for him to get a glimpse of field, part of it fenced. Beyond a silhouette of trees were the distinctive cupola of a small mosque and a stout three-story building, around which were more elegant rooflines of shorter buildings. The draft of air into the clammy box was cold; wherever they were was at a much higher altitude than Wonobo.

Udin jumped up into the back and attacked Isaac, his fist crunching into Isaac's chest and belly and shoulders while he shouted at him to keep the blindfold in place. "I'll teach you a lesson," he said, and smacked Isaac with such a stunning blow to the face that Isaac thought his right cheekbone had cracked. He fell to the floor of the box, holding his hands over his head.

"Let him be," Tanto said, scrambling into the box and getting between them.

Isaac cried. He wanted to be stoic and brave, but the pain and fear were too much for him to keep at bay. "What have I done to you?" he sobbed.

"Be quiet," Tanto told him. Isaac took a deep breath and put a clamp on his sniffles. Tanto fixed the blindfold and helped him down out of the box and across the field. The ground was soft and chilly under Isaac's bare feet. Crickets chirped. The odor of mud and cow was strong on the nippy air. A gate creaked opened and then a door, accompanied by annoyed snorts and the shuffling of hooves. Isaac's bare feet now scraped on rough cement. Tanto pulled him to a stop and removed the blindfold. Udin held a flashlight. They were in a large shed, divided in two by a half wall of split planks. A bulky, two-wheeled cart took up most of one side. The flashlight glinted off a tin-sheeted roof and plywood walls. On the other side of the half wall were two bulls in ox stalls. They weren't happy with Isaac's presence. They blew air and swung their horns.

"Get in the cart," Tanto ordered. "It will be your new home for a while."

He put a clamp on Isaac's left wrist. The clamp was a large U bolt with a padlocked pin attached to a heavy iron chain. It was meant to be attached to the cart to prevent anyone from making off with it. The other end of the chain was banded onto a stout coconut log stump on which the front of the cart rested.

"I'd be quiet if I were you," Tanto said. "These Madurese racing bulls don't like the smell of bulé."

Udin shined the flashlight in their direction. Isaac saw red eyeballs and wicked horn tips.

"See that bucket on the ground there? That's your toilet," Tanto went on. "Try to keep your clothes clean; those are the last clothes you're getting."

Isaac was quiet. His right eye was swelling rapidly. Somebody was bound to show up to take care of the bulls. He would beg to be released or at least to have a message taken to the cops.

Tanto and Udin left without another word.

Isaac's thirst returned. It was a convenient focal point for his thoughts, which if given free rein would have overwhelmed him, reducing him to hysteria. He did not know how long he sat in the cart before a malarial fever spiked again. He heard in his hallucinations a man chanting in Arabic. "Ar-Razzaz, Al-Fattah, Al-Alim, Al-Basit . . . no, no, not Al-Basit. Al-Qabiz. Al-Qabiz. Al-Qabiz before Al-Basit, Al-Qabiz and then Al-Basit, you stupid brain of mine." Isaac opened his good eye and saw a man as squat as a toadstool holding a kerosene lantern high, studying him.

"Hello, Pak," Isaac said as courteously as he could. "How are you tonight?"

The man said nothing. He was a hunchback. He had no neck. It looked as though his head had been placed onto a pit in his shoulders. His eyes were sunken pools rimmed by thick bone and adorned by heavy brows. He had a thin, twisted nose. He looked like a creature that a fevered imagination would produce.

Isaac asked, "My parents, are they okay?"

The hunchback did not reply. Isaac's mind swirled away. When he next came back to consciousness, two faces drifted in the unstable vision of his good eye. One was the heavy-browed and sharp-nosed hunchback, still holding his lantern high. The other was a woman in a green jilbab headdress that emphasized the roundness of her face, which bobbed around like a balloon.

The hunchback said to her in Javanese, "He was shaking so much, the chain was clanking. Something's wrong with him. I'll keep an eye on him like Mas Tanto said, yes, but not to watch him die."

The woman lifted Isaac's chained wrist. Her fingers were cool and strong. She took his other wrist and counted his pulse. She put the palm of her hand to his neck to gauge his temperature. She bent closer to study the crow peck on his cheek and his swollen right eye.

"That Tanto," she said. "He pretends he's a bin Laden militant and forgets he's a cultured Javanese. You shouldn't even treat an animal like this. And he's burning up. Malaria, probably." She lowered Isaac's wrist. "Thank you, Mas Bengkok. Let's get him out of here. Mas Tanto gave you a key to this lock, didn't he?"

The hunchback nodded. "But what if Imam Ali finds out we've moved this boy?"

The woman pondered briefly. "I'll tell the kiai," she said. "If the honored teacher takes an interest in this boy, which I think he will, then there is not much that group can do. Please, remove the shackle."

The hunchback obeyed. Isaac moaned and touched his wrist, already cut from the shackle's chafing.

The woman said, "We'll put him in the second-floor *mushollah* in the tower. Only the first-floor bathrooms are still being used. It's a perfect place to keep him. But we'll have to sneak him in. The children haven't gone to bed. If they see a bulé child, *aiyah,* they'd be worse than a pack of Balinese dogs barking at a jinn."

Mas Bengkok put a large burlap feed bag onto a trolley with wooden wheels and told Isaac to get into the bag. The woman helped him, smiling reassuringly. She wore a matronly blouse and a full skirt that grazed the ground, both the same shade of green as her headdress. She said in the same soothing tones she would use for an injured animal, not knowing he could understand, "Don't be frightened. We're moving you to a more comfortable place where we can take better care of you."

The hunchback, who still hadn't said a word to Isaac, said to the woman, "He speaks Javanese."

The woman's brows rose in surprise.

"My parents," Isaac whispered, looking up at her from the bag. "Are they okay?"

"Oh, you do speak Javanese," the woman said. She said to the hunchback, "I'll go ahead and get the room ready."

"Please. My parents."

"You must be quiet," the woman said, not unkindly.

The hunchback pulled the bag over Isaac's head. The gates to the shed creaked open. It seemed that the hunchback pushed the trolley over every rut and bump he could find. The air in the bag was rank with remnants of decaying hay. But a little bit more misery on top of Isaac's fever and pains meant nothing.

The hunchback began muttering in that gravelly voice of his, "Start at Al-Mumit, and what comes after Al-Mumit is Al-Haiy, Al-Qaiyum, Al-Wajid, Al-Wahid, Al-Qadir—no, no, no, not Al-Qadir. As-Samad, As-Samad, As-Samad! Aiyah, start from the beginning again: Allah Ar-Rahman, Ar-Rahim, Al-Malik . . ."

A creaking of a gate, some more rough bumps, and then sounds familiar from the American Academy boarders' dorm, of rambunctious children expending their last bit of energy just before bed. There was a thwack of a ball being kicked and then the thump of the ball as it hit the trolley. A boy shouted, "Beware the hunchback, for a jinn rides upon his shoulders."

The hunchback shouted back, "The insult of a eunuch is praise to a real man's ears."

The fragrance of night blooming jasmine, the earthy mustiness of turned dirt, and the biting odor of fertilizer penetrated the sack, as did the pleasantly bitter scent of roasting coffee. A radio, or possibly a television, blared its evening news from Jakarta. The woman broadcaster talked of looming war and of ambassadors being summoned here and there to receive warnings and complaints. She mentioned military aircraft and airspace intrusions and spoke of crashed helicopters and a missing American child and the Wonobo Tragedy.

The hunchback pushed on, resuming his recital of Arabic. He got stuck. "What comes next?" he muttered. "What a dung heap of a brain I have." He sighed and a moment later opened the top of the burlap sack. "We're at the stairs. You take this blanket and pull it over your head, and then you hurry up those stairs. I'll be right behind you, so no tricks."

Isaac did as he was told. It was too dark to see the steps. His head was spinning by the time they got to the second-floor landing. He panted with ragged gasps. He was so weak, the hunchback had to hold him up. He reached around Isaac and opened the unlocked door. He half carried, half dragged Isaac down a dark, empty, echoey corridor and into a tiny room lit by a round fluorescent bulb. The round-faced woman in green helped him onto a canvas cot.

"I have something here for you to drink," the woman said. "It is for your malaria and will help you sleep."

She held the teacup to his lips. Her fingers were blunt and calloused. Her right forefinger was crooked from an old and poorly mended break. The brew was bitter enough that he grimaced and tried to turn away, but she forced the green liquid down him. She gave him a glass of warm boiled water to rinse his mouth.

"You'll sleep now," the woman said.

The *jamu* had a quick effect on Isaac's shrunken stomach. The circuits of his brain shut off. When they came back on, it was with the sensation that time had passed, but everything was still the same, including the round-faced woman, ready with more jamu. "So, your name is Isak. That is a good name from the Book. I am

Ibu Halimah, named after a woman of a desert tribe who had the great honor of becoming the Prophet's wet nurse when the Prophet, *salla allahu alaihi wa sallam,* was still a baby. He suckled at Halimah's breast, along with her own child."

Ibu Halimah lifted a cup to Isaac's mouth. He drank the thick, grassy liquid. He closed his eyes and was taken away to a world of twirling figures, snippets of words, echoes of screams, hints of heat, and carrion birds perched on barkless branches of dead trees. Then that world vanished into the sweet nothingness of unconscious sleep.

Several woozy days passed, the equilibrium between parasite and herbal medicine sloshing back and forth from one side of the battlefield to the other. Isaac drifted in and out of his stupor. Every time the jamu wore off, something with glittering eyes chased him back to wakefulness.

When he next came to, Tanto stood brooding over him. "I only find out now that you moved him," he said to Ibu Halimah. He was wearing a gardening uniform of shorts, dirty T-shirt, and bare feet. "You didn't even tell me. I nearly raised the alarm when I saw the empty shed."

Ibu Halimah's natural posture of authority stiffened to regal imperiousness. She said, "If I had told you, you would have told Imam Ali. Now that the kiai knows he is here, you can't take him away, can you?"

Tanto snorted. "A single woman is able to destroy paradise," he said.

Ibu Halimah harrumphed. "It takes years to learn the ways of a Madurese racing bull but only one day to learn about men. And from what I saw, the bulls were getting better treatment than this child. Shame on you."

"The shed was not going to harm him," Tanto said. "And he needed a little lesson in the harsh things of life. Didn't you, Isak? Life is hard outside those compound walls of the mission."

Isaac stared at the gardener.

Tanto said to Ibu Halimah, "A million Javanese children get sick with malaria every year, and most of them don't get even half the attention you are giving this bulé boy."

"He is a special boy. The Tuan Guru says that Allah has chosen him for a special purpose."

"Maybe we should just circumcise him, make him say the *shahadah,* and get it over with."

Isaac rose on his elbow. He croaked, "Mas Tanto, what's happened to my parents?"

Tanto scowled. "Why didn't your parents leave on the helicopter?"

"They're doctors, they help the sick and the poor and—"

"They are Christians trying to convert Muslims. In true Muslim countries you would have all been beheaded."

"Is that why you made that secret gate in the wall? So you could sneak in at night and kill us?"

Tanto growled and said, "We're not murderers."

"So why did you make the gate?"

"We were planning a raid, to put you on a boat to Singapore

quietly and without fuss. We didn't expect helicopters, but they did the job for us, praise be to Allah. Your parents should have gone on them."

"Why did you rob the church?"

"Rob? We were merely collecting the infidel tax."

"Then why are you wearing Reverend Biggs's watch?"

Tanto immediately covered the watch with his left hand.

Ibu Halimah arched her left eyebrow. "So that is where you got it," she said.

"I could have kept the Chinaman's gold Rolex," Tanto said. "This watch is hardly worth anything."

"If it's part of the tax, then it doesn't belong to you," Ibu Halimah said. She held out her hand. The two adults glared at each other. Tanto lost the battle of wills. He stripped off the watch and tossed it at her.

"I don't know why I don't divorce you," he growled. "Other wives are dutiful and respectful, but you are like the thorns of a cactus plant."

He stomped out of the room without another word.

Isaac said to Ibu Halimah, "You two are married to each other?"

"Fifteen years. We have one son. About your age. My boy is smart, but my husband—well, he has the stout heart of a bull, and sometimes the brain of one."

From the noises that had filtered into his periods of semi-consciousness, and from the sweet coolness of the air, he knew that he was at an Islamic school, a *pesantren* run by the Nahdlatul

Umat Islam, high in the mountains. But he asked anyway, "Where am I?"

"In a safe place," Ibu Halimah said.

"What's going to happen to me?"

"Nothing bad. We will all be told in time."

"Do you know anything about my parents, Ibu?"

"Don't worry, Isak. Mas Tanto did not allow anyone to harm them."

Isaac waited for a flood of happiness at the news. All that came was a little trickle of relief that he did not have to worry about his parents. "When will I see them again?"

"When Allah wills. No more questions."

Another woman in green robes and headdress brought in a tray with a bowl of steaming rice porridge flavored with chicken broth and a glass of sweet lukewarm tea. Beside the bowl was a spoon wrapped inside half a paper napkin. She also had a small Garuda Airlines cabin bag over her shoulder. She placed the tray on the seat of the chair and hung the bag on its back. She left.

Ibu Halimah said, "Eat now."

The rice porridge was ambrosia. But after only half the bowl he began to feel as stuffed as a Thanksgiving turkey. He pushed the bowl aside.

Ibu Halimah said, "Finish the food. Your stomach can take it. And you need the strength to start your studies tomorrow. The kiai himself will teach you." She beamed as though Isaac were most fortunate and favored.

"My studies?"

"Certainly. You are in a school, are you not?"

Isaac contemplated this startling revelation. Something dark grew within his heart. "I don't want to study anything here," he said.

Ibu Halimah sighed as though she had heard this sort of truculence before from many reluctant scholars. "Isak, this is a difficult time for you. It is foolish to pretend otherwise. You can't exactly keep busy in here, so you need something to occupy your thoughts."

"But I'm still sick."

"Yes, it is a nasty malaria you have, but your attacks are getting less severe."

"What am I going to be studying?"

"Why, the Holy Qur'an, of course. This is an Islamic school."

Isaac stiffened. "But I'm a Christian."

"Of course you are. That does not mean you cannot study the Holy Qur'an. Finish the porridge and drink your tea."

Isaac did so, after which Ibu Halimah said, "Now you will bathe. Starting tomorrow it will be first the bath and then *magrib* evening prayers and then dinner. In that bag are a small towel, soap, a toothbrush, and a change of clothes. The *mandi* is on the first floor. Mas Bengkok will take you there and back. You shouldn't be seeing anyone, but if you do, do not speak to them. Not one word. Understand?"

Isaac understood.

Isaac left his cell for the first time, escorted by Mas Bengkok, who was camping out in the hall. By the door was a cot similar to

Isaac's, and on the floor beside it was a thermos of tea and an old radio.

One end of the hallway was blocked with construction plywood; just this side of it was an indoor stairway. Mas Bengkok led Isaac down the cobwebby steps. Isaac's muscles were weak. He descended the steps at half speed, putting both feet on each tread before moving down to the next.

Mas Bengkok was chanting again: "Allah Ar-Rahman, Ar-Rahim, Al-Malik, Al-Quddus, As-Salam . . ."

They came to the bottom landing. Mas Bengkok ceased his chanting and slowly peered around the corner. Satisfied, he stepped out into the corridor and motioned Isaac to follow. He pointed to a tin-sheeted door. Isaac pushed it open and entered a washroom about the size of two phone booths illuminated by a flickering bulb. The rough cinder-block walls were coated with thin whitewash. Built into the corner was a cement water cistern with a brass tap plugged into the wall. A plastic dipper floated in the water. Algae grew in the corners of the unevenly tiled floor. A squat toilet—two cement footpads on either side of a hole—graced the spot between the cistern and the near wall. Nailed into the space above the toilet was a small wooden platform.

Isaac closed the door and put the Garuda bag on the platform. He squatted over the hole. On the other side of the mandi wall somebody was moving around. He immediately thought about hollering for help, but what good would that do?

Isaac bathed, using harsh lye soap he found in the Garuda bag. He also found a cheap plastic toothbrush and a small tube of hotel toothpaste, along with a pair of used but clean gym shorts and a T-shirt with a faded judo club logo on it. There was no underwear. The thin towel hardly dried off all of him, and damp spots appeared all over the clothes, including an embarrassing spot on the crotch. But what was there to be embarrassed about? Nobody was going to see it except a hunchback.

Mas Bengkok knocked loudly.

"Okay, okay," Isaac said, smearing his hair down with his hands before opening the door.

Mas Bengkok took one look at him and said, "You have a toilet in there, and you still manage to piss in your pants." He marched Isaac back up the stairs, once more chanting the sequence of Arabic words as though it were a litany. Once again he stumbled over a word and roundly cursed himself.

"What is that you keep saying?" Isaac asked. He repeated a sequence.

The hunchback's eyes widened. "You pronounce those perfectly."

"So what are they?"

"Those are the first seven names of Allah. There are ninety-two more."

The hunchback locked Isaac into the mushollah cell. His footsteps scurried away down the hall. Moments later a loudspeaker came to life somewhere near the mushollah, broadcasting the call to prayer.

Isaac put his good eye to the crack in the shutters. He was on the second floor above a well-tended garden crisscrossed with graveled paths leading toward a one-story building of glass and marble and pale blue roof tiles. Above the teak doors of the entrance was a sign with a one-line scrawl of Arabic, a verse from the Qur'an. The Indonesian translation said: MY LORD! INCREASE IN ME KNOWLEDGE.

Through the building's open windows, Isaac saw a single room, devoid of any furniture, which was too large to be a classroom. The room was brightly lit with fluorescent lights. Children knelt at prayer on their mats. The boys wore brown sarongs and white shirts. In their half of the room, segregated by a cloth screen, the girls were dressed in white from head to toe.

A short while later, after the prayers were finished, Mas Bengkok unlocked and threw open the door to Isaac's cell, holding a radio. "Listen, this is Australia's Indonesian service. We're on international news," he said excitedly. The crackly voice of the radio's newscaster said, "The American State Department spokesperson referred to the Nahdlatul Umat Islam as a terrorist organization and said that there would be direct consequences if the abducted schoolboy was not immediately freed unharmed. Meanwhile, Major General Rachman of the Indonesian police stated that his men were continuing their search for the twelve-year-old boy. Isaac Williams's parents issued a new plea for his release."

Graham Williams's hoarse voice came over the waves. He spoke in slow Indonesian. "We plead with whoever has our son, we beg you to release him to us. He has been gone from us almost one full week now. Allah has given all parents the gift of children, regardless of race or religion, and we ask that our son be returned to us, which is surely according to Allah's will."

Mas Bengkok switched off the news and grinned at Isaac. "You are a star," he said. "They even have your picture in the newspapers. Maybe someday I'm going to be interviewed about you. I'll say, 'I taught Isak the ninety-nine names of Allah.'"

Hearing his father's voice on the radio was strange. Isaac wished he could reassure his parents that he was okay. It was distressing to hear his father so distressed.

A half hour later Ibu Halimah put Isaac to bed with another cup of bitter herbs that Isaac eagerly drank. With its sedative, he would not dream.

Chapter Eleven

FTER FRIDAY NOON PRAYERS Ibu Halimah woke Isaac from a shallow nap. Her round face beamed. "The honorable *kiai* is here to start your lessons."

The honorable *kiai* stood at the doorway. Isaac found himself looking into the gentle eyes of Mr. Suherman. He backed up on the cot until he was against the wall. Mr. Suherman's calm expression did not change. Isaac's gaze became riveted on the large Gucci leather case dangling from the teacher's shoulder. Isaac said to Ibu Halimah, "Tell him to go away. Tell him to leave me alone."

Ibu Halimah said, "Isak, what is the matter with you?"

"He's a terrorist; he'll kill me."

"That's ridiculous, child, that's—"

"He had a bomb at the school, he was going to blow us up, he's one of those terrorists, he's got a bomb in that bag!"

Ibu Halimah grabbed him by the shoulders, peered into his eyes, felt his cheeks. "You're delirious again."

"I am not. Mr. Summerton had a photo of him. Please, Ibu Halimah, don't leave me alone with him."

Mr. Suherman sat down in the chair. He said to Ibu Halimah, "Stay a moment for the boy's sake. Isaac misunderstands, but he has reason enough to be afraid." He opened the case and withdrew a Qur'an, its cover soft leather embossed with calligraphy.

Ibu Halimah crossed her arms, regarding Isaac with a displeased frown.

Mr. Suherman draped his right leg over his left and said, "Righto, let me get my bad cards out on the table. Eight years ago, as a newly fervent and radicalized Muslim, I went to Afghanistan and attended one of bin Laden's Al-Qaeda training camps. I wanted war against the West. I wanted to become a martyr for the cause of Allah and Islam. But the organization forbade me to become a martyr. They had other tasks for me. I was sent to Jakarta to launder Al-Qaeda money, as my father did in London for the Suharto regime. There I met Tuan Guru Haji Abdullah Abubakar. I learned from the Tuan Guru a better Islam, a truer Islam. The Tuan Guru is to bin Laden what the tree of life is to a shriveled weed. Instead of being an Al-Qaeda jihad warrior seeking the death of American infidels, I am now training to be a Nahdlatul Umat Islam missionary to save their souls."

Isaac's gaze inched upward to Mr. Suherman's face. The teacher grinned. "Does that sound familiar?"

"You weren't trying to bomb us?"

"Absolutely not."

"There was a bomb at the hospital."

"But not at the school. I made sure of that."

Isaac didn't know what to make of such a baffling statement. Was Mr. Suherman implying that there had been plans to bomb the school? "So you were trying to convert us instead of blow us up?"

"In a manner of speaking, yes. But mostly, I was at the school to learn about American Christianity."

"Why?"

"I want to learn how to contextualize Islam to the American culture. To paraphrase something your Reverend Biggs said, I see in America a wheat field ripe unto harvest for Allah."

Isaac felt dizzy, as though six had become nine. "But Mr. Summerton had a picture of you—the State Department says you're a terrorist. No way they'll let you into America."

"It's just a matter of negotiations." Mr. Suherman rubbed the bottom of his lip and studied Isaac. "I have certain information that perhaps I could trade for a green card. As your Bible says, be innocent as doves but wise as serpents."

Isaac said, "The State Department says the Nahdlatul Umat Islam is a terrorist organization." He touched his eye. "The Nahdlatul Umat Islam did this to me."

Mr. Suherman sighed. "That is a good start for our first lesson. The word 'Islam,' Isaac, means 'surrender to Allah.' It is not a religion, but a way of life. The straight path. Some Muslims walk it true, and some meander off the edges into sin at times. It is no different in Christianity. There are Christians who are convinced that God has called them to kill homosexuals, there are pastors who urge violent war against abortionists. So it is in Islam, even in the Nahdlatul Umat Islam."

"Like Udin?"

"The sullen boy with the scruffy beard? I apologize for him. Violence against children is always a sin."

"And Mas Tanto?"

Mr. Suherman glanced at Ibu Halimah.

She harrumphed and let her arms drop, moving to the door. "I'll leave you two gentlemen to discuss my husband in private."

After she left, Mr. Suherman said, "Mas Tanto means well, but he is easily led by misguided rhetoric, such as Imam Ali's—" He cut himself off. "You are sidetracking me. And I am sure you do not want to hear about the inner politics of the Nahdlatul Umat Islam. Now, before we continue, I want to show you something."

Mr. Suherman led Isaac out into the hallway, where Mas Bengkok had placed a bucket of water on a plastic mat. He said, "You've seen Muslims wash up at the mosques before prayers? That's called *rukun wudu*. I'll show you how in a minute. But first, you did have a bath this morning?"

"No, I take them in the afternoons," Isaac said.

"I suppose that will have to do. You washed everywhere?"

Isaac nodded.

"Even your private parts?"

Isaac flushed. "Yes. And behind my ears, too. Look, Mr. Suherman, I'm a Christian. To do this ritual would insult my religion and yours."

Mr. Suherman laughed and shook his groomed head. "Is it true that you are uncircumcised?"

Isaac's blush deepened. "What does that matter?"

Mr. Suherman ignored that. "Have you reached puberty? Do you have hair around your genitals?"

Isaac's face burned. "A little."

"Have you ever experienced a nocturnal emission?"

"Nocturnal emission? What's that?"

Mr. Suherman said dryly, "If you have to ask, then you haven't. So, you are still in puberty and uncircumcised. By tradition, impure. Since being uncircumcised is an impurity that wudu cannot remove, then what you are about to do is not true wudu and insults neither Christianity nor Islam. Learn it for the sake of cultural knowledge. Is that acceptable?"

"I guess so," Isaac said, listening for God's still small voice that would tell him if it weren't. He didn't hear it.

Mr. Suherman showed Isaac the procedure of ablution. Hands, mouth, nose, face, forearms, head, ears, neck, and feet were rinsed in a precise way. Puddles began to grow on the plastic mat.

When he was done, Isaac said, "I don't feel a whole lot cleaner."

"As I said, the rite is only symbolic. Its true effectiveness is when it is done in the spirit of prayer."

They returned to the cell and sat down cross-legged on prayer mats that Mr. Suherman had folded up inside his large bag. The teacher began his lesson. "The way of Islam is the way to salvation. God in His great mercy has given us two guideposts. One is the Holy Qur'an, the word of Allah, and the other is the Sunnah, or the way the Blessed Prophet lived his life, which is a practical example of how a holy life should be lived. In these lessons we shall concentrate on the Holy Qur'an."

Mr. Suherman paused. It was a teacher's pause. Sure enough, he asked a question, smiling at his not altogether eager student.

"What do you know about the Holy Qur'an, Isaac?"

"It is the Muslim Scripture written by Muhammad a long time ago, sometime after Christ."

"When you speak of Muhammad to a Muslim, Isaac, it is polite to say 'peace and blessings upon him.' Muhammad, peace and blessings upon him. Muhammad, *salla allahu alaihi wa sallam,* which means the peace and blessings of Allah be upon him. *Salla allahu alaihi wa sallam.* Repeat, please."

"Salla allahu alaihi wa sallam."

Mr. Suherman nodded approvingly. "You have an ear for languages. Most Westerners would find that a true tongue twister. Now, you have said that Muhammad, peace and blessings upon him, wrote the Holy Qur'an. That is a common misconception of non-Muslims and sometimes a deliberate one. Nothing could be further from the truth. The Blessed Prophet was no more the author of the Holy Qur'an than I am the creator of the universe. The Holy Qur'an was revealed to blessed Muhammad by Allah As-Samad Al-Awwal Al-Akhir, Allah the Eternal, the First, and the Last, who, over a span of years and through His angel Gabriel, gave His prophet His word, syllable by syllable, in such glorious and thrilling language as was never before heard in the world and which we have with us to this very day in unbroken and uncorrupted transmission. This Holy Qur'an in front of me is exactly the same, syllable for syllable, as what Allah revealed to His prophet Muhammad, peace and blessings be upon him, over a millennium ago. We can be confident that this Holy Qur'an, this very one in front of me, is the word of God without corruption. It was given in history to one man, but it is nonetheless the true and eternal word of God. It is living Scripture, vital and vibrant. It is Allah's greatest blessing to our ancestors, to us, to our descendants, forever and forever. The Qur'an purifies our thoughts, corrects our behavior, and molds our lifestyles. It enriches our inner being, it lights up our hearts and souls. But this is possible, Isaac, only if we study the Holy Qur'an and meditate on it."

Isaac stared at Mr. Suherman, the Muslim kiai, with frank amazement. He had just heard, in the mellifluent tones of Oxford, a short sermon that he had heard many times before. Except those sermons had been about the Holy Bible. Mr. Suherman had a radiant glow on his face that Isaac had seen before on those anointed of God. The last time he had seen a similar expression, it had been on the face of Reverend Biggs. He said, "You sound like you're talking about the Bible."

"I'm afraid not. The original revelations to the early prophets such as Moses, Abraham, and Jesus were indeed the words of God. But those revelations were distorted, altered, and occasionally purposefully adulterated by the followers of these prophets. The Holy Qur'an makes this very clear. There is truth in the Bible, but it is not the Truth."

Isaac stiffened.

Mr. Suherman said, "This is a hard thing I say, for Christianity is your tradition. I don't ask you to believe me. Instead, meditate on the Holy Qur'an, and it will speak the Truth to you in ways that I cannot."

Isaac blinked. How many times had he heard the same thing said of the Bible?

Mr. Suherman withdrew from the Gucci bag a paperback Qur'an.

Isaac stared at the book being held out to him.

Mr. Suherman wiggled it. "Go on, it won't bite."

Isaac reluctantly took it. The cover had a border of intricate calligraphy. The book looked to be well thumbed.

"Please be careful with it. This Pickthall edition is out of print and hard to find."

Isaac had countless times heard the Qur'an being recited and had seen the calligraphy of Qur'anic verses, but this was the first time he had actually held a Qur'an.

Mr. Suherman said, "Let's find a verse. Chapter—we call it a sura—sura 11, verses 69 to 73."

Isaac did not move.

"Isaac, the Qur'an is a miraculous book, but it is not going to open its covers of its own accord. Sura 11, please."

Isaac shook his head, without looking at Mr. Suherman. "I am a Christian. It'd be a sin to read the Qur'an."

Mr. Suherman jerked back, whether in genuine shock or mock show, Isaac couldn't tell. "Nonsense! How could it be a sin to read the Qur'an? This is a thought from Satan."

"You don't understand. From what you have said about the Bible and the Qur'an, one of them must be wrong. And since I am a Christian and believe the Bible is true, how could I dare open the Qur'an, even if I am wrong?"

Mr. Suherman studied Isaac without expression. Then he lifted his face to the ceiling and laughed with rib-shaking humor. He said,

"Isaac, Isaac! You have the talent to be a scholar of Islamic law. *Aduh,* I did not intend to put you between the desert and the devil. That is not the case. Are there not Qur'ans in your Christian universities for your Christian scholars to study? And do they feel as though they commit sin when they read the Qur'an? Certainly not! If nothing else, Isaac, read and study the Qur'an to expand your horizons, to extend your intelligence and knowledge of other religions, to appreciate the beauty of the Qur'an as magnificent literature. Are not these things *halal,* or permitted, in Christianity?"

"Well, yeah," Isaac said slowly.

"Surely they are. You don't have to agree with the Qur'an, but don't ever mock it. Mocking things you don't believe in is a fool's game. Now, wouldn't you like to know what the Qur'an has to say about your namesake, the prophet Isaac, peace be upon him? If you would open your Qur'an to sura 11, verses 69 to 73."

Isaac opened the cover. Nothing with claws whooshed into his soul to possess him. The heavens were not rendered. His heart beat as before. He flipped some pages. The fresh whiteness of original publication had long acquired an aged tint, and the top corner of each page was shiny from constant thumbing. The left-hand pages contained the verses in English, presented like the Bible. The right-hand pages were covered with flowing Arabic script. He took a deep breath, feeling as though he were about to plunge into a strange pool of dark water and unknown depth. He read aloud:

"And our messengers came unto Abraham with good news.
They said: Peace! He answered: Peace! and delayed not to bring

a roasted calf. And when he saw their hands reached not to it, he mistrusted them and conceived a fear of them. They said: Fear not. Lo, we are sent unto the folk of Lot. And his wife, standing by, laughed when We gave her good tidings of the birth of Isaac, and after Isaac, of Jacob. She said: Oh, woe is me! Shall I bear a child when I am an old woman, and this my husband is an old man? Lo! this is a strange thing! They said: Wonderest thou at the commandment of Allah? The mercy of Allah and His blessings be upon you, O people of the house! Lo! He is the Owner of Praise, Owner of Glory!"

As Isaac read this he found that the pool he had dived into was not so strange and alien after all. This was nearly the same story that was in the Bible. Aside from the quaint language of the translation, the Qur'an was a lot more user-friendly than he would have thought.

Mr. Suherman grinned. "What do you think, Isaac?"

"It's like the Bible," Isaac said. "It's even written in King James English, which nobody ever speaks anymore. Isn't there a more modern translation?"

"This is the Pickthall translation," Mr. Suherman said. "It is closest to the majestic harmony and melody of the original Arabic. Listen."

Mr. Suherman composed himself, took a breath, and began reciting in Arabic the latter passage of Abraham's sacrifice in the ululating cadence that Qur'anic Scripture readers use. In Mr. Suherman's recital was the majestic harmony he spoke of, which began to register itself on Isaac's ear and mind, trained to the scaled melodies of Western songs and hymns.

Isaac's wonderment must have been written on his face, for when Mr. Suherman finished, he smiled softly and asked, "Do you hear some of the heavenly music? Can you imagine what it must have been like fourteen hundred years ago for the first listeners of blessed Muhammad's terrible ecstasies?"

"Terrible?"

"Indeed. He did not seek them. They were forced upon him. It is said that he felt as though his soul were being torn from him. He was, initially, a most reluctant prophet."

Isaac said, "I don't know Arabic. I do know English, and this English doesn't sound majestic. It sounds thick and hard to understand. It'd be more interesting for me to read a more modern translation."

Mr. Suherman was frowning, but not in displeasure. He was thinking. "Would you say that someone from the Bible Belt of America might find another translation of the Holy Qur'an more interesting to read?"

"If there is anyone there who wants to read a Qur'an in the first place, yeah."

Mr. Suherman said, "You don't think anyone there would?"

Isaac chose his words carefully. "It would be unusual. Islam is a totally different culture."

Mr. Suherman's "No!" rang loudly. "Not a culture, but the straight path. It is the Truth of Allah, and He will find those whom He will, even in the Bible Belt of America."

"Still, a lot of them couldn't read this English."

Mr. Suherman pondered this, measuring out his thoughts

with slow distinct nods of his square chin. "Isaac, I do believe that Allah has brought you into my life just as much as He has brought me into yours. I never thought of this. Thank you."

"It's nothing," Isaac said, perplexed by Mr. Suherman's gratitude. His suggestion wasn't all that much to be grateful for. Most Americans wouldn't be interested in reading any version of the Qur'an. Isaac was quite literally a captive audience. He had no choice in the matter.

"This is enough for today, I think. You look tired." Mr. Suherman took out a ruled notebook and a pen from the Gucci case. He jotted down something. He ripped off the sheet and handed it to Isaac. "I want you to read and study these verses before our next lesson tomorrow."

Isaac took the sheet reluctantly. He was sick, locked up, separated from his family, not knowing what was going to happen, and now, on top of all that, he had homework to do.

"Any questions?" Mr. Suherman asked, like a teacher.

And Isaac, like a student, knew better than to ask any. Except there was one that had nothing to do with the Qur'an. "What's the Tuan Guru really like?"

"The Tuan Guru is the father I wish I'd had. He is strict and stern yet loving. He is a . . ." Mr. Suherman paused, searching for appropriate words.

"A kidnapper," Isaac said.

"Excuse me?" Mr. Suherman said, and then understood. His eyes hardened in anger. He said, with words cold-rolled from the steely press of his anger, "Tuan Guru Haji Abdullah Abubakar is a true servant of Allah, and whatever he does in the name of Allah is just and righteous. You are here because it is God's will. There is no reason other than that. Do not speak evil of the Tuan Guru, for the evil will come back to you."

"Sorry," Isaac said again.

Mr. Suherman put his Qur'an back in the leather case. He rose from the chair. Isaac, like a well-bred Javanese boy, automatically followed suit from his cot, his head respectfully bowed. "Don't forget to study those verses," Mr. Suherman said. It was a warning rather than a reminder. At the door he paused. His face was still rigid. Then he sighed, and his facial muscles relaxed. "Come here," he said. Isaac obeyed. Mr. Suherman blew into his right hand and passed the palm of it over Isaac's neck and chest, lingering over the heart. He recited something in Arabic and then said in English, "O Allah! Lord of the People, Remover of Trouble! Heal this sick one with the healing that leaves no ailment, for You are the healer, and You alone." Mr. Suherman smiled at his student. "And for the sake of your tradition, Isaac, I add: For yours is the kingdom and the power and the glory. Amen."

Mr. Suherman left. Isaac sat down on the cot, perplexed. Mr. Suherman had meant well, but did God count that prayer for healing as a witch's spell to be abhorred?

"I didn't ask for it," Isaac said loudly, reminding God of that.

Later Ibu Halimah asked, "What do you think of Kiai Suherman?"

Isaac answered politely, "He is a good teacher."

"Yes. He is one of the best and brightest young men we have. He is going to be the Nahdlatul Umat Islam's first missionary to America."

"He told me."

"The Americans want to bomb Afghanistan and kill Muslims. But Kiai Suherman wants to go to America and tell Americans about the straight path of Allah. That, Isak, is true Islam."

Chapter Twelve

MR. SUHERMAN SAID, "YOU have read those verses I gave to you to read?"

Isaac said, "They were about Jesus. The Qur'an says that God created him out of dust. That's wrong. Jesus is the Son of God. God the Father, God the Son, God the—"

"Nonsense! Is Allah some commonplace fornicator of the flesh to have a child with a woman? A monstrous thought! Sura 112, verses 1 to 4 say in the translation of Pickthall, 'Say He is Allah, the One! Allah the eternally Besought of all. He begetteth not nor was begotten, and there is none comparable unto Him.' The Christians claim they believe in one god, yet they actually believe in three."

Isaac, recalling one of Pastor Cornelius's favorite analogies, said, "But three in one, like a rope that is a single rope but made of three strands."

"Sophistry. Your own Scriptures show how you believe in three gods. In the Bible story about Jesus being baptized, you have a god in heaven and you have a god as a dove and you have a god in the water. Don't use semantics to try to wiggle out of it. There are three gods in three different places at one time. By Allah, what sort of monotheism is this? How can your Bible as it is today be considered holy with such monstrous corruptions in it?"

Isaac felt as he always did in the presence of a grown-up who was telling him something for his own good, whether he believed it or not.

Mr. Suherman said, "You are scowling, Isaac."

"If Islam is such a wonderful religion, why do you convert others at the point of the sword and behead those who refuse to convert? Do you have a sword packed for America?"

Amazement stretched across Mr. Suherman's handsome face. He said, "I have been warned that Americans have a common misconception of Islam being the religion of a bunch of bloodthirsty fanatics. You grew up in Java, and yet you ask such a question?"

"Mr. Suherman, Muslims robbed us. Muslims burned my church. And this," he said, touching his finger to his healing eye, "all this happened in Java. By Muslims."

Mr. Suherman expelled a breath and rubbed his hands on his knees. "Isaac, I have told you that unfortunately there are many misguided, immature Muslims, easily confused and deceived. Muslims can and do sin and perform deeds that Allah condemns. The U.S. State Department calls the Nahdlatul Umat Islam a terrorist organization, but what else would the Great Satan say about faithful Muslims struggling and fighting for the cause of Allah against Christian missionaries from America who actively seek to turn Muslims into apostates? This is a very serious matter that I am not sure a young boy can understand, but you must try."

Isaac exclaimed, "But the doctors, my parents—they are nobody's enemies. They are here to help the poor and the sick."

"The poor and the sick and the oppressed are always the easiest prey. I have nothing personal against your parents, and, Isaac, Isaac, I would welcome them with wide arms were they purely humanitarian doctors who worshipped their Jesus within the confines of their own religious community. But they are proselytizers, and so they are not welcome here. This is partly the fault of the Muslims who have allowed them to be here and of the Muslims who do not take care of their own poor and sick. Nonetheless, the presence of a Baptist mission with a subversive hidden purpose of converting Muslims is intolerable. This is a gross sin against Islam, which no true Muslim can tolerate. However, as the Tuan Guru explained to some of our hotheads, the Nahdlatul Umat Islam is not a *komando* jihad group, and he was not about to issue a *resolusi* jihad for holy warfare."

"But you want to be a missionary yourself."

"I bring the true Word, Isaac. I bring, in the message of the prophet Muhammad, peace and blessings upon him, the culmination of what Jesus *alaihi as-salam* originally taught."

"So what's going to happen to me, now that I know about Islam? Are you going to let me go on my merry way as a Christian?"

"Are you willing to surrender to Allah?"

"To Islam? No."

The kiai tugged his ear as he pondered something and then said slowly and reflectively, "It would be wrong for me to pretend there are no differences of opinions, even strong beliefs, among Muslims about the faith. The Shiites and the Sunni, for example.

And we of the Nahdlatul Umat Islam are Sunni; yet even within the Nahdlatul Umat Islam, there are differences of opinion, and you, my boy, have stirred up a major debate. What should we do with you? Why has Allah seen fit to give us this opportunity to make you an example to the world?"

Isaac really didn't like the sound of that. To be made an example wasn't, as far as he knew, a generally positive experience.

The kiai continued in a reflective mood, "There are those who argue that you should be forced into Islam as a lesson, as outright punishment against the Union of American Baptists' mission for its sins in Wonobo."

Isaac stared at him in horror. There came to this chamber the sound of wings beating on air. The room darkened. The beast was at the door. Isaac felt faint, his blood as thin and poisonous as turpentine.

"Isaac! Isaac!" Mr. Suherman said sharply. "By Allah, you stare at me as if I am a ghoul about to devour you! You are safe with us. It is only a few of our ignorant and tempestuous members who speak so foolishly. The Holy Qur'an says that there is no compulsion in religion and that punishment for disbelief in Islam is for Allah Himself to administer in the hereafter. You are safe here. I'm sorry I spoke so bluntly, I forgot that you are only a child."

Isaac said faintly, "So I won't be beheaded?"

"Beheaded? Who has said anything about beheading?"

"You won't force me into saying the Muslim creed?"

"Of course not. That would not make you a Muslim. We are

not laboratory rats, that if we press this button, we get this reward. When we accept Islam, we must accept, not grudgingly, but with love: You must love Allah first, with all your heart, all your mind, all your soul. Sound familiar?"

So familiar that again Isaac slipped into a déjà vu moment.

"And this, Isaac, is how the *shahadah* should be said." Mr. Suherman paused, withdrawing deep into a stillness. His eyes closed. He inhaled softly, and then words came out of his mouth, but not words, a cry, but not a cry, an ululation of song, but not a song. It was a soul taking wing to its creator.

"Ashhadu anna la illaha illa allah wa ashhadu anna muhammadan rasul allah."

Isaac had heard this creed sung many times over mosque speakers and by Muslims in prayer, but he had never heard it as he heard it at this moment, swelling to fill the small room and then echoing up to the very ramparts of heaven. Isaac's scalp prickled. Tears came to his eyes, and he was pierced with a swift longing to experience the certainty and the ecstasy of Mr. Suherman, who, for that moment, was in communion with his God.

As for Isaac, nothing filled the vacuum that was his soul.

On Tuesday, Ibu Halimah said, "I know your mother. She has treated some of our women. She's a very good doctor." Then she made a face. "But she's a Christian. The Tuan Guru was very angry when he heard about those visits."

"She's trying to help people, is all."

Ibu Halimah replied in the same refrain as Mr. Suherman, with the same notes of holy righteousness: "She and the others are trying to convert Muslims to Christianity, and that is nearly the most wicked thing you can do. I myself was a warrior in the jihad of prayer against the American Christians. I spent many hours in prayer, and Allah has heard and has driven them away." Her tone softened. "I know they are your people, Isak. We are not cruel, but we must do what is right."

"So how much longer am I going to be held captive?"

"Captive? That is not the word to use; you are here at Allah's will. You will be released according to His time. But keep your spirits up. Your malaria is nearly cured, I'd say."

That prompted a memory. "Ibu, last night there were mosquitoes in the room. Can I have some repellent tonight?"

"We don't have mosquitoes here. We spray regularly."

"Truly, there were mosquitoes. Please, can I have at least some mosquito coils to burn? And the medicine you give me isn't helping me sleep as well as before."

"That's because I'm reducing the dosage. It can be addictive."

"No, please don't reduce the dosage."

Her high, arched eyebrows arched higher yet, nearly meeting the forehead band of her veil. "Surely you aren't addicted yet."

"I only want to sleep without dreams."

The eyebrows fell back into place with a clunk of understanding. "It is necessary to dream," she said. "There are bad dreams from the devil, yes, and when those come, seek the shelter of Allah with prayer. But also remember that the hadith says that good dreams come from Allah and that the truest dreams are those that come at dawn."

"What happens when we die?" Isaac asked Mr. Suherman during his lesson later that day. He had meant to ask what Muslims think happens when we die, because he, Isaac, actually knew the truth of it. But he was tired and those were the words he said.

Mr. Suherman said, "Sura 32:11 says, 'The angel of death, who hath charge concerning you, will gather you.' In other words, not only is death an inevitable fate for all people, but it is also a planned and purposeful fate. All humans have souls, and when we die, our souls await the Day of Judgment, when Allah will decide which souls are to be punished in hell and which souls shall enter paradise."

He paused, and then continued. "One of my favorite verses says, 'That day will faces be resplendent, looking toward their Lord.' In this life we perceive Allah only in part and with desperately longing glimpses, yet in the hereafter His presence will be full and glorious. Oh, to be in the presence of Allah, eternally bathed in the light of His glory and in His love."

The longing that had crept into Mr. Suherman's voice trailed its fingers across Isaac's heart.

"And hell?" Isaac said.

Mr. Suherman gestured to the page of the Qur'an that Isaac had read from. "It says there that it is a place of fire and desolation. Yet God is love and mercy still, and there is a saying I love that says the doors of hell will one day sway crookedly in the wind like those of an abandoned and empty house. Even Satan will be forgiven." A soft smile of wonder and joy tugged at the corners of Mr. Suherman's lips. "Is not such a merciful and compassionate God worthy of our full love and devotion, Isaac?"

Isaac thought but did not say, *My God damns forever.*

Chapter Thirteen

HAT EVENING MAS BENGKOK brought Isaac his medicine and a box of slow-burning mosquito coils. "Ibu Halimah said you wanted these," Mas Bengkok said. He lit one of the green coils with a match, stuck it on its tiny aluminum stand, and placed it under Isaac's cot. White smoke curled up and spilled upward from around the cot's edges, its heavy fragrance spreading throughout the room.

There was enough sedative in the medicine to soon make Isaac drowsy but not enough to put him into a deep sleep. He found himself in a ravaged land, dotted with broken-backed helicopters and demented mobs. With a jerk, he woke up. The lightbulb was still burning overhead. A rooster crowed. His arm was draped over the side of the cot, its wood frame digging into his forearm.

Claws scraped on the outside staircase, accompanied by rasping breaths. From under the mushollah door wafted the faint stench of a carrion eater.

The beast of his dreams was getting closer.

Isaac listened with mounting horror. "Mas Bengkok, help!" he shouted. "Mas Bengkok, please get me out of here!

Something shook him and shook him again. "What? Who?" Isaac said, and now the words were full and real in his mouth. Mas

Bengkok stood over him, a dark but familiar outline in the unlit room. Isaac looked around with blurred eyes.

"You were shouting. What's wrong?"

Isaac took a light-headed breath. He was sweating. His heart still thudded in his chest. He said, "I heard something out on the landing. Could you check? Please, Mas Bengkok, please."

The hunchback shrugged and went out into the hall. He returned a moment later. "Nothing there."

Isaac's heart quieted. He thought about what Ibu Halimah had said about dreams, about how the truest dreams come at dawn.

He wondered if she was right in ways she did not know.

At his morning Qur'an lesson Isaac had such difficulty concentrating that Mr. Suherman finally asked, "Is the malaria bothering you?"

"I didn't sleep well last night," Isaac said. He didn't intend to say anything more but found himself blurting, "I'm having awfully bad nightmares."

Mr. Suherman said, "Isaac, I promise that no harm is going to come to you."

Isaac said, "Something evil keeps chasing me."

Mr. Suherman said nothing. His penetrating gaze seemed to search both Isaac's mind and heart. Then he picked up his Qur'an and with both hands held it over Isaac's head. He murmured a prayer in Arabic.

When he put down the Qur'an, there stole over Isaac's heart a calmness that was not there before, enough to make him wonder: *Could Islam really be a wide road to hell for everybody who travels on it?* He asked, "Mr. Suherman, how do Muslims become saved? Are they saved when they say the confession of faith?"

"What do you mean by 'saved'?"

"Well, eternal salvation, saved from hell and given eternal life in heaven."

"Ah. Is salvation then a matter of punishment and reward? Do you seek God because you fear hell and wish for heaven?"

Isaac was silent.

Mr. Suherman said, "A famous saint in Islam once walked the streets of her city crying out, 'I want to set heaven ablaze and extinguish the fires of hell so that we know who is praying to God out of love and not out of fear of hell or hope for paradise.'"

Isaac said, "I am saved, not because I want to go to heaven, but because Jesus died on the cross for my sins, and I believe in him." Approved words of piety that tripped off the top of his brain but were as lifeless as he was himself empty of emotions.

"How hard Christians make it for Almighty Allah to forgive sins," Mr. Suherman said. "Requiring blood sacrifices and death and gore. Allah is Allah the Forgiver and the Forgiving. It is as easy for Him to forgive entire seas of sin as it is for a mother to kiss her baby. There is no such thing as original sin. We are born pure and perfect and inheritors of paradise, yet we can choose to disobey Allah and to sin, again and again. But Allah is compassionate and forgives with extravagant mercy."

The school loudspeaker broke into Mr. Suherman's words with

the call to noon prayer. Mr. Suherman reacted immediately. He murmured a brief prayer in Arabic and then went outside for the ritual washing. He returned to pray in the former mushollah. He ignored Isaac as though Isaac were not there. He stood facing Mecca. With his eyes closed and his hands clasped together at his waist, he recited several Qur'an verses in Arabic. He raised his hands with palms outward to either side of his face, thumbs touching his earlobes, and with a louder voice said, *"Allahu akbar!"* He bowed at the waist and then knelt and bent forward until his forehead touched the prayer rug. This he did twice, each time crying aloud, *"Allahu akbar!"* He straightened his back, and with his hands resting on each bent knee and with his right forefinger elevated as though in emphasis, he recited the confession of faith. *"Ashhadu anna la illaha illa allah wa ashhadu anna muhammadan rasul allah":* "I confess that there is no God but Allah, and Muhammad is His prophet."

Isaac followed in his mind the familiar flow and tilt of the Arabic words. He knew them by heart; he traced them out in his mind without saying them.

After a silence Mr. Suherman continued his prayers in English, from his kneeling position: "Praise be to God, Lord of All the Worlds. The Compassionate, the Merciful. King of the Day of Reckoning. You only do we worship, and to you only do we cry for help. Guide us in the straight path, the path of those to whom you have been gracious, with whom you are not angry, and who go not astray."

After another brief meditative pause Mr. Suherman went on.

"Allah the Compassionate, the Merciful, you have chosen this child Isaac according to your purpose so that your glory may be shown to the world. This child Isaac is a child of the Book, and I pray that you, O Allah, the Merciful and the Compassionate, grant him mercy and compassion and protect him from the Evil One in the hours of his waking and in the hours of his sleep so that your purpose may be fulfilled on the day you have ordained. Amen."

The effect of Mr. Suherman's prayer on Isaac was the same as that of Reverend Biggs's Evacuation Eve prophecy. It was rain on parched soil—not enough of it to soak deep, but it was the first rain in a long time. Where had it come from? It could only have come from God, the God of Abraham and Isaac and Jacob. The God of Ishmael.

Isaac desperately wished for the strength of Mr. Suherman's faith, the simplicity of his prayers and adoration. Why was his God so distant?

While waiting for his supper Wednesday evening, Isaac sat cross-legged on the prayer rug, reading the Qur'an, which he'd put on the bookstand in the cone of light spreading from the overhead bulb.

Behind him the door opened. Mr. Suherman said, "This is a sight to warm my heart."

Isaac expected a flush of guilt in his Christian soul, but none came. Still, as a matter of face, he said, "Got nothing else better to do."

"You have a special visitor." Mr. Suherman stepped inside the room and motioned for somebody out in the hall to come inside.

The visitor who shuffled in barefoot and with downcast eyes was a boy in a clean sarong and neatly mended tunic. He carried a plastic bag.

"Hey, Isak," he muttered.

"Is that how we greet each other?" Mr. Suherman scolded. "*Al-salamu alaikum,* Isak."

Isaac rose uncertainly to his feet. "*Alaikum as-salam,* Ismail."

Mr. Suherman left the cell, closing the door behind him.

Ismail glanced at Isaac. Ismail's face flushed, and he lowered his gaze again. "You look fat and healthy," he said, a meaningless throwaway phrase commonly used as a casual greeting.

Isaac should have replied in kind, but he said, "I'm skinny and I'm not that healthy. I got malaria."

Ismail nodded, swinging the plastic bag in his hands. "I heard."

Isaac said, "You remember the treasure hunt on the river, those mosquitoes? That's where I got the malaria from."

Ismail nodded again. The plastic bag stopped swinging. He was biting his lips, but a giggle escaped anyway. "You should have seen yourself, a big old bulé cow swinging his arms like a crazy propeller—" Ismail caught himself. He coughed and said, "Sorry."

"Yeah, well, malaria isn't any fun." But Isaac was smiling too. "*Aduh,* my mother was angry when I got home."

"And my father was furious," Ismail said. "He spanked me with the broom. My sister laughed until she farted."

The two boys stared at each other and then burst out laughing themselves. Isaac plopped down on his cot. He gestured to the chair. "Sit down. Sorry I don't have anything to offer you for a drink, but, well, you know . . ." He gestured at the walls around him.

"I hope they let you go soon," Ismail said.

"Me too. Say, that coin we found, what did you do with it?"

"I had to hide it," Ismail said. "Imam Ali told me it was a wicked thing and ordered me to throw it away, but I hid it instead, up in the *jambu* tree."

"Imam Ali," Isaac said. The name inserted itself between the two boys, bringing with it a silence. Isaac fidgeted on the cot. He didn't know what to say; rather, he had a lot of things to say, questions to ask, but he didn't know the right *first* thing to say.

Ismail abruptly opened the plastic bag. He put a cardboard box on the floor. "For you," he said.

Isaac leaned over and lifted the top. Nestled inside was a new pair of red-trimmed Reeboks. He picked them out, staring with wonder at Ismail.

Ismail, looking down at his lap, said in a flat and formal voice, "I humbly apologize with all my heart for taking your shoes. I have made *istighfar* before God, and now I seek your pardon." He fell silent. He pressed his thin lips together until they blanched. He released them and said, "I'm sorry, Isak, I really am." He looked at Isaac, blinking his eyes.

Isaac said, "They're new."

"I couldn't get yours out of that glue trap. They're probably still stuck there in the middle of the road."

Richard Lewis

The two boys were silent for a moment and then began laughing so hard again that Mas Bengkok opened the door to tell them to shut up, that they could be heard in the dorms. Ismail wiped his eyes and said, "I got the money to buy these working for Kiai Suherman, doing errands and stuff. He's strict, but he pays like an American." He smiled his old Ismail smile, an electric current zinging across his face and brightening his eyes. "So, you're going to become a Muslim? That would be great if you did. Just think of all the fun we could have together."

Isaac looked at Ismail. He thought of their forays into the cane fields, their swims in the irrigation canals, the time they'd dragged a monitor lizard into Ismail's sister's room when she was napping. Yet over all these memories was another that Isaac didn't want to remember but that cast its shadow regardless.

Ismail asked, "What's wrong?"

"Nothing."

"But there is something."

"Really, Ismail, it's nothing."

"I've said I'm sorry. I mean it, I truly do. I want to be friends again. But something's still not right, is it?"

Isaac opened his mouth, shut it, and then opened it again. "During the riot you carried a poster of my head on a spike."

Ismail frowned absently, not recalling, and then blood rushed to his face, burning the skin to a mottled auburn ash Isaac had never seen before. "I—I—I'm sorry," he stuttered. "I'm sorry, I wasn't thinking, I was . . . amok, I was amok, I didn't mean it. I—" He shut his mouth so hard that his teeth clicked. He flung himself down on the rug. For a second Isaac thought Ismail was prostrating before him, but Ismail was in prayer, pleading, *"Astaghfir allah al-azim,* grant me forgiveness, O Allah." He repeated this several times. He sat up, took a quavering breath, and then turned his head and smiled tentatively at Isaac. "You forgive me too, please?"

Isaac pursed his lips thoughtfully. He said, "You're a terrible artist. It didn't look like me at all."

A crack of a shared smile, followed by another round of helpless laughter. For a second time Mas Bengkok had to step in the room to shush the boys.

When Ismail left, he did so with a promise that he'd visit again as soon as he could. They would plan their next adventure.

Chapter Fourteen

THE NEXT DAY A dozen men sat on prayer rugs laid out in the large hall, the bright midafternoon light bringing out the rich reds and browns of the rugs' weave. Mas Tanto and the bully Udin were among those listening intently to Imam Ali of the Al-Furqon Mosque. Despite the small numbers of attendees, the Imam was using a microphone and speaker to address his audience. His yellow eyes glowed; his long narrow tongue flickered as he spoke.

Isaac worried that the Imam would be able to sniff out his presence, trace the odor of Christian bulé boy wafting from the hole in the shutter. He shouldn't be watching, but he couldn't tear himself away.

The Imam said, "The Americans call me a militant and a terrorist. If being a militant Muslim means wanting to remove from our own land this incredible insult of arrogant American infidels trying to seduce our own people to leave the straight path, then, yes indeed, I am a militant! And if the Americans want to call me a terrorist, why, I suppose I am indeed a terror to the enemies of Allah! Words of praise, indeed, brothers, that I am called a militant and a terrorist!"

The others chuckled and nodded their agreement.

"Brothers, when the infidels seek to overcome Islam, then the purpose of *tabligh,* the teaching of Islam and the strengthening of faith of the Muslim *ummah,* becomes the tabligh of the sword. The Holy Qur'an repeatedly says"—and here the Imam recited verses in Arabic, which he translated into Indonesian—"'Slay them, slay them, behead the kafir. Smite them on the neck.'"

He looked at each of the men and then cried out, "Praise be to Allah, Ruler of All Worlds! Brothers, may I speak frankly? We have in our hands the means to demonstrate to our weaker brothers in the Nahdlatul Umat Islam, and to the Islamic world, and to the world of the infidels, our devotion to Allah and to His cause and purpose. I speak of the infidel child. Allah's stern word is very clear regarding the fate of infidels should they refuse to believe in Him and His Prophet, peace and blessings be upon him. Indeed, let us give this child a reasonable opportunity to believe, but as far as appeals and negotiations regarding his release, they are of no more worth than a dog's vomit. Are we to listen to the counsel of the confused minds and the half blind? If it becomes necessary, who among us is willing and ready to wield the terrible sword?"

Tanto's visage filled Isaac's vision. A thoughtful look was on that square, stern face. He turned his head, swiveling his gaze as unerringly as a radar beam until it was upon the shutter. Isaac could not close his eyes. After several seconds Tanto released that locked-in gaze and bent his head to whisper to his companion Udin. Udin's scraggly chin straightened. His gaze too swung out and up.

Isaac flung himself away from the shutter.

Richard Lewis

The Imam closed the meeting by reciting the confession of faith: *"Ashhadu anna la illaha illa allah wa ashhadu anna muhammadan rasul allah!"* The words, the lilt, and the cadence were the same as Mr. Suherman's, whose confession Isaac had found so moving and alluring, but the Imam's confession was cold and brutal, like the bite of sharp metal on skin, slicing through jugular and spinal cord.

"There is no compulsion in Islam," Mr. Suherman had said to Isaac in this very room. "Do not worry, you are safe," he had said. These remembered words and the remembrance of Mr. Suherman's assurance calmed Isaac's fright. Surely Imam Ali had been speaking with the same hyperbolic indulgence that a sports fan employs when advocating the execution of a referee.

He lay down on the cot. A commotion erupted in the hallway outside. In a loud voice Udin ordered Mas Bengkok to open the door. Mas Bengkok protested.

"We are here on the Tuan Guru's business," Udin said. "Open this door immediately."

"Open it yourself," Mas Bengkok said sourly.

The door burst open, and Tanto strode into the cell, followed by Udin. Udin reached behind him and shoved the door shut on Mas Bengkok's face. Isaac cowered on the cot. Tanto took the three steps to the window and looked out the hole in the shutter, taking his time to see what could be seen.

Udin twirled the hairs on his chin with dirty fingers. "They are treating you very well up here in this little hideaway, bulé boy. A little resort of your own, eh? There's some of us been wondering where you were. Mas Tanto finally let the cat out the bag."

Tanto turned and looked at Isaac with a face as expressionless as plywood.

"You should show some gratitude to the Tuan Guru," Udin continued, "and the best way to do that is, of course, to become a Muslim. It is very easy to become a Muslim. This is what you say, *Ashhadu anna la illaha illa allah wa ashhadu anna muhammadan rasul allah,* in the presence of two Muslim witnesses. And here we are! Can you say that, bulé boy?"

Isaac warily shook his head.

"And after you say that, you confirm it by being circumcised, which we all know you aren't. Or you can be circumcised first and then say it. It doesn't really matter, I don't think. What do you think, Mas Tanto?"

Mas Tanto had no thoughts to share.

"I thank the Tuan Guru deeply for his hospitality," Isaac said.

"Such politeness! Have you ever heard such a polite boy, Mas Tanto?" Udin suddenly dropped the pose. "Say the *shahadah,* bulé boy. And for a dog like you it is best said when you are kneeling on the floor."

Isaac shook his head again, fear putting agitation into the movement.

Udin grabbed Isaac's upper arm, digging hard with his fingers. Isaac levitated off the cot, trying to ease the agony of Udin's upward pull. Udin dragged him to the prayer rug. His other hand clamped around Isaac's neck. Crying and sputtering, Isaac tried to fight back, but it was as useless as spitting into a monsoon wind.

Udin forced him downward, kicking at his legs until they

gave way and he was kneeling on the hard rug. Udin continued forcing Isaac's head down until his forehead touched the rug. The grip on his neck eased enough to allow Isaac's vocal cords to operate.

"Say it," Udin hissed. "Repeat after me: *Ashhadu anna la illaha illa allah wa ashhadu anna muhammadan rasul allah.*"

"No, I can't, I can't, I won't, I can't." Isaac was not aware in what language he was wailing out his resistance.

Udin shook him as a terrier would a rat. "Say it! *Ashhadu anna la illaha illa allah wa ashhadu anna muhammadan rasul allah.*"

"No," Isaac croaked.

Udin tightened his grip, blocking off Isaac's windpipe. Isaac gagged and tried to pry off Udin's fingers. The door opened, and Mas Bengkok charged into the room. Udin's grip momentarily eased. Isaac broke free with a lunging, twisting effort that sent him sprawling forward on the floor. Udin's dirty fingernails clawed tracks into the skin of his neck as he tore loose.

"What's going on?" Mas Bengkok demanded.

Isaac crabbed up against the wall, crying and gagging.

"We're only trying to supplement Kiai Suherman's Qur'an instruction," Udin said.

"Mas Tanto I know, but who are you?" Mas Bengkok said directly and thus, for a Javanese, very rudely. "You are not a teacher of any kind, you're nothing more than a cowboy."

"I am a member of the NUI."

Mas Bengkok snorted. "That so? You aren't behaving like one. This boy's in my charge."

Mas Tanto stirred at last. "I put him in your charge," he said.

"Indeed you did, Mas Tanto," the hunchback said with more civility. "But higher authorities have taken a direct interest in the boy, and I am now responsible to them and not to you."

Udin hooted in derision. "Kiai Suherman is not a high authority. He wants to be an American."

"Oh, to be young and wise again like you," the hunchback said. "Now leave."

As he left the room with Tanto, Udin stooped to snatch up the new Reeboks Ismail had given Isaac.

Mas Bengkok looked at Isaac. "Might as well take you down for your bath," he said. The hunchback recited the names of Allah on the way down the stairs and kept reciting as he stood guard outside the door.

When Isaac was done, Mas Bengkok escorted him back up the stairs. Each step was another name of God. "Al-Badi. Al-Baqis. Al-Wadi." His steps faltered as the names came slower and finally stopped altogether. He pounded his head with the flat of his palm. "Allah! I nearly had it, nearly had it. Aiyah aiyah, what comes next, what comes next?"

"Ar-Rashid," Isaac said.

Mas Bengkok pounded both sides of his head. "Of course. Stupid. Stupid! I nearly did it too. So close, I've never been so close."

He locked Isaac back in his cell, muttering all the time about how he came so close and then forgot the ninety-eighth name of God.

He returned with the dinner tray, once more reciting the

names of God. This time the names came smoothly and without hesitation. "Al-Muti, Al-Mani, Az-Zarr, An-Nafi." He unlocked and opened the door. "An-Nur, Al-Hadi." He entered. "Al-Badi, Al-Baqi, Al-Waris." He placed the tray down on the bed. "Ar-Rashid."

He paused and took a deep breath.

"As-Sabur."

The ninety-ninth name of Allah.

He shifted his gaze beyond Isaac's shoulder, as though hoping to see the gates of heaven opening and the angels of Allah descending. No celestial rewards? Ah, no matter. A broad smile appeared and then faded to a somber but pleased expression. "I've done it at last, Isak," he said. He stepped forward, placed both hands on Isaac's shoulders, and drew him close for a Javanese kiss on both cheeks.

"Eat all this food," he said. "The Tuan Guru Haji has declared tomorrow a fasting day for the Nahdlatul Umat Islam, sunrise to sunset. He does this sometimes when something special is going to happen."

Isaac did not respond to Mas Bengkok's smile, which evaporated. The hunchback left without saying good night, starting again on a cycle of Allah's ninety-nine names.

Isaac still felt the hunchback's moist, oaty breath on his cheeks. He rubbed both of them with his hands and sat down in the chair. He stared at the food, a larger mound of rice than usual, colored with various sauces and the most savory of meats.

The pebble of loneliness and fear rattled around in the empty chambers of his heart. He said, "Mom? Dad? Where are you? I miss you. I've had enough here. I want to go home."

The words broke no dam of pent-up tears. No flood of anguish or other heartbroken emotion roared down to flush him away from this burned and sterile place.

At last he lay down on his cot. And after a while he slept.

He slept a waiting sleep. The hours passed. His dreams felt no fetid presence of the Lord of the Crows and raised no alarm.

In the distance an impatient rooster crowed. Isaac heard an echo of Ibu Halimah whispering, "The truest dreams are those that come at dawn."

What he dreamed of, half awake and half asleep, was the red-lipped girl at the dangdut show. A warmth spread in the hollows of his bones and in his groin. His penis stiffened until it was agonizingly distended. Isaac moaned. His penis twitched and spasmed. Something warm, like urine, but much more sticky, spurted onto his thighs.

At that moment the door crashed down. Five or six men rushed into the room, led by Udin. Mas Tanto was at their rear. "Grab him, quick," Udin said.

Isaac had no time to react. Two men seized his arms and slammed them onto the cot. Two other men grabbed his ankles and forced them down against the canvas.

"Let me go!" Isaac cried out. "What do you want? Let me go!"

Imam Ali materialized at the doorway. His bright crow's eyes glittered. His narrow tongue flicked across his thin lips. Isaac's muscles lost all strength and his blood turned to vapor. "Please don't kill me," he gibbered. "No, please, don't behead me."

"Behead you?" Udin said. "It's not your head we're cutting off."

The others guffawed.

Udin said in an unctuously soothing voice, "Don't worry, Isak, today you shall become a Muslim. There is one little detail that we are taking care of first."

Imam Ali stepped forward. The two men holding Isaac's ankles spread them apart. Imam Ali moved in and stood at the foot of the cot between Isaac's legs. He lifted Isaac's sarong until Isaac was fully exposed.

Isaac squirmed, but the men held him tight. One of them said, "It's dark in here. Are you going to do it by feel?"

The Imam chuckled and in his cackling voice told Udin to turn on the overhead light.

"Mas Bengkok!" Isaac shouted, straining to lift his head. "Mas Bengkok! Help me!"

The Imam said, "Quiet down, boy. This is standard procedure. It will only hurt you if you let it hurt you."

Mas Tanto had taken a place behind Isaac's head. Isaac tilted his head backward, trying to catch a glimpse of him. "Mas Tanto! Please, you know me, please help me. Please."

"Ah," Imam Ali said. "What do we have here? Do you know this is the first white worm in its blanket that I have ever seen? What a pitiful-looking thing. Like a starving grub." He flicked it with his finger as the other men laughed. "A slimy, starving grub. He's just finished masturbating, would you believe." He chuckled as the others laughed uproariously.

Isaac screamed, "Mas Tanto, please!"

Tanto stepped forward and clamped a rough, calloused hand over his mouth, pressing down hard so that Isaac could not open it to bite his fingers.

Imam Ali used Isaac's sarong to clean the penis, still chuckling and shaking his head. "Boys will be boys, eh?" he said. He took Isaac's cleaned penis in his fingers. He stretched out the foreskin as far as it would go. Isaac tried to kick his legs to shake the Imam loose, but the men's grip was too strong. "I think it could stretch out farther," the Imam said.

Without warning, he pulled back the foreskin, slipping it over the glans of Isaac's penis. The foreskin resisted for a moment. The Imam tugged harder, and tissues that connected the inner foreskin to the glans tore loose. The pain was excruciating. A million volts of electricity stabbed into the center of Isaac's spinal cord, and his back arched off the bed. Huge beads of sweat popped to the surface of his forehead. He screamed so violently that his lungs seemed to rip loose from their anchors. Tanto's thick hand muffled the noise.

"Quite a bit of bleeding," the Imam said conversationally. "A boy his age, I would have expected some more looseness there, less attachment."

"Maybe he hasn't masturbated enough," Udin said, to another round of laughter.

Imam Ali stretched out the incandescently painful foreskin. Isaac moaned in agony. "That's better," the Imam said. He put a hand inside a small bag that he carried over his shoulder and

Richard Lewis

withdrew an object that he pressed onto the glans of Isaac's penis. "I'm almost tempted not to use the shield and try a little freehand cutting," he said. "Maybe on my next infidel child." He next withdrew a razor knife.

"Let go of his mouth," Udin told Tanto. "I want to hear him scream this time."

Tanto did not release his hand.

"Let go," Udin said.

Tanto let go.

Imam Ali pinched Isaac's foreskin with his fingers. Holding the razor in his right hand, he sliced the foreskin along the edge of the shield.

What had been excruciating before was now beyond all adjectives of pain. Isaac's scream was instinctive and primal. His muscles seized so violently that his left leg shook off its holder, and the Imam had to cease his cutting to put his weight on the flailing limb until the man got his hold back again.

Tanto quickly clamped down hard on Isaac's mouth to silence him.

"Allah, I've never heard it hurt so bad. Even a stuck pig doesn't squeal that loud," Udin said, shaken by the intensity of Isaac's pain. He regained his composure. "I guess bulés can't take pain the way we can."

Tanto growled, "We're not using any antiseptic cream. I tell you, this is not a good idea. The Tuan Guru has said nothing about—"

"I said I'll take the responsibility," Imam Ali said, cutting again as Isaac swooned. "Didn't you hear me?"

Another cut and the Imam was done. He stuffed toilet tissue over the raw and bleeding glans and placed over that a bamboo cod-piece, which he strapped in place with nylon string. Isaac barely noticed. His eyes fluttered, Imam Ali's face unsteady in their view. The foul monster that had been chasing him all these nights was no figment of his imagination, a summoned illusion, but was as real as the pain he was feeling and had taken bodily shape in the form of this crow-eyed, beak-faced, thin-lipped man whose breath smelled like scalded chicken feathers. This was no Imam.

This was the Lord of the Crows himself, in human guise.

"The next step," the Imam said, "is for you to recite the confession of faith in the presence of two pious Muslims. Now, we would do, of course, but we shall give you an even more grand and glorious occasion in which to become a Muslim. Why, thousands of Muslims shall witness this, and the whole world will watch. Rejoice, little Isak, that you have been granted this glorious opportunity to become a Muslim in front of the whole world."

Isaac summoned all the residue of his evaporated faith and hissed something through teeth gritted against the pain.

"What's that?"

"I don't want to become a Muslim."

The Imam patted his cheek. "Of course you do. You haven't gone through all this pain for nothing, have you?"

Ibu Halimah bustled into the room. "What outrage is this?" she boomed. "Get away from that boy!" She shoved the two men holding Isaac's feet away from the cot. With hands on her hips, she stared angrily at Imam Ali.

He stiffened. "Don't you know who I am?"

"I know poisonous mushrooms from good. Get away from him." She pushed the Imam to the side and caught sight of Isaac's groin. "*Iyallah!* What have you done!"

"Be calm, woman," the Imam said. "It is only a circumcision."

"Does the Tuan Guru know of this? No, I think not. You men with your overblown egos and stiff-necked pride, taking it out on a little boy. Shame on you. Now go."

The Imam said to Tanto, "Brother, who rules in your house?"

Tanto did not answer. He trailed out after the others, his head bent under the weight of his wife's anger.

Alone with Isaac, Ibu Halimah became brusque and efficient. She removed the codpiece. She clucked at what she saw. "Butcher," she muttered under her breath, not intending for Isaac to overhear. "Let me go get my medicine bag," she said. "I'll be back in a minute. Don't move."

Isaac lay still. The searing flames of pain were receding to a steady glow.

When she came back, she had a cup of jamu in her hands. "Drink this, it'll help the pain, calm you down."

Isaac feebly waved away the cup. "Thank you, but I don't need it."

"But, Isak—"

"I don't need it. My dream came true at dawn, and so now I don't need it."

She considered Isaac. "As you wish," she finally said. "But I must clean and treat your wound." She started with an anesthetic that bit fiercely before it took effect, reducing the pain of Isaac's penis to a sting, tolerable if he thought of other things. What he thought of was a Hutu beheading a Tutsi.

"*Aiyah,* this is a shame," she said as she worked. "A circumcision should be a time of joy and celebration. A little bit of hurt, but then singing and feasting. A circumcision to a boy should be what a wedding night is to a maiden. But this, what sort of circumcision has this been?"

Isaac said nothing.

The Hutu's blade still glistened shiny smooth even after passing through the Tutsi's neck.

When Ibu Halimah was finished, she said, speaking more gently than she ever had, like a mother would, "You don't have to be brave. You can cry."

Isaac blinked once, twice. "I've no more tears," he said. "No more tears."

Richard Lewis

Chapter Fifteen

A FEW HOURS LATER Mr. Suherman studied the bloodstains on the cot. His face hardened but his voice remained soft as he said, "Listen to me, Isaac. This has nothing to do with Islam."

Isaac said nothing. He sat on the chair with his legs carefully splayed, staring at the crack in the shutter.

Mr. Suherman sighed. "Allah will hold Imam Ali accountable for all he has done. And, *in sha'a allah,* so will I. But what he has done cannot be changed. It is time to go. Follow me."

Isaac did so, his throbbing penis protected by the codpiece from the weight and shift of the sarong he'd been given to wear, along with a white tunic. Mr. Suherman left the door to the cell standing wide open. "We are not returning," he said.

Mas Bengkok's cot was gone. A bucket of clean water stood next to the wall. Mr. Suherman performed wudu and then asked that Isaac do the same. "I know you are wounded in your heart as well as body," he said gently. "Do it as best you can."

Isaac went through the motions. When he was done, Mr. Suherman said, "I'm going to blindfold you. There are some men standing outside the door. They will not hurt you. They will put you in a car." Mr. Suherman took the black sash that was around his shoulders and tied it around Isaac's eyes. He knocked on the door at the end of hall. It whisked open. Brusque but kind hands gathered up Isaac and took him down the stairs. The men joked good-naturedly at his bent, spread-knee shuffle. He was guided onto the comfortable rear seat of a sedan. Two minders sat on either side of him.

As the car descended into the familiar lowland heat, public bus conductors chanted out the names of their destinations. Isaac's current minders did not realize just how well he knew the province. His mind made a map, traced out a route, and circled the town where they had started.

Dogs and boys have an uncanny ability to scent home. Isaac scratched his nose, bumping up the lower edge of his blindfold for a peek. The sky was at last a scintillating blue. Isaac saw on his right the charcoaled ruins of a two-story storefront. Pedestrians hurried past without giving it a glance.

Gideon Wira's shop.

There fell into Isaac's heart the absolute certainty that Mr. Wira was dead, killed by the mindless, murderous mob.

Isaac let the blindfold drop.

A few minutes later the car's tires crunched on gravel and then stopped. The doors flung open. His keepers got him out and hustled him along. Isaac grimaced from the pain of his jostled penis. He stumbled up a short flight of four steps. A door opened. "Take off your sandals," one of his guardians said. Isaac kicked them off his feet, and he was pushed through the door, which closed behind him. None of the men followed him.

Isaac stood there not knowing what to do.

A resonant voice said, "Remove your blindfold."

Isaac obeyed, squinting against bright light flooding in from a window. He was in a small room painted pure white. Turkish rugs covered most of the marble floor. Across from him was another door. Beside it was a low dais; on that dais rested a thin red cushion; and on that cushion sat an old man with sunken cheeks, bushy white eyebrows, and a tuft of a beard. He was swaddled in white and wore a white turban. He looked at Isaac with a gaze that burned.

Isaac's mouth went dry. His vision grew dim at the edges.

The old man lifted his right arm, and a hand appeared out of the voluminous sleeve of his blouse. A scrawny finger with a cracked, yellowed nail beckoned him closer.

Even seated on the dais, the Tuan Guru was still a head shorter than Isaac. With a vigorous movement, he hoisted Isaac's sarong with both hands, exposing the codpiece. He lifted the codpiece without unstrapping it. He cricked his head left and right, inspecting the wound. His expression changed not at all. Letting the sarong drop, he motioned impatiently for Isaac to step back and then appeared to lose all interest in him. His gaze turned inward with the self-assurance of a man accustomed to himself as he sat in judgment of others.

Mr. Suherman entered the room. He handed Isaac a rolled prayer rug. He said, "We will go out in a few moments. Sit where I put you, on that rug, in the Islamic manner. Sit quietly. You will be told what to do, so listen carefully at all times and obey what you are told. Your ordeal is nearly finished; there is only the one more step to take."

The words echoed in Isaac's brain. *Only the one more step, one more step, one more step.*

Mr. Suherman opened the other door. He motioned Isaac to go through first. Before Isaac was a vast, soaring chamber, with an immense congregation of men, women, and children sitting on its floor.

He was, as he already knew, in the Grand Mosque of Wonobo. Thousands of Wonobo's faithful had gathered together for Friday's noon worship, row after row after row of worshippers lined up in ranks spaced by the length of a prostrate body, the symmetry of their ranks broken only by the marble-faced columns that towered from the floor to a distant ceiling. The majority were men, dressed in somber-colored sarongs and blouses. The women were segregated to the left side, separated by a low white screen. They were garbed in white from head to toe, leaving only their brown faces exposed.

At Isaac's appearance the worshippers' whispered praying ceased. Mr. Suherman put his hand on the small of Isaac's back. He kept applying a slight pressure, guiding Isaac across the floor into the silence.

In the center of the front row sat Imam Ali with his crow face. He looked upon Isaac with a beneficent smile. Udin sat beside him. His smile was much more hungry.

Just outside the prayer hall on the northern colonnade, Isaac glimpsed a discreetly placed video camera on a metal tripod. The cameraman, a headset clamped to his ears, wore prayer dress. From far beyond the mosque's grand entrance came the faint yet unmistakable braying of a press mob being held at bay from their news.

"Eyes down," Mr. Suherman whispered.

Isaac lowered his gaze. His ribs were slick with sweat. The kiai indicated for him to put down his prayer rug at the right end of the first row, in two spaces clearly reserved for them. Mr. Suherman put his rug down beside Isaac's.

Isaac sat down carefully, nursing his groin. Once seated, he took a deep breath. He felt very far away from his own body. The only thing that seemed to connect him to his flesh was the twinge of pain beneath the codpiece.

In the center of the front row Imam Ali resumed his murmurs of Scripture.

The muezzin of the Grand Mosque approached the microphone that stood in front. With his back to the congregation, he lifted his hands to the sides of his head, palms outward, and began reciting the call to prayer.

As the last echoes swirled and died Tuan Guru Haji Abdullah Abubakar strode out the door Isaac had just used. He paused and surveyed the hall. In that brief sweep of his penetrating and all-seeing eyes, it seemed that he not only knew and recognized each person present, but also read the words of their minds and the writings on their hearts. Some of the congregants shifted uncomfortably on their rugs. Others, like Imam Ali, glowed with the Tuan Guru's unspoken blessing.

The Tuan Guru's gaze rested on Isaac. Again Isaac felt pierced by that hot, merciless, knowing stare.

"*As-salamu alaikum,*" the Tuan Guru said in a strong voice, wishing peace upon the assembled worshippers.

No peace fell upon Isaac.

The Tuan Guru ascended the three short steps to the pulpit, which was a marvel of workmanship in rosewood with enamel and mother-of-pearl inlay. He sat down cross-legged on its small, rug-covered platform. He began his sermon with the familiar Arabic words, "*Bismillah Ar-Rahman Ar-Rahim!* In the name of God the Compassionate, the Merciful. Praise be to Allah Almighty to whom none can be compared. His being transcends all of space and all of time. He is Ruler of Worlds. The Lord of Might. The Master of Destiny. The Owner of All Praise. He lifts up the lowly whom He will and reduces the mighty whom He will. Praise be to the hearer of our prayers, to the All-Seeing and All-Knowing. There is none like Allah. He guides whom He will, and His path is straight and complete to perfection. *Ashhadu anna la illaha illa allah wa ashhadu anna muhammadan rasul allah!* May Allah have mercy upon the Prophet's descendants and upon his companions. May Allah grant them peace.

"Today I wish to speak of the completeness of Islam, the indivisible oneness of the straight path within which there is no crookedness. There are some who say, I am of the party of this Imam, or I follow the teaching of that *alim*. And there are some that say, I am a follower of Tuan Guru Haji Abdullah Abubakar. There are some of you who are confident they know what I am going to say. Therefore, it seems to me that one of you who knows this should take my place on this *minbar* and speak to the others who do not know. Is there anyone willing to do so? To grant this tired tongue some rest?"

The Tuan Guru fell silent as he searched the large and quiet hall for this volunteer who might replace him. His gaze lingered upon Imam Ali. No one moved, least of all the Imam.

"Very well. I shall speak myself, then, of the completeness and indivisibility of Islam. And let me start with the obvious, which is plain for all of us to see: the presence in our midst of a child of the unbelievers."

The Tuan Guru pointedly looked to his left at Isaac. The congregation was galvanized by these last words. The air became charged with electricity. A surge of heat suffused Isaac. He began sweating again. He stole a glance at Imam Ali and then at Mr. Suherman. Imam Ali had an eager, expectant look on his beaklike face; Mr. Suherman's was impassive.

The Tuan Guru said, "Praise be to Allah, who ordains as He pleases! He in His Wisdom delivered this boy into our hands, He has placed him there according to His purpose. And what is His desire in this regard?"

Isaac concentrated on the pain radiating from his penis. He did not want to hear the fate that the Tuan Guru had decided for him. The Tuan Guru spoke with great emotion and with bristling of his eyebrows. At last one sentence cut through the barrier of pain that Isaac had erected around himself.

"Isak, would you please stand before me."

The Tuan Guru's command was softly spoken but had the terrible clarity of a suddenly drawn sword. The congregation stirred and then hushed with anticipation.

Isaac felt faint. His mutilated groin throbbed. Mr. Suherman took his elbow. Isaac was so light that Mr. Suherman's mere touch seemed to lift him to his feet. They moved forward, with a thousand pairs of eyes once more upon them. The silence clung to Isaac, making his steps difficult.

He came to the foot of the pulpit. Isaac stared at the finely veined marble underneath his bare feet. *I am a Christian. I must not reject my faith. Dear God, help me.*

But God was silent, and in his fear and pain Isaac knew the awful truth: He did not want to die, not even for his faith.

The Tuan Guru leaned forward and said, "Child, look at me." His command had such power that Isaac could not resist. The Tuan Guru caught and held Isaac's helpless gaze. The burning heat was there as before, but Isaac was suddenly confused, because he saw something else that he could not name until the Tuan Guru did so himself, crying out, *"Bismillah Ar-Rahman Ar-Rahim!"*

Compassion. Mercy.

"We humbly beg you, young Isak, to come to common terms with us, to accept Islam and become part of our family."

Isaac stood there as dumb as a calf before the slaughter. *God, help me.* God's silence became even more profound. In Isaac's fright blossomed a pricking of anger. He no longer wanted to be a pawn in either earthly or heavenly games, pushed this way and that. He forced sounds to his lips. *"Ndak isa."* I cannot.

The Tuan Guru said nothing. Isaac quailed. Then the Tuan Guru smiled, an astonishing smile of warmth and humanity, and said clear enough for all in the mosque and those beyond to hear, "Allah calls whomsoever He wills, and there is no denying His call. Who is to say when He shall call you, young Isak? Until then, the Qur'an is clear in teaching that there is no compulsion in Islam. Looking upon you, I am reminded of a verse that is addressed to captives." He sang the Arabic and then said in ringing Indonesian, "O Prophet! Say to those captives who are in your hands: If Allah knows any good in your hearts, He will give you better than that which has been taken from you and will forgive you. For Allah is forgiving, merciful."

The Tuan Guru raised his gaze to the congregation and said, "Truly, the straight path is of an indivisible oneness. The very plain wording of this *ayah* is also echoed by Abu Musa, who said that the Prophet said, 'Free the captives, feed the hungry, and pay a visit to the sick.' Who among you can deny that the purpose of Allah regarding this child Isak is not this very clear and plain commandment, to release him whom fate has placed as a captive in our hands and to say to the world that is watching us even this moment: Islam gifts you all with the great and priceless pearl that is peace, if only you will accept it."

A murmur of agreement swept the packed mosque like an ocean wave running along the sand. The Tuan Guru let the silence linger before he spoke again to Isaac.

"Isak, you are a child of the Book, a creature of Almighty God. You have in your heart the goodness for which Allah searches." He paused and then murmured, "May you receive from Allah that which is better than what was taken." He let his compassionate gaze linger on Isaac. "I will shortly release you to your parents with my blessing, but first, Imam Ali, will you please come forward. Yes, I mean you, Imam Ali."

The Tuan Guru descended from the pulpit. Imam Ali approached, his yeasty smell raising the hair on Isaac's nape. He came into Isaac's peripheral view. Isaac adjusted his stance to lose sight of the man.

The Tuan Guru said to both Mr. Suherman and Imam Ali, in a voice strong enough to carry to the most distant person of the stunned congregation, "I wish for you to salam this boy with me, for he is Allah's creation."

The Tuan Guru turned slightly to face Isaac. He bent at the waist, extending his clasped hands. Isaac automatically caught the Tuan Guru's calloused hands between his palms. *"Allah umina amin,* Isak," he said, his eyes twinkling.

Mr. Suherman salamed Isaac. He was smiling broadly and winked. *"Allah umina amin.* The peace of God be upon you," he whispered.

That left Imam Ali. Isaac flicked a quick glance at the Imam's face. It was suffused with anger and humiliation. He did not extend his hands. The Tuan Guru rested his eyes upon the Imam, saying nothing. Imam Ali's dark face grew duskier yet with blood, and with great effort, he extended his hands. Isaac was equally loath to take them, these hands that only hours previously had mutilated him, but he did so, for there was nothing else he could do. He barely touched the Imam's scaly skin and then let his hands drop.

The entire congregation, the thousands of men and women and children, rose to their feet and, in one ringing voice that swirled out to infinity and crossed the bridge to paradise, proclaimed to Isaac, "The peace of God be upon you."

Mr. Suherman led Isaac out of the prayer hall and down the northern arcade, shaded by the scalloped folds of the roof's overhang. A man with a video camera followed their progress. The walkway, made of patterned marble, stretched the length of the mosque. The open air to the left was curtained off by a thick and brilliant sunlight, transforming the arcade into a tunnel of shadow.

"Isak! Isak!" Ismail, in prayer garb, rushed out of the main prayer hall toward Isaac, his narrow face lively with a happy smile. Isaac stopped. "The Tuan Guru let you go," Ismail said excitedly. "You know what that means? That means we can be friends again. Listen, how about I come by this afternoon? You know, the same place, the tree."

Isaac glanced down at the bulge in his sarong.

Ismail's gaze followed, his smile turning into a frown. "Oh. That. It'll take a couple days before you feel like playing, I guess." His smile returned. "But next week, okay? There's a great *wayang kulit* show . . ." Ismail's voice trailed off. "What's wrong?"

"Go away," Isaac said. "Just leave me alone."

Mr. Suherman said, "Ismail, you are missing your prayers. Go back in and join the others."

Ismail backed away, confusion pinching his face.

Mr. Suherman put his hand on Isaac's back and moved him

forward. "There," he said, gesturing with his other hand toward the end of the arcade. "Your parents are waiting there. Do you see them?" And then he vanished.

Beyond the far front steps of the mosque was a mass of people milling behind a sawhorse barricade. Most of them aimed cameras or held boom microphones. Upon seeing Isaac, they surged, with a barrage of firing cameras. A host of khaki-uniformed policemen held them back. In the front of the commotion stood Graham and Mary Williams, still as statues. Then Mary pulled her hand away from her husband's and climbed over the sawhorse barricade to run toward Isaac. She opened her arms, and her familiar warm fragrance enveloped him. She released the embrace to hold his face in her hands, kissing him on his right cheek and his left cheek. His black cap toppled off his head. She was crying, her tears destroying the makeup that she had put on for this occasion. "Isaac, oh, Isaac."

Graham Williams stepped up beside her, extending his hand. "Let's go home, Isaac."

Richard Lewis

Chapter Sixteen

ISAAC, DRAPED IN A hospital gown, stood by the window of a fourth-story hospital room that overlooked the alley and the residential compound beyond.

Reverend Biggs had prayed, "We shall know the place we left and know it joyously, as home."

Aside from fresh plywood on the garage roof that replaced the burned patches and the "H" still visible on the front lawn, the compound was untouched. His house looked as it always had.

Maybe the tape of history could be played backward, the helicopters landing in reverse on that "H," the staff and students descending backward from the ramps, into their former lives, no different from when they had left.

Except for Isaac, who would have been divided irrevocably into two. An uncircumcised Isaac would scramble backward to his perch in the flame tree, and from there, he would stare across the gap of time and of immutable events to a fourth-floor VIP room in the hospital occupied by the circumcised Isaac, who would return the stare.

If he climbed up to that perch now, what would he see? The tree had survived the rioting unharmed, but was it the same tree, created by God for the pleasures of children? It had lost most of its red blossoms. No leaves had sprouted. Its nude branches looked not bare, but barren.

"I kept the faith," Isaac whispered. "I said no."

The reunion of American Christian parents with their son abducted by Indonesian Muslims was a headline news item, blending international politics and religious tensions with a human interest story that had, for the most part, a happy ending.

Later that evening, once he was released to the care of his parents and allowed to return home, Isaac watched that happy ending on CNN. The video cameras had captured his march down the exterior arcade toward his waiting parents. The cameras zoomed in on Mary scrambling over the sawhorse and sweeping her son into her arms for her embrace. They showed the world her tears and Isaac's own dry eyes.

It took a long time for Isaac to fall asleep that night, but when he did, it was a sound sleep. The Lord of the Crows had not been vanquished, that Isaac well knew, but the creature had, for the moment, gone elsewhere.

The dawn azan from the Al-Furqon Mosque woke him. The call to prayer was considerably more muted than those broadcast several weeks ago. Isaac lay awake on his bed, legs spread to help relieve the throbbing of his swollen penis. The sliding door to the porch below whisked open. His mother was going outside for her dawn devotional. Isaac smelled the fragrance of her hot coffee. There rose the sibilant whisper of her prayer, the rising notes of her distress: "Lord, I have a wounded son. He hurts and needs help that I can't seem to provide. What am I to do?"

Isaac got out of bed and slipped into his sarong and a T-shirt. He shuffled barefoot to the toolshed on the perimeter of the residence side of the compound. He searched in the musty corners until he found what he wanted. He made his slow, pained way to the flame tree. Dawn had broken behind gray clouds gathered around the volcanic peaks far to the west. The tree's bare branches looked sick and spindly against an uncertain sky. He loosely tucked the hem of the sarong into the waist fold. Holding the tool with one hand, he awkwardly climbed the flame tree. The scab on his penis broke. He ignored the blood dripping down his thigh and onto the branches that he climbed upon.

For a minute he sat on his perch.

At the Al-Furqon Mosque the Muslims of the community gathered once more, but instead of engaging in the spiritual warfare of *kunut nazilah,* they performed *salat al-istisqa,* the ritual prayer for rain. The speakers on the minaret were silent, but Isaac could hear on the still and turgid air the new Imam reciting the Qur'an and the people responding earnestly with *"Allahumma asqina."* O Allah, send down rain upon us.

Isaac got up from his perch. He found a steady position and began to cut the branches of his perch with the saw in his hand.

A boy left the mosque and crossed the street. He stood underneath the tree and called up to Isaac. Isaac ignored him and continued sawing. One branch after another fell to the ground. When all the perch branches had fallen, Isaac glanced down at the sidewalk. Ismail was gone.

Chapter Seventeen

A MASS OF GRAY CLOUDS swirling low to the earth diluted Sunday's sunrise. An hour later it was drizzling. Isaac attended church with his parents. His shield put a peculiar bulge in the crotch of his trousers, so he wore a straight-cut batik shirt, the hem of which came down near his knees.

Canvas tenting stretched over the burned remains of the Maranatha Church. The congregation sat on folding metal chairs. The air still had the acrid scent of smoke and ash. Empty holes in the scorched brickwork marked where windows had once been. The beautiful stained-glass artwork was now colorful shards sprinkled in the piles of rubble by the irrigation ditch.

"God has answered our prayers for rain," Pastor Cornelius said.

Isaac assumed that the Muslims of the Al-Furqon Mosque were also taking credit.

He did not sing the hymns, nor did he stand for the prayers. His mother whispered for him to, but he shook his head. During the closing benediction she sat with him, holding his hand.

The rain fell steadily, not a flooding rain, but a blessing rain that was avidly drunk by a thirsty land. The rain kept falling without a break. Sometime in the night a tremendous crack rent the sodden evening, followed immediately by an earthshaking thud. The noise jolted awake the entire neighborhood, still skittery about unexpected events and alarms. Graham Williams rushed outside in his pajamas. Isaac waddled as fast he could behind him. The security guards were already out in the schoolyard, their high-intensity flashlights shooting blazing beams that reflected off the falling motes of water. They quickly found the cause of the noise.

The flame tree had drunk too greedily of the miraculous groundwater. The first major branch, about five feet in diameter, had sheared off under its own gluttonous weight. It lay on the ground like a savagely severed appendage. Splayed splinters the size of a man's forearm marked where branch and tree had joined.

By early morning the rain had ceased. Before going to the hospital, Graham sat down on the edge of Isaac's bed. He said, "Trees don't live forever, Isaac. They get old and die like people. We're going to have to cut down the rest of the flame tree before more of it falls and hurts somebody."

Isaac rolled the edge of the bedsheet between his fingers. "I know," he said.

Graham watched Isaac's restless fingers. "About you going to America—there isn't really any other alternative."

"What grade am I going to be in?"

A long silence, broken at last by Graham's sigh. "I don't know." He glanced at his watch. "I have to go. See you tonight."

Isaac watched the work crew cut down the wounded tree. He sat on the steps of the closed school, his knees spread under his sarong. The workmen used ropes and double-handed pull saws. The tree was not toppled, but dismantled branch by branch.

It took all day for the work crew to cut down the tree. Isaac watched the last load leave in the hospital's rusty pickup. The pickup returned with a load of rich loamy dirt escorted by the new gardener, a young, crinkly-haired Christian. Isaac didn't know his name. He started to mend the gaping hole in the ground that the uprooted stump had left.

Isaac watched the gardener fill in the hole. Burying the dead, in a way, although there'd be no tombstone here.

That afternoon somebody delivered a package to the security post. The guards thought it was a bomb. Isaac, who saw the commotion and heard the description of the man who had dropped it off, marched over. To the guards' spluttering horror, he ripped open the taped folds of the wrapping paper. "See, it's just a book." He riffled the pages.

"Why, it's the Qur'an," Mr. Theophilus said.

Not just any Qur'an but Mr. Suherman's copy of Pickthall's translation. On the first page Mr. Suherman had written, *To Isaac, a child of the Book: May you grow in the grace of Almighty God, and may you do so in peace wherever you live.*

Isaac took the Qur'an up to his room. He put it down next to his devotional Bible, which he hadn't touched since he'd come home. Nothing happened. There was no annihilation of matter and antimatter. He left the Qur'an where it was.

What kept Isaac awake that night was neither pain nor

nightmares, but the Qur'an on the dresser. Isaac was a usurper in this room, trying to sleep a usurper's sleep. One day the real uncircumcised Isaac was going to return and exclaim, *Who's been sleeping in my bed? Who's brought strange Scriptures into my room?*

He must have slept for some time that night, but he once again was awake before dawn. His mother was on the porch below. She was angry at somebody. Even though she spoke quietly so that Isaac could not make out the words, he knew that tone of voice, full of his mother's famed and monumental anger.

He stole down the stairs and to the end of the darkened hallway leading to the garden porch. Mary sat on her rattan chair, her Bible open on her lap under the porch lamp, and spoke out into the gathering light. She said in that flat-trajectoried, armor-piercing tone, "You say that you are close to the brokenhearted and that you save those who are crushed in spirit. It says so right here in your holy word." She tapped the page. "Well? Where are you? Is this verse meaningless, then? I think so. I've been waiting and waiting. I don't think this verse belongs in the Bible. I'll just remove it." She ripped the page, crumpled it in her fist, and tossed it aside. It landed next to another crumpled page.

"And what about this promise of yours?" she said, turning to another passage. "'Do not fear, for I am with you.' Oh?" The "oh" was a parody of surprise. Mary ripped this page out of her devotional Bible too, crumpled it and threw it.

Isaac cringed, waiting for the terrible whirlwind of fire. Nothing happened. Mary inexorably continued with her list of judgments. She continued to weigh God according to His stated promises and found Him wanting. With each judgment, she ripped out another a page of her Bible.

Finally and most awfully, she accused Him of lying: "This is what you said: 'Never will I leave you, never will I forsake you.'" She was quiet for a moment, staring at her mutilated Bible, the pages torn from it littered around her feet, and then at the last torn page still in her hand. She lifted her head and in a quiet and terrible voice said, "Where were you for my son? Where are you for me? Why have you abandoned us?"

The words and his mother's anguish settled in the crevasses of Isaac's own soul. But if God would not give her comfort, how could he? If God would not answer, what words could he give?

Then he knew. He knew what was needed, both for him and for her. The knowledge came with urgency. He pushed open the door. "Mom, Mom, get dressed, we have to go."

For a moment she stared blankly at him. "Isaac?"

He grabbed her hand and tugged it, trying to pull her out of the chair. "Get dressed, we have to go."

"Go? Go where?"

"We have to go see the Tuan Guru right now."

"The Tuan Guru?" A heartbeat. "The Tuan Guru," she breathed out, and the exhalation dried her moist eyes and changed them to disks of slate. She stood. "Where is he?"

"Up in the mountains, at a pesantren school. Hurry up, let's go."

"Isaac, as much as I want to confront the man, I'm not about to take you back into that lion's den."

"I want to see him."

"Isaac—"

"Please, Mom. He's not going to hurt me. He's not going to let anybody hurt me. He let me go, didn't he?" His mother was still shaking her head. Isaac said, "Mom. I *need* to see him."

Her head stilled. She studied Isaac and then said, "Perhaps you do."

Fifteen minutes later Mary and Isaac Williams were in the Kijang van with the darkened windows, heading down Hayam Wuruk Avenue. She had put on a business suit and jewelry and makeup. She drove swiftly. Isaac put together the route out of town in his head, recalling the cries of bus conductors, tracing a line backward until they came to the foot of the mountains and then up into them.

Two hours into their drive, they caught up to a truck with a load of young Madurese racing bulls tethered in the back, swaying and scrabbling to keep their balance as the truck took the curves.

On the outskirts of the town of Gambang a gaggle of girls in full green dresses and green jilbabs descended from a hired bus, out on a picnic to a nearby waterfall advertised by a large roadside sign. Girls from a Nahdlatul Umat Islam pesantren.

"We're getting close," Isaac murmured, staring at them.

Up here on the higher mountain slopes the weather-beaten houses and mosques hunkered down to the earth in a land that was closer and more susceptible to the capricious elements of water and fire. Scents and colors were crisper, even the stinks and the mud-mottled hues. The sky was so clear that it seemed to be tinged with the purple of the upper atmosphere.

They passed a mosque that proudly stood in splendor of spotless whitewash, immaculate green paint, and gleaming silver dome. A banner urged parents to enroll children in the mosque's Qur'an and Arabic classes, taught by qualified teachers from the Nahdlatul Umat Islam pesantren. In fact, classes were being held that morning. They were presently in recess. Young children played games in the front yard, supervised by older girls and women in full dresses and green jilbabs.

One round-faced woman caught a wayward volleyball and tossed it back to a circle of screeching children. As she did so she caught sight of the Kijang driving past. She paused and stared at the car's occupants.

Mary and Isaac followed the truck, rattling over a one-lane bridge that spanned a mossy, boulder-strewn stream flowing at the bottom of a deep crevasse with ferny sides. A hundred yards beyond the bridge land had been cleared into pasture. A rutted vehicle track led from the asphalt road to stables and a few smaller shacks. To the right of the stables was a bamboo-fenced paddock. To the left of the stables, behind square-topped hedges and a row of coffee trees, were the low, graceful buildings of the Nahdlatul Umat Islam pesantren, graciously proportioned out of gleaming whitewashed walls and wide slabs of glass. But in the middle of the elegant complex there rose an ugly, three-story building, something that the Dutch might have built a century previously. Isaac saw on the outside of the building the stairs that he had laboriously climbed, trembling with malaria, and descended two weeks later, equally laboriously, with a codpiece under his sarong. The building was now roofless and a throng of construction workers swarmed over the top story, knocking down walls.

Mary stopped the car on the edge of the road. The truck they had followed trundled across the unfenced field to the stables. The trainer, dressed in sarong and rubber sandals and chewing betel nut, was already waiting. He spat a thick stream of red fluid onto the ground. The driver got out and, after a quick hello and a yawning stretch, lowered the truck's rear gate. He dragged a ramp from the side of the truck bed and put that in place.

A group of pesantren adults strolled through the coffee trees, heading for the truck. They were all male, dressed in the flowing garments of Islamic scholars. Leading them, a half step in front, was Tuan Guru Haji Abdullah Abubakar, his turban-wrapped head as unmistakable as a lighthouse.

Mary slowly exhaled.

The Tuan Guru walked up the ramp at the rear of the truck with the agility and balance of a much younger man. He had a quick look at the bulls and their tethering. Satisfied, he descended and gestured to the trainer to start unloading them one by one for a closer examination.

The first young bull descended, and the old man began running his hands over its muscles.

Mary Williams tilted the rearview mirror and examined her makeup. Her war paint was still without blemish. The scent of her perfume had become the pheromones of battle. "Let's go have a chat with him, shall we?" she murmured.

They got out of the car and began walking across the expanse of grass in the humped middle of the vehicle ruts. Mary kept her attention on the Tuan Guru, avoiding stumbles and a couple of cow pies with nearly extrasensory perception.

The men gathered around the bulls did not at first notice their approach. One lifted his head and saw the tall blond woman striding toward him, and the joke he was making dribbled into silence without the punch line. The others followed his gaze, and they, too, fell silent.

The Tuan Guru did not look up. He continued his examination of the animal's chest, tapping it with a cupped hand.

Mary halted several feet from the Tuan Guru's back. Isaac stood close to her. She stared at the Tuan Guru's turbaned head. The other men stared at her. The Tuan Guru gave no indication that he was aware of her and Isaac's presence.

The trainer put his hand to his mouth and cleared his throat, but before he could say anything to alert the old man, the Tuan Guru said into the animal's ear, *"Al-salamu alaikum,* Isak."

Isaac answered automatically, *"Alaikum as-salam,* Tuan Guru."

Still addressing the animal, the Tuan Guru said in Indonesian, "Is this your mother you have brought with you?" He shifted his tapping hand to another spot on the calf's chest.

"Inggih, Tuan Guru."

"Al-salamu alaikum, Ibu Isak," he said, addressing Mary as Isaac's mother.

Mary Williams said nothing.

The Tuan Guru continued to speak as he tapped the calf's

Richard Lewis

chest. "You are a doctor, Ibu Isak. You know something of mammal physiology. These Madurese racing bulls are a lowland animal, but I bring them up here to train at high altitude to increase their stamina."

He gave the calf one last chest tap and then turned around to face Mary. Their gazes locked. He was at least two heads shorter than her, turban included, yet such was the strength of his presence that they seemed to be looking at each other on the same eye level.

He said, "Some years ago I read about Olympic athletes training at high altitude. I thought what works for humans must work for bulls. If I may ask, what is your considered and expert opinion? Am I correct in making this assumption?"

Mary inclined her head in acknowledgment of his addressing her. She spoke in her slow but fluent Indonesian. "A proper training program at this altitude should increase the animal's red blood cell count, yes," she said. "That should lead to increased stamina. But that does not necessarily translate into extra swiftness. And there must be some drawbacks. Do these bulls acclimatize to the cooler weather, or do they become more susceptible to other illnesses?"

The Tuan Guru stroked the underside of his chin with a long thumbnail. The rasp of the cuticle on tough skin and thick hair was overridden by the whine of a scooter coming down the road. "Some do become sick," he said. "But those that don't prove to be superlative racers. Madurese bull racing is, you see, a hobby of mine."

Mary inclined her head again, the very picture of polite graciousness. "It is good for a busy man like yourself to have a relaxing hobby."

The Tuan Guru's white eyebrows wriggled. He laughed, a dry barking sound, "Relaxing!" he exclaimed. "This hobby causes more tense moments and raised blood pressure than any of my work. I speak of the races, of course. I do not gamble, as that is forbidden by Allah, but I still like to win, and that is a pleasure Allah permits."

"I am sure that is so."

The Tuan Guru said, "However, it is rude to attend to my hobby when a person of esteem seeks an audience with me. This is your purpose, no? Unless you have come here to admire these fine young bulls for some reason?"

A woman in Islamic garb and green jilbab driving a scooter came into view. She braked to a stop and parked the scooter in front of the Williamses' car. She hurried along the vehicle rut toward the group of men, boy, woman, and bull, a broad smile on her face.

"It *is* you," Ibu Halimah said, swooping Isaac up in an embrace and sniffing both cheeks with sharp inhalations. "How are you, child? Are you well?"

"*Inggih,*" Isaac said politely.

But his mother said, "No, my son is not well. He was physically abused and tortured by some of your people." She said the last directly at the Tuan Guru. Her anger was building again. Everyone present, Ibu Halimah and the Tuan Guru and the trainer and the casual onlookers, tightened into a tense stillness. Even the bull swung its soft liquid eyes to Mary in alarm.

The Tuan Guru spoke. "Ibu Isak, I would be extremely rude to keep an esteemed woman and outraged mother standing here in the sun and the wind and the smell of the stables."

The wind was indeed stiffening. What had been seeping over the high volcanic ridges as a breeze was beginning to trickle down in greater volume, the pressure of a building storm behind it. The sunlight was no longer clear and weightless; a faint cataract of nearly invisible mist was filming over the sky and adding a milkiness to the blue.

The Tuan Guru spoke to one of his caftan-robed men, who had pallid skin and nervous eyes, magnified by thick lenses in wire-framed glasses. The Tuan Guru said to Mary, "My librarian will take you to my office. I shall be a moment seeing to the stabling of these bulls." He spotted something in her eyes, for he added, "You have sought my audience, and I shall grant it."

The librarian escorted them through the hedges that marked out the various sections of the pesantren. The roofs of the dorms poked over the flat hedge tops. Children played raucously. One boy raised his voice to say, "Beware the hunchback, for he stinks worse than his brethren, the twice-humped camels."

A familiar voice snorted, "The man who farts conquers the boy scented with cologne."

The librarian ushered them along a trellised walkway with offshoot paths that led to classrooms, empty at this time of day. He shepherded them to the grand entrance of the main building. A dozen schoolboys swarmed over one of the coffee trees that lined the wide driveway to the left. They were joking as they picked the tree's beans, but as soon as they spotted the librarian, they quieted and worked in industrious silence.

The librarian tugged open one of two thick doors. Spacious indoor gardens flanked the marble foyer. Two wide halls continued left and right. Four closed office doors with frosted windows fanned out in an arc opposite them. The librarian led them to the far door on the right.

Beyond this door was a secretary's outer office. The desk was cluttered with phone, computer, and stacks of paperwork and correspondence. The sooty ashtray on the desk and the lack of feminine touches suggested that the secretary was a male chainsmoker. An Islamic calendar with a picture of the sacred Kaaba at Mecca was the only decorative touch on the walls. The door to the inner office had been replaced by a hanging curtain woven in an oriental design with lots of tassels on its edges.

"Take off your shoes," the librarian said. He neatly lined the three pairs beside the curtained doorway. He held the curtain to the side for the two guests. They padded into a large, inner office whose trappings of desk, chairs, cabinets, and shelves had been shoved up against the far wall. Rugs had been placed in the cleared space. In the center was a plain teak coffee table surrounded by large, hard cushions. Two Moorish arched windows were set in the wall to the right. The light outside was rapidly becoming tarnished.

The librarian went to one window and opened it. A breeze gusted through and chased out the stuffy warmth piled up in the corners of the room. "Please sit," he said.

Mary and Isaac sat on one the rugs. Isaac crossed his legs. His mother tucked hers to the side underneath her skirt. The librarian sat down with them. Before long the hanging curtain stirred, pushed aside by the Tuan Guru's skeletal and freshly washed hand. The librarian rose. Isaac began to stand as well, but Mary held him down. This was deliberate rudeness.

The Tuan Guru appeared not to notice. He said to the librarian, "Did you offer our guests some chairs? They may not be accustomed to sitting on the floor in this manner."

The librarian looked crestfallen. The Tuan Guru sighed. He said to Mary, "Would you prefer to sit on those chairs?"

"I am already seated."

The Tuan Guru inclined his head. He sat down on the red cushion opposite the Williamses, with the low coffee table between them. He motioned the librarian to his side with a crook of his finger. The librarian bent low, and the Tuan Guru whispered an instruction into his ear. The librarian left the room.

The Tuan Guru said, "I trust you are not too uncomfortable. I myself do not like chairs. A lifetime of study and prayer on cushions and rugs and floors has seen to that. I find chairs too tempting. An old man like me could soon succumb to the easy convenience of chairs. My bones and muscles would sing praises to Allah for chairs and would protest at having to lower themselves to hard floors."

"Are chairs a sin, then?" Mary Williams asked.

"Only if one sits upon them in the presence of Allah. The Blessed Prophet taught us the proper positions of prayer, those of humbleness and submission. Other than that, chairs are merely a habit, and at my age I don't have the time or the inclination to change habits."

The curtain stirred. Ibu Halimah entered and placed a silver tray on the coffee table. She unloaded its contents of small cups, a long-necked copper pot that looked like Aladdin's genie lamp, and a filigreed silver bowl mounded with sugar. She poured the steaming coffee, as thick and black as printer's ink. Its rich aroma filled the room. She withdrew from the room, not having met anyone's eye or having said a word.

"Arabica coffee," the Tuan Guru said. "From our own trees here. Did you see the children picking the beans? That is part of their chores. They also help tend the gardens and the vegetable beds. Please, drink."

Mary Williams took a polite sip. Isaac, curious, tasted his. The hot liquid had an exotic richness to it, as though it had been brewed in a Bedouin tent. An Islamic coffee.

The Tuan Guru held his cup by its lip, pinching it between thumb and forefinger. He slurped a mouthful, looking at Mary Williams as he did so. He lowered the cup and said, "So, Ibu. You have sought an audience with me."

She nodded. "Someone must be held accountable for the deeds that were done in the name of the Nahdlatul Umat Islam, but I am not here for that. I am here with a mother's heart, to hold *you* accountable for what was done to my son by men of your organization."

The Tuan Guru put his cup down on the table. "There is a saying: The man seeking vengeance does not disturb my sleep; the woman seeking vengeance puts me on guard throughout the night; the mother seeking vengeance sends me running to

Richard Lewis

hide in the tiger's den. So. You seek vengeance."

"I seek justice. For my son's abuse and torture."

The Tuan Guru nodded. He said something in Arabic, which he then translated into Indonesian. "Allah desires not any injustice to living beings. To Allah belongs all that is in the heavens and the earth, and unto Him all matters are returned." The Tuan Guru stared at Mary, who had fallen into a dangerous calm across the coffee table from him. He said, "Allah is Allah, whether He is the God of Muslims or of Christians or of Jews. You are my honored guest and offered my full hospitality without malice and deceit, but you are not and cannot be my friend. We, Christians and Muslims, are a family, but it is within families that the deepest schisms run. Yet as family, we are most alike in many ways, and foremost is the same Supreme Lord who reigns with His will over you and me. The Allah that these ayat refer to is the same Tuhan of the Bible and the same Jehovah of the Torah. You are a daughter of the Book. You say you honor Him. Tell me, Ibu Isak, are you submitted to Almighty Allah?"

The blunt and powerful question was of the kind that old and wise shepherds who brook no shilly-shally evasions ask of their flock. Mary blinked. "Yes, I am submitted to my God."

The Tuan Guru said, "Even though we believe differently, your God is my God. Can you not leave this matter of justice in Allah's hands? For these ayat are as validly addressed to you as they are to me."

Mary smiled without warmth. "Indeed, I can leave this in God's hands. Or in those of the authorities He has ordained to act on His behalf. Men like Lieutenant Nugroho."

"Ah. And the lieutenant's punishment—perhaps a jail sentence of a year or two—that would suffice as justice?"

"Yes."

The Tuan Guru's reply was swift, delivered as incisively as a scalpel cut. "You lie."

The coffee cup trembled in her right hand. She cupped it with her left.

The Tuan Guru continued, "You are full of anger. Not just anger against me. Not just against those who harmed your son. You are full of anger against Allah, who would allow harm to come to Isak."

The fragile handle of Mary's cup snapped off. Coffee jostled onto her blouse. She gave a small cry of alarm. The Tuan Guru slipped a hand into the depths of his caftan and withdrew a plain handkerchief that he handed to her. She dabbed at the spill.

"You are angry at our God," the Tuan Guru repeated. "The one and only God, neither begotten nor begetting." He sipped his coffee again. "Tell me, Ibu Isak, if you blame God for what happened to your son, then who gets the praise for saving his life during that terrible helicopter crash?"

Mary's hand ceased moving. Her lowered eyes glanced left toward the curtained door, as though seeking for a way of escape.

The curtain moved and the librarian entered. He nodded at the Tuan Guru, who returned the nod. The librarian held aside the curtain. Tanto shuffled into the room, followed by a nervous Udin. Behind these two came Imam Ali, whose steps were stiff and indignant. The Tuan Guru did not invite them to sit. They stood in a row at the side of the room.

Tanto wore shorts and a singlet dirty from interrupted gardening. Udin and Imam Ali wore sarongs and shirts. A white haji's cap perched on Imam Ali's narrow head. A black cap was crammed onto Udin's head, which slipped an inch as he bowed toward the Tuan Guru. Beads of sweat popped out on his forehead. Tanto had pulled himself within his shell, an impervious and impassive mask locked into place on his face. Imam Ali glanced at Isaac and Mary Williams, and his lip curled. He did not look at them again and stared somewhere beyond the window opposite him. Isaac tried not to look at the Imam. The oxygen in the air seemed to thin. It was harder to take a breath.

The Tuan Guru said to Mary, "Allah ordains as He wills, and it is clear that He has decreed this moment and has called you to it from your Christian castle in Wonobo. He has directed us all to be here, and what I only moments ago assumed to be coincidence of presence and schedule I now see is His doing." He lifted a hand, indicating the three men. "These are the men who forcibly circumcised your son Isak. This I did not condone." The Tuan Guru spoke as offhandedly as though he were mentioning the naughty antics of his racing bulls. Under his bristling eyebrows, though, his eyes were keenly gauging Mary's reaction.

Mary shifted and turned toward her son with a questioning look that asked him to confirm these identities. But Isaac was now looking fully and helplessly at Imam Ali, his breath coming in quiet, agitated pants. A color rose in Mary's face that was far more than the rosy heat of blood, and her own breathing seemed to cease altogether. She turned her gaze to the men, her blue eyes having become vacant holes of violet, her anger growing and raising the temperature of the room a degree.

Udin's throat convulsed. Imam Ali's small eyes flickered her way. Tanto bent his head and stared at his feet.

Mary exhaled. It was a terrible sound, all mercy being expelled from her soul. She rose from her cushion.

"You wish to destroy these men," the Tuan Guru said, also rising to his feet. He came around the coffee table and stood to the side, between her and them. But he was not there to protect these disciples of his. "I give you leave to slaughter them, if you wish, to satisfy the lust of your vengeance. I will not lift a finger to save them."

Imam Ali snarled. "By Allah! I can save myself from this stinking Christian bitch."

"Silence!" The Tuan Guru did not raise his voice, but it had a shattering power to it. Imam Ali fell silent.

Mary's hand flashed out. Her palm slapped Imam Ali's cheek with enough force to leave an imprint as deep and seared as that from a red-hot brand. Tears of pain came to his eyes. He clenched his fists and took a menacing step forward.

"Be still!" The Tuan Guru's command bound and held the Imam. After a second the old man turned and said to Mary, "Did that feel pleasurable? Did that feel true and righteous?"

Mary closed her eyes. She trembled.

The Tuan Guru moved closer to her. "Allah ordains as He

wills, and I see that He has called you here to this moment, has chosen this place and this time, to speak to you. He, who has been hidden from your heart's eyes and silent to your soul's ear, is speaking to you now. What is it He is saying? What was the word that He gave His prophet Isa, whom you revere as Yesus Kristus, to speak to the Jews of his age, and that Isa speaks through the ages to you now? What is this word that Allah murmurs to you?"

Mary, with her eyes still closed, lowered her head, clenching her jaw.

"Vengeance?" The Tuan Guru's one-word question was a burning whisper.

Mary shook her head. She opened her eyes, looking at the Tuan Guru through brimming tears. She whispered softer yet, "Forgiveness."

"Ahhh." The Tuan Guru sighed deeply. "Forgiveness. And can you forgive the abuser of your son, Ibu Isak?"

She cried out, "I don't know!"

"Don't seek the forgiveness in yourself, then, but turn to Allah for His help, for He forgives as easily and freely as a baby smiles."

Mary Williams flicked away a tear. She murmured, in English, "Lord God, help me." She took a deep breath and looked at Tanto. "I forgive you," she said.

Tanto looked down at his feet. Mary turned to Udin, who shrank and gulped at this towering bulé woman who had cause to want him obliterated from the face of the earth and who still looked capable of carrying out this desire. "I forgive you," she said.

Slowly, she faced Imam Ali, whose expression remained as unyielding as a tombstone. She extended her hand. Her fingers brushed his branded cheek. "I am sorry I struck you," she said in Indonesian. She looked Imam Ali fully in the eyes. She bit her lower lip until its blanched skin seemed on the verge of tearing. The tears that had filled her eyes turned to sharp and dangerous shards ready to sunder flesh. She closed her eyes. "Help me," she whispered again in English. She opened her eyes and said unevenly, "And I forgive you for what you did to my son Isaac." She inhaled again, drawing the air through her nostrils. "I forgive you," she repeated. The words came more easily, but they were still stilted and empty, without meaning. Suddenly, though, something flashed through her eyes. "I forgive you," she said yet a third time, and now there was life to these words.

She turned to the Tuan Guru. "I forgive you all," she said, a hesitant joy rising in her face. But it halted as the Tuan Guru slowly shook his head.

"That is well, an honest start," he said. "Yet there is one more thing that must be done, the hardest forgiveness to be granted."

She said, with some bewilderment, "You mean God? God does not need my forgiveness any more than the ocean needs salt."

"No, Ibu," the old man said. "I am not referring to forgiving God, who, as you say, needs no forgiveness from His creatures." He held out both his hands and took hers, pulling them unresistingly from her body. The brown leathery hands that had all his adult life been surrendered in the service of Allah the Most Exalted, the one incomparable Supreme Being who begetteth not and was not begotten, gently held the paler, softer ones of a doctor who had dedicated her life and career to God the Father, God the Son, and God the Holy Spirit. "The hardest forgiveness of all is the one that you must seek for yourself." His gaze dropped briefly upon Isaac before returning to her.

Mary Williams gazed searchingly into the Tuan Guru's eyes. Her own filled with tears as she slowly nodded. She gently withdrew her hands from his and turned to Isaac. She took a deep breath and began to speak in English. "Isaac, I've done you a very great wrong. When I decided to stay here while you got on that helicopter, I thought I was following the Lord's will, putting His calling first. But I wasn't. I was putting my pride first. I put my pride before my love and duty to you. You feel I abandoned you . . ." Mary Williams's words began to teeter, as though they were stumbling on a downhill run through a rocky field, barely keeping their balance. ". . . and you are right, I did abandon you. I should have been with you the whole time, I should have . . . I should have . . ." The words tumbled to a halt. In the smallest of voices forced across the longest of distances, she said, "I was so very wrong. Please forgive me."

Isaac stared at his mother. He'd never seen her like this. He knew without wanting to know it that he had the power to hurt her cruelly. And heaven help him, for a moment there burned a fierce desire in him to do so. She *had* abandoned him. But he loved her. He trembled briefly, as if shaken by an inner wind, and the moment passed. "You didn't know what was going to happen," he said. "Of course I forgive you."

She gathered him up in a hug.

"Mom," he said, embarrassed.

She released him and wiped her tears away with the back of her hand. She said wonderingly to the Tuan Guru, "Who would have thought . . . you are truly a man of God. I don't understand it, and I won't try to. God bless you. It may not be possible for us to be friends, but God bless you."

The Tuan Guru solemnly nodded. "And to you, *Allah umina amin.*"

Mary Williams stepped up to Tanto and said, "I haven't thanked you for what you did to save the hospital and the compound from being looted and destroyed. That took the true courage of a good man. I thank you now, Mas Tanto."

Tanto, this most reserved and unemotional of men, could not keep bottled up his pleasure at Mary Williams's praise. He flushed darkly, and his embarrassment at flushing only deepened the color. He muttered down to the area where his right foot was squirming into the carpet, "You're welcome."

Imam Ali glared at Tanto.

Mary Williams took Isaac's hand and left the room. Isaac, however, felt a pull on the back of his head, as though a heavy hand had clamped on his skull with squeezing fingers and was rotating his head against unwilling muscles. He found himself staring into Imam Ali's beady eyes, and he recalled a spooky line he'd read somewhere, that when you gaze into the abyss, the abyss gazes back at you. The skin of his neck crawled, his penis shrank with an achy sensation, and the rest of him shuddered.

His mother might have forgiven Imam Ali, but he couldn't. Not ever.

Chapter Eighteen

WHEN HE AND HIS mother returned home late that afternoon, Isaac wandered to the schoolyard and stood on the circle of ground where the flame tree had once grown. The grass that had been planted over the scar left by the stump removal was already taking good root. Nothing indicated that a great and memorable tree had once soared to the sky here.

He had stood in front of the whole world and kept the faith, but God had not kept faith with him. But perhaps God knew that if the Tuan Guru had brought out the beheading sword, Isaac would have recited the *shahadah* and become a Muslim. Perhaps this was why God was silent and the place that He had occupied in Isaac's heart had been ripped out. What did this make Isaac? Maybe, just like he was neither a Javanese nor an American, he was no longer a Christian, but not quite a Muslim.

He stared up at the sky. The sun was an ugly blob of dull orange. That awful yellow smog was returning to Wonobo.

And into Isaac's heart came that old familiar fear.

The Lord of the Crows was on his way.

That evening at dinner Isaac declined the sandwiches and barely touched his soup. Graham Williams told Mary of something that

Mr. Ali, the business manager, had passed on to him, that Ibu Hajjah Yanti had seen Ruth in the Wonobo market and that Ruth had told Ibu Yanti, who told Mr. Ali, who told Graham, that she was deeply regretful that she had walked out of the Williamses' household. This circuitous message passing was a time-honored Javanese method of communication between two aggrieved parties.

Isaac went up to his room and got ready for bed. He eyed the Qur'an on top of his dresser. He opened the cover of the book and read again the inscription: *May you grow in the grace of Almighty God, and may you do so in peace wherever you live.* Ha. In the distance a stray dog yelped. The fragrance of jasmine mingled with the metallic odor of smog.

The Lord of the Crows was coming, headed straight for this room. Isaac had no doubt at all of that. There was unfinished business at hand.

Even though he knew it was futile, he made sure his windows were shut and the door to the porch locked. He pulled the curtains and stretched out on his bed.

He promptly fell asleep. Not a deep sleep, but deep enough for him to revisit the day's events as though experiencing them all over again. The recounting slowed down the closer he got to the Tuan Guru's carpeted office, slower and slower yet as he was inside it, and then it halted altogether as Imam Ali walked into the room, Isaac's perspective frozen onto the carpet in front of him, unable to look up at the Imam, who, he knew, had shed his human form, revealing his true and monstrous identity, which was a lot more pointy and beaked.

There came from somewhere outside the dream a sharp sound, like a giant mousetrap snapping, and his eyes flew open. The fuse box had blown. A moment later his dad stomped down the stairs. Isaac was in blackness thicker than anything he could dream. He couldn't even see the hand that he brought up and waved in front of his face. With the fan dead, sweat began to gather on his forehead and under his arms. Fear trailed a fingernail across his heart.

A photon pinged upon his retina, then another. This was no normal light. He lifted his head. On the top of his dresser the shut pages of the Qur'an gleamed palely between the dark covers.

Isaac rose from his bed. He held his hand above the Qur'an's front cover. He felt no radiating heat. He put his forefinger under the lip of the cover and flicked it open.

No burst of flame enveloped him.

He drew closer and noticed that the front page was glowing in splotches. He picked up the paperback and riffled the pages, finding similar splotches throughout the book. Where the splotches were the brightest, he could read the words printed on top of them. It was most peculiar, but it was assuredly a natural phenomenon. Maybe a fluorescent fungus, but natural.

From somewhere behind him, someone breathed out his name.

"Isak."

Isaac whirled around, clutching the Qur'an to his chest. The voice that cawed his name, the Muslim pronunciation of his name, came from far away, too far away for mortal voices. Isaac shivered. He listened with strained ears. He did not hear his name again, but once was enough. He wanted to flee, wanted desperately to flee, but he made himself reach for his desk chair. He pulled it out and sat down, facing the closed door to the porch.

He waited.

"Please," he pleaded quietly, "I don't want to go through this night after night."

"*Isak.*"

The voice was closer, much closer, as close as the porch outside, the curtains quivering to the hoarse timbre.

"*Isak.*"

There was a movement of air as the locked door to the porch opened with a slight creak. A musty odor wafted into the room. Isaac nearly swooned with a terror huge enough to annihilate him. His bladder squeezed and his penis jerked, and it was this that saved him from surrendering to that terror. A part of his mind clung to a determination not to pee in his pants. He wasn't going to suffer that humiliation.

"Isak."

The voice was now distinctly present. It sounded like Imam Ali's voice, a voice that Isaac would never forget, but yet it was somehow transformed.

Someone—or something—stepped into the room with a clacking of feet. The blackness grew even thicker, making it impossible to see anything. "Good boy, Isak, waiting so patiently for me." The words were raspy and moist.

"*Inggih,*" Isaac said in a shaky voice.

"I am pleased to see you hold the Holy Qur'an in your hand."

"Inggih."

"So. It is time, my boy."

"Yes, time to finish this." Isaac's initial terror was receding. The vise on his bladder decreased its pressure.

"Finish this? Ah, no, my beautiful boy, this is just the start, the new life that begins when you say the confession of faith. You do remember the words of the *shahadah*? I am sure you do. You are a bright boy who remembers such things."

"'There is no God but Allah, and Muhammad is His prophet.' There, I've said it, now leave me be."

A moist rasp of humor. "A clever boy too. Not in English, you know that. In the Arabic. I am sure you remember the Arabic."

Oh, yes. *Ashhadu anna la illaha illa allah wa ashhadu anna muhammadan rasul allah.* "There must be two witnesses."

"They are here."

"I cannot see them."

"They are here."

Isaac lifted the Qur'an, holding it edgewise in front of him, allowing the rim of glowing pages to illuminate whomever or whatever was before him. The soft beam seemed to melt away into nothing. "I don't see them," he repeated. "I don't see you."

Again that chuckle. "Do you really want to see me?"

Isaac's terror flooded back. He said nothing.

"I thought not. And as for the witnesses, listen."

Udin's sly voice said, "Isak, how are you?"

The reedy voice of Ibu Ruth said, "I am here."

Isaac said, with trembling defiance, "I refuse your witnesses.

They must be Muslims of good standing, not bullies or wishy-washy apostates."

That moist chuckle again, but not so amused this time. "Let's not waste any more time with lawyering, Isak. You are conveniently holding the Holy Qur'an, so place your right hand on it and recite the syahadat."

"I can't. I'm a Christian."

"No, you are not. No longer. You have deserted that faith. Or should I say, it has deserted you. Where is your Jesus now, hmm? He has never been, not when you were born, not when you were baptized, not when you were sick, not when you were in that mushollah cell. Come to Allah, Isak. Surrender yourself to Him. Submit yourself to Him in Islam."

"You are no Muslim! You are a demon, a shaitan, and there are no witnesses, you are making them up—"

"Silence!" The voice did not roar, but it grabbed Isaac's heart and shook it. The smell intensified into a stench, and there shimmered before him the outlines of a hulking figure that might have been that of a man, except that for the fleetest of moments Isaac saw the black shape of a huge oblong head and a wickedly curved protuberance that could only have been an outsized beak.

The Lord of the Crows.

The shahadah, Isak. Say it now. The voice was now inside Isaac's head.

Isaac remained silent.

Say it now!

Isaac knew with awful certainty that his confession would

make no difference. This Lord was going to take him anyway, whether he made the confession or not. His consciousness was fading. There blinked into his dying awareness a white speck of light, too dim and distant to grant any hope, but it was something for his mind to grab hold of.

"But I do have a choice," he murmured. The light brightened and grew near.

Say the confession! The voice was wrought with fury beyond description. *Say the confession, you miserable, stupid boy. You have forfeited your faith. You belong to me. Say it!*

The light was bright enough for Isaac to feel its strengthening warmth. He realized with wonder that it was a light within himself. "I choose to forgive you," he said. "I really do forgive you."

With a roar so immense as to be soundless, the Lord of the Crows reared to strike, but the blow never came. The light within Isaac exploded into a brilliance that changed the roar into a shriek of alarm, and through the light's blinding whiteness, Isaac saw a black form blown back and falling, falling, falling into a bottomless void.

Isaac blinked his eyes rapidly as his physical senses equilibrated to the ordinary surroundings of his bedroom. He was sprawled on his mattress. That awful, holy radiance faded into ordinary light.

The electricity had come on.

He spotted something on the wooden floor beside the desk, fluttering to the sudden breeze of the fan. He got up and bent to retrieve it. It was a shiny black feather. A crow's feather, each part of it perfectly formed, from tip to quill. But that was all it was. A crow's feather. Isaac dropped it into the wastebasket and went back to bed. His heart was whole once more, and within him a still small voice said, *My son, in whom I am well pleased.*

Chapter Nineteen

LMOST A YEAR LATER Isaac returned to the schoolyard, which was still a schoolyard, but no longer for children. The American Academy of Wonobo had permanently closed its doors, and its buildings had been taken over by the Nurse and Village Health Worker Training Institute of East Java. Several trainee nurses in stiff white uniforms, one of them male, bustled across the yard, glancing curiously at this odd bulé boy who was grinning at a tree sapling over by the wall.

Isaac stood where the flame tree had once soared. Another baby flame tree was growing in its place. Deliberately planted, of course, but Isaac had the pleasing notion that it was the spirit of the old tree that was budding out of the ground. Over time this sapling would grow tall and stout for boys to climb. But not Isaac. This was not his tree. Nonetheless, he squatted and ran two fingers up the side of the slender trunk. He paused the fingers where two tiny branches overlapped. He laughed. "I'm the first to climb this tree," he said. But he'd leave it for another boy to carve his initials in the wood.

It was time to do something else. He returned to the house and got from his old room a long, narrow cardboard box. He walked across the residential compound and out the hospital gate, carrying it over his shoulder.

"Isak, stop."

Isaac turned around. Mr. Theophilus strode up to him and said, "Where are you going?" He still had the height to look down at Isaac, but not as far down as on that day last August, so very long ago and in a different lifetime.

"Out for a walk," Isaac said.

Mr. Theophilus eyed his blond hair and blue eyes, his new button-down shirt and baggy cargo pants, his Birkenstock sandals, the long narrow package. "You are not to leave the compound, your mother said."

"That was months and months ago." And a different Isaac.

Mr. Theophilus narrowed his pale yellow eyes and then nodded. He withdrew a cell phone from his blue trouser pocket. "Wonobo's been quiet, but take this just in case."

Isaac thanked him and slipped the cell phone into one of his many cargo pockets. He strolled down Hayam Wuruk Avenue, passing the same shops, dodging the same crowds, smelling the same scents of Java, overhearing and understanding the same snatches of Javanese conversation as he had done countless times before. Yet something was different, and it wasn't Wonobo. The world that Isaac now knew, a world that stretched all the way back to Connecticut and the Ash Institute for Gifted Children, did not diminish. The bone-and-blood familiar Javanese world in which he ambled did not pull him in and transform him.

He was neither American nor Javanese, but that did not mean he was nothing. He was who he was, Isaac Williams.

The first two months in the States had been a black hole of

homesickness. But the hole had slowly filled up with simple everyday things: what buses and subways went where; the museums and the best times to go; Sunday-morning services at the cheery Presbyterian church; reruns of *I Dream of Jeannie,* which was his favorite television show out of the bewildering number of them; the community library and its constant supply of new books; and more recently at Ash, Andy Mills, with whom Isaac studied calculus and played chess and on Saturdays searched for monsters in the hallways of the Museum of Natural History.

And Tara Conway, too, with her spiked hair and her belly button ring and her smile that was half friendly, half mystery. In her last e-mail she'd asked him to bring her back some real Javanese tea.

The steady trade winds of the dry southeast monsoon scrubbed the blue sky with balls of cotton cumulus. The curling breeze had tangy hints of sea spray carried from waves breaking on Java's southern coral reefs. This was the Javanese weather Isaac loved most, and he luxuriated in it now, but there was strong in his mind the recent memory of his first wondrous snowfall.

Life was big and grand, and Isaac was growing into an intention of experiencing as much of it as he could.

Graham Williams had told Isaac that in the middle of the night the previous week a gang of men had stolen three frangipani trees out of the old Muslim cemetery, no doubt to be sold to a new golf course somewhere. These trees had been by the avenue's fence. A crew of neighborhood men was fixing the last of the gouges that the thieves had left in the ground. One of the men pounded the dirt fill with an iron tamper. Isaac watched for a second, then said, *"Al-salamu alaikum,* Bapak Trisno."

Bapak Trisno straightened and stretched his back, looking at Isaac. *"Alaikum as-salam,* Isak. So you are back?"

"Not to stay."

Bapak Trisno nodded. "Ismail is at home, if you are looking for him."

"Thank you."

Bapak Trisno nodded again and, without another word, returned to his work of placating the outraged dead.

In the clear space that the stolen frangipani trees had left, a young boy flew a kite in the trade wind. The kite was a darting mote in the sky, enjoying its unhindered play. Ironically, for all its appearance of soaring freedom, it was its tether that kept it aloft. If the string broke, the kite would swoop and sway uncontrolled to the ground.

Isaac stepped behind one of the untouched trees for a pee, propping the package up against a branch. He studied the pink tip of his penis held between his fingers, ringed by the brighter pink of healed flesh. After twelve years of intimacy with a foreskin, this sight had for a time startled Isaac with its unfamiliarity. But he was now accustomed to it. Imam Ali may have been brutal, but he had cut properly and the wound had healed normally.

Isaac climbed the cemetery's far fence and walked down Ismail's street, quiet this time of day. His heart pounded with each step. Once he came in sight of Ismail's house, his steps slowed. One house away he ceased walking altogether. He did not see the white goose that charged out from the yard behind him, but he heard its angry hiss and skittered away just in time to avoid a nasty nip. His momentum took him to the front of Ismail's house and died away, leaving him stranded in front of the closed gate. The house's front door was open, but the living room was empty. The television was off.

A Nahdlatul Umat Islam sticker was still plastered to the veranda railing. The visage of Tuan Guru Haji Abdullah Abubakar silently watched Isaac but raised no alarm within his heart.

A narrow face flashed in the small window of the bedroom that Ismail shared with his brothers and sisters. Ibu Trisno walked around the corner of the house, her hands dusty from freshly milled rice flour. She stopped, blinked, and then said, "Isak, is that you?" A delighted smile blossomed. "Why, of course it is, come in, come in."

Isaac opened the gate and stepped into the yard. "Is Ismail home?"

In answer Ismail appeared in the front doorway at the top of the veranda steps. He was as scrawny as ever, his shorts and mended shirt still too big for him. He looked at Isaac without speaking, his thin face blank, unplugged to any current.

Isaac held out the package. "I got you something from America," he said.

Ismail glanced at the package and then returned his gaze to Isaac's face. A smile trickled onto his own and into his dark eyes. "You're looking fat and pale, like an infidel grub."

Ibu Trisno put her knuckles on her hips. "Ismail!"

Isaac said, "And you're looking like something even a

Richard Lewis

garbageman wouldn't pick out of the gutter."

Ismail laughed, a full 220 volts dancing on his face. He trotted down the stairs and slapped Isaac across the shoulder, grinning. "Didn't I tell you to take me to America next time you went? So why'd you go without me?"

Ibu Trisno shook her head in mock exasperation and returned to her kitchen.

Isaac wiggled the package. "But I brought something back for you."

Ismail took the long narrow box. He shook it. "What is it?"

"Open it," Isaac said.

Ismail pried open the cardboard flaps and pulled out a long plastic rod, a curved red handle on one end and on the other a gray ring. "Still the same question," he said. "What is it?"

"A treasure finder," Isaac said.

Ismail's eyes widened.

Isaac stuck a hand in one of his cargo pockets. "But it doesn't use a jinn. It uses batteries. Here." He gave Ismail a two-pack of nine-volt Duracells.

Ismail quivered with excitement. Isaac put in the batteries and showed him how to use it.

"Wait, wait," Ismail said, handing the detector over for Isaac to hold. He darted to the side of the yard and climbed to the second branch of the *jambu* tree. When he descended, he had an old Chinese coin in his hand, the one the boys had found in the bed of the Brantas River. He scooped out a hole in the yard, dropped the coin into it, and shoved the dirt over it. "Okay, let's try," he said.

Isaac gave him the detector. Ismail clicked the ON button and swept the sensor ring over the covered hole. It buzzed. "Wow, it works, it really works!" Ismail dug out the coin. He brushed it off on his shorts and gave it to Isaac. "You keep it," he said. "Take it back to America for good luck." He wiggled the detector, his eyes shining. "Let's go down to the river, Isak."

And because hope always rises triumphant in the hearts of boys at the prospect of finding treasure, Isaac grinned and said, "This time, gold."

Glossary

Alaikum as-salam: reply to Islamic greeting of *Al-salamu alaikum,* both meaning "Peace be upon you"

aiyah: exclamation of surprise or frustration

alim: An Islamic scholar or teacher

Ambonese: a person from the city of Ambon in Maluku, East Indonesia

arak: potent alcoholic drink

Awas lo: "Be careful"

ayat: verse, as in a verse from the Holy Qur'an

azan: the Muslim call to prayer, generally broadcast from mosques

bapak: means "father"; also respectful form of address for a male Indonesian

bemo: public transport jitney

bencong: transvestite

bismillah: Arabic term for "in the name of Allah"

Bugis: a seafaring people from the island of Sulawesi, with many communities established throughout the archipelago

bulé: slang for white person

dangdut: a form of popular music with Arabian and Hindu influences

dukun santet: witch doctor

gamelan: an Indonesian orchestra made up chiefly of percussion instruments

hadith: the words and deeds of the prophet Muhammad as reported by his contemporaries and collected by Islamic scholars as an ancilliary Scripture to the Holy Qur'an

haji: a male Muslim who has made the obligatory pilgrimage to Mecca; also an honorific title used to address such a male

hajjah: a female Muslim who has made the obligatory pilgrimage to Mecca; also an honorific title used to address such a female

halal: permitted by Islamic law

Hutu: African tribe

ibu: means "mother"; also respectful form of address for a female Indonesian

Imam: a title of respect for a Muslim religious leader; also the leader of the congregational prayers

inggih: Javanese word for "yes"

Irianese: a person from the island of New Guinea

istighfar: begging for God's pardon

Iyallah: exclamation commonly translated as "Oh, God"

jambu: a type of fruit tree

jamu: medicinal herb

jihad: the concept of striving toward religious purpose, sometimes narrowly taken to mean a holy war *jilbab:* head covering in which the entire head except the face is covered

jinn: a type of supernatural creature

jizyah: tax paid by non-Muslims to a Muslim state (in early Islam)

kafir: infidel; person who does not believe in Islam

kampung: village

kepeng: old Chinese coin

kiai: an Islamic religious scholar; also respectful form of address for such a scholar

Kijang: a local brand name for a Toyota; means "deer" in Indonesian

komando jihad: warrior

kris: a wavy blade, often considered magical

kunut nazilah: a type of jihad against a spiritual foe that usually takes the form of prayer

magrib: one of the five daily prayers prayed early in the evening, near sunset

mandi: to bathe; a bathroom

mas: Javanese title for a man

ma sha'allah: expression of strong disapproval

minbar: pulpit

mosque: Muslim place of worship

mushollah: a prayer room, usually in a public building

Nahdlatul Umat Islam: fictional organization, translates as Renaissance of the Islamic Community

pak: Javanese title for a man

peci: rimless, oval cap, usually black

pesantren: boarding school for Muslim children, with a heavy emphasis on Qur'anic studies

resolusi jihad: a resolution by an Indonesian Islamic organization for holy warfare

rukun wudu: the rite of ritual washing before prayers

salat al-istisqa: a special prayer for rain

Al-salamu alaikum: Islamic greeting, meaning "Peace be upon you"

sambal: hot chili sauce

shahadah: the Islamic confession of faith

shariah: Islamic law

tabligh: using instruction to increase understanding of Islam

Tuan Guru: title of respect for Muslim leader

Tutsi: African tribe

ulamah: Islamic scholars or teachers

ummah: congregation

wayang kulit: shadow puppet, or the puppet show itself, usually depicting an Indian epic